Read on!
Tina
Susedik

Table of Contents

Acknowledgments
Chapter One
Chapter Two
Chapter Three
Chapter Four
Chapter Five
Chapter Six
Chapter Seven
Chapter Eight
Chapter Nine
Chapter Ten
Chapter Eleven
Chapter Twelve
Chapter Thirteen
Chapter Fourteen
Chapter Fifteen
Chapter Sixteen
Chapter Seventeen
Chapter Eighteen
Chapter Nineteen
Chapter Twenty
Chapter Twenty-One
Chapter Twenty-Two
Chapter Twenty-Three
Chapter Twenty-Four

Chapter Twenty-Five
Excerpt from "The Balcony Girl"
About Tina Susedik
Books by Tina Susedik

The School Marm by Tina Susedik

Cover Design by: Staral Ink

This is a work of fiction. The names, characters, places, and incidents are the products of the author's imagination or are used fictitiously. Any resemblance to actual events, business establishments, locales, or persons, living or dead, is entirely coincidental.

All rights reserved. No part of this publication may be reproduced, stored in a retrieval system, or transmitted in any form or by any means (electronic, mechanical, photocopying, recording, or otherwise) without the prior consent of the author. The only exception is brief quotations in printed reviews.

The scanning, uploading, and distribution of this book via the Internet or via any other means without the permission of the author is illegal and punishable by law. Please purchase only authorized electronic editions, and do not participate in or encourage electronic piracy of copyrighted materials.

Your support of this author's rights is appreciated.

Published in the United States of America by

Tina Susedik

Copyright © 2020 by Tina Susedik

Acknowledgements

After writing so many books and stories, it's difficult coming up with people to thank. You know who you are. So, this one goes to my cat, Nikki. If it weren't for your treading across my keyboard, trying to take a nap on my lap while I'm writing, and whining for treats, my stories would be done a lot sooner. I love you anyway.

And, as always to Al. If the sun refused to shine, I would still be loving you. If the Mountains crumble to the sea, there would still be you and me. (From our song, "Thank You" by Led Zepplin.

Prologue

September 26, 1879

The smell of smoke grew stronger as Suzanna Lindstrom, Deadwood's schoolteacher, stood on the front steps of the small house she and her sister, Julia, shared. She wrapped a shawl over her nightgown and shivered in the crisp fall air.

A boom awakened her from a deep sleep where she'd been dreaming about King Winson. A glow from the direction of downtown Deadwood caught her attention. Was someone having a bonfire? A large explosion shook the ground. She grabbed the doorjamb to keep her balance. What was wrong? She had to wake Julia.

Holding the edges of her shawl at her neck, she raced across their living room and threw Julia's door open wide. "Julia, Julia," she yelled, approaching the bed. With the blankets pulled over her head, like she usually slept, it was hard to tell where to push at her sister.

Another explosion rocked the house. At this point she didn't care if she poked her sister in the eye, they had to find out what was going on and see if anyone needed help. She nudged the blankets. "C'mon, Julia, wake up."

Her sister didn't move. She prodded Julia again. When there was no response, she took hold of the blanket and threw it back. "What on Earth?" Beneath the blanket was nothing but a pile of pillows lumped together and shaped to look like a body.

"Oh, my God." She pushed the pillows to the floor, then ran from the room. Maybe she was in the kitchen having a late-night snack. When she found the room empty, she snapped her fingers. The necessary. She raced to the front door.

Outside, the smoke was thicker and the glow in the sky brighter. She pounded on the outhouse door. "Julia," she screamed. "Come out. Something is happening in town." No answer. She yanked open the door to an empty building. "Where the hell is she?" If her mother were here, she'd be firmly chastised for swearing.

Lifting her nightgown above her bare feet, Suzanna ran past the schoolhouse to the end of the street. A roar unlike any she ever heard before greeted her. The air was thick with smoke and heat. Surely the hounds of hell had come to destroy Deadwood. She sank to the ground and covered her face. "Julia," she sobbed into her hands. "Where are you?"

KINGSTON WINSON TUGGED Julia Lindstrom down the smoke-filled street. Heat licked at their heels. People ran from buildings, yelling, screaming. Horses, pigs, and dogs, all who once roamed at their will, charged around them. A woman wearing nothing more than a sheer nightgown, eyes wide with fear, headed up the hill.

"We need to get to Hattie's," Julia hollered into his ear.

Like a steam engine, the fire roared behind them. "No, you need to get up the hill like everyone else."

"Hattie usually takes something to help her sleep." Tears streaked her soot-covered face. "We can't let her and the other girls die."

They passed the bank where King's best friend, Daniel Iverson, had his office and room. Smoke coursed from the windows. Glass shattered, pelting them with sharp shards. An explosion rocked the ground.

"What happened?" Julia asked, gripping his arm with steel fingers.

"It sounded like the fire set off kegs of gunpowder at Jensen and Bliss' Hardware Store, which will only make things worse." He pushed her forward. "Let's get moving. We need to get to the hills."

"Julia?" A deep voice called out from the door of the bank.

Daniel. Thank God he'd gotten out from the burning building.

"What?" Julia yelled over the snarl of the flames.

"What the hell are you doing here dressed like that?"

"There's no time to question her," King said, slapping at an ember smoldering on his shirt. "Right now, we need to help people from the buildings and up the hill."

"I'll go to Hattie's and help them get out."

Daniel captured her elbow. "You'll do no such thing. Go back to your house. The fire isn't headed toward it."

Julia yanked her arm from his hand. "I'll do no such thing, Daniel Iverson. You can't tell me what to do." Without another glance, she ran toward Hattie's.

"Damn woman," Daniel muttered, chasing after her.

King charged behind him. "A damn *fine* woman. Head to the hills," he shouted at people crying, screaming, and having no idea what to do. While rushing up the stairs of Hattie's brothel, he prayed all the town residents would make it out safely. He peered over his shoulder. Sparks jumped from building to building, setting more wooden structures aflame. His back was so hot, surely his shirt was on fire.

He and Daniel threw open the doors to Hattie's as Julia disappeared up the stairs. *Shit.* While he was concerned about Julia, she was Daniel's worry right now. But where was her sister, Suzanna? Had she remained at the schoolhouse on the other side of town? Or was she among those heading to safety? He said a short prayer for her.

By the time they reached the second floor, Julia had already pounded on the first two doors to the right of the stairway.

"You follow Julia, I'll take these rooms." King pointed in the opposite direction. "Fire! Get out now," he yelled, beating on the first door. Holding wrappers to their chests and followed by men in their union suits, Hattie's girls appeared from their rooms.

"Run," King yelled. "Get out of here and head for the hills. The entire town is on fire." He yanked a pair of pants away from a man jumping on one foot while trying to put them on. "There's no time for modesty. Get the hell out of here." Eyes wide with panic, the man did as he was told. "Idiot," King muttered.

The heat had intensified by the time he'd reached the last room. From the other end, Dorrie's voice screamed to get Hattie out of the building. With all the rooms emptied, he headed for the door, covering his mouth and nose with his handkerchief. His eyes watered and nose burned. A man he recognized as a pious churchgoer who owned a haberdashery and had five children, charged down the stairs.

"Hurry up," he screamed when Julia, followed by Daniel with Hattie over his shoulder, appeared through the smoke. The roof creaked and swayed. The walls vibrated as if they were trying to shake off the flames. The stairwell to the alley filled with smoke. If they didn't get out of here soon, they'd all perish. Even now, it was getting difficult to breathe.

King's hopes of sucking in fresh air when they left the building were dashed. The air was smokier and hotter. Daniel stopped and glanced over his shoulder. "Go on," King yelled. "I'm right behind you."

Stopping to help several people who'd fallen behind, made the trek up the hill longer and more treacherous. By the time they reached the top and joined the crowd, he could barely catch his breath. The smoke wasn't as bad at the top, but it still filled his lungs with each breath.

All around him people stared at the disaster playing out below. As each building fell, an owner or resident cried in dismay. Several people, both men and women, simply stared in shock, the fire reflected in their wide eyes. Others called for friends and loved ones.

King squatted in front of Hattie. "Is everyone accounted for?"

"I . . . I don't know."

"I see Dorrie with Ivy," Julia said, wiping her forearm across her forehead. "I'll send them over here and help search for the others."

Another explosion rocked the town. King stared down the hill and tried to place where the individual buildings had once stood. "Must be Colin's store," he said to no one in particular. He didn't want to, really he didn't, but he turned his attention to where he thought his restaurant and hotel were. Nothing. There was nothing but flames, smoke, and . . . nothing. Deadwood was destroyed.

The one person he hadn't seen was the new schoolteacher, Julia's sister, Suzanna. She had to be safe. "I'm going to head to Suzanna's to make sure she's all right," King said, rising to his feet, his knees creaking as he stretched to his full height. If there was such a thing as a heavy heart, that's what he had. He'd only known the teacher a short time but knew without a doubt she was the one for him.

"How're you going to do that with the entire town burning?"

"I'll follow the top of the hill. When I'm above their place, I'll head down. I need to make sure she's all right and didn't go to town to help."

"What about your restaurant and Leona?" Daniel asked.

A tear rolled down King's face as he gazed at the inferno below. "Thankfully, Leona was in Lead visiting friends." He shook his head. "And there's not a damn thing I can do about the restaurant." With those last words, his legs still shaky from the rescue and running to safety, he disappeared among the people waiting out the firestorm

Chapter One

Three months earlier, June 1879
Deadwood, Dakota Territory

The stagecoach driver's voice rose above the creaking of the coach, calling for the team of eight horses to stop. Cramped between her sister and a man with whom she'd had a running battle over his roving hands, nineteen-year-old Suzanna Lindstrom peered around her older sister, Julia, hoping for a glimpse of the outside world.

Lord, she hoped they were almost to Deadwood. The exhausting, dirty, frightful ride from her family home in Iowa hadn't been romantic like all the newspaper articles made it out to be. And if Mr. Silverstone beside her ever washed a day in his life, she'd smelled no sign of it. Along with his body odor and the swaying of the coach, a few times she thought she'd lose what little food she'd managed to eat during their quick stops to change horses.

The only redeeming factor had been the lovely lady sitting across from them. A proper lady, a banker's wife, who didn't seem to sweat under the layers of her striking red skirt and jacket. The only signs of Mrs. Woods' discomfort were a fan she flicked back and forth across her face, a speck of dirt on the lacy collar of her white blouse, and the removal of her gloves.

Suzanna held back a sigh and refrained from glancing down at her homespun brown skirt and short-sleeve gingham blouse, both flecked with dust and dirt. In view of the heat, she'd removed her bonnet and held it in her lap. The darn thing wasn't managing to keep her blasted thick, curly, blonde hair in place anyway. Every morning, she'd twist it in a bun, and within a few hours, the strands were tangling over her shoulders. What would it take to look like Mrs. Woods instead of the poor farmer's daughter from a ramshackle house filled with too many siblings?

Before Julia lifted the canvas window covering failing dismally in its duty to keep out dust, the driver's sidekick opened the door. The driver held his rifle over one shoulder and tipped his hat. "Thought you might like a look at your new home, Mrs. Woods. The view from here is one you don't want to miss."

In the days since boarding the third stagecoach on their trip, it never failed to amaze her how someone as disreputable looking as the driver had such perfect elocution. But then the gold rush had brought people from all walks of life to the Black Hills, including lawyers, bankers, teachers, and, of course, thieves.

"Well, let's make it quick," Mrs. Woods said, sniffing haughtily then offering her hand to the man.

The coach tipped as the stocky woman stepped out, giving Mr. Silverstone an excuse to rub against Suzanna. She shoved his hands away. "You touch me one more time, you'll regret it." She kept her voice to a whisper. She didn't need anyone to find out how the man had pawed at her. The future schoolteacher of Deadwood couldn't afford a bad reputation.

Suzanna followed Julia from the coach. Over the course of their trip, she and Julia had seen many types of landscape. Prairies, hills, woods, and mountains galore. The stagecoach had wound its way through gorges and narrow passages. The valley here opened up between the ridges, revealing the bustling city of Deadwood.

From their height, the people in Deadwood resembled scurrying ants. The sun reflected off what she assumed were signs hanging from more buildings than she'd seen in her life. This time she couldn't hold back a sigh. Here was a town filled with excitement. Coming from a small farm stuck out in the middle of nowhere, with too many children for her parents to support, things had been boring. Maybe life in Deadwood would be more interesting.

Maybe she'd be invited to tea with Mrs. Woods and the other society women. Once she was able to wash and change into more suitable clothes, surely the woman would see Suzanna was meant to be part of Deadwood's society. Though her family had little, her mother had come from a well-to-do family out East and made sure her daughters were schooled in proper etiquette. With Julia being a seamstress, they had several outfits fit for more than poor farm girls.

"Isn't it gorgeous?" Julia said, taking Suzanna by the arm. "Look at the size of those trees. They must have been here for thousands of years."

Suzanna wasn't sure about thousands of years, but she had to admit the pines were impressive. A thought came to her. "What are the chances we'll find husbands here?"

Julia jerked Suzanna's arm. "Remember, we're not here to get hitched," Julia hissed. "Do you want a passel of kids like Mama? You agreed to teach for one year. If you get married, you'll have to quit, and then all you'll be is someone's indentured servant."

Suzanna stuck her nose in the air and jerked her arm away from her sister's hand. "Well, I don't plan on marrying a dirt farmer. I'm going to find a rich man."

"Don't forget where you came from." Julia nudged Suzanna. "I'm not sure where you get these lofty ideas. All you talk about is Mrs. Woods, her refined manners, clothing, hair, voice. You're not in Mrs. Woods' league and never will be."

"We'll see about that. Deadwood is our new future." Suzanna swept up her skirt and headed back to the coach, leaving her sister behind. Why was Julia so set on them not getting above themselves? Here, no one knew they'd come from humble beginnings. Thanks to their mother making sure they went to school they were educated. In fact, educated enough for her to teach the town's young. When so many of her friends her age were married with at least one child, she was starting fresh. And she planned on making the best of it. The man she'd marry would be sophisticated, smart, and, most of all, rich. She'd have a large house with servants, host lavish teas and parties, and forget about the life she'd left behind. Surely, those things could be found in Deadwood, couldn't they?

KING SLOGGED THROUGH the mud, avoiding horses, oxen-driven wagons, and drunks. It was only ten in the morning, but there was an abundance of all three. Mud splattered on his already filthy clothes. With the spring thaw, water from the hills congregated on Deadwood's main street.

He scraped his hand over the week-old, scruffy hair on his face. He needed a shave, a bath, and clean clothes before he went to meet the weekly stagecoach set to arrive, he glanced at the town clock hanging near the bank—in an hour.

As he plodded his way across the street to King's Inn, his restaurant and hotel, he avoided a particularly large pile of ox dung. A horse raced down the street, slinging mud in every direction.

"Stagecoach is a-comin'," the man yelled, slapping his hat against the horse's hindquarters.

With his foot in the air to sidestep the horse droppings, King couldn't move quick enough to get out of the way. Why was the arrival of the stagecoach garnering such excitement when it had been coming to Deadwood for three years?

As the horse passed, its tail whipped across King's face. Arms flailing, foot waving in the air, King's leg went out from beneath him. Rump first, he landed in the pile of manure he'd been trying so desperately to avoid.

Someone falling in the street was not an uncommon occurrence, so luckily no one paid any attention. No one, except for his best friend, Daniel Iverson.

"Well, don't just stand there laughing like a hyena, help me up." The mud was slippery, slimy, and disgusting. Without anything to grip to pull himself up, he kept tumbling back into the mire.

"Catch." From his place on the wooden sidewalk Dan tossed him one end of a rope. "I'll pull you up."

There was no way he was going to let his friend reel him in like a floundering fish. "Just hold on to it." He tugged on the rope with slick and gooey hands.

"Wait," Dan said. "You're going to drag me in with you. I'll tie it to a post."

King eyed the rickety post holding up an equally rickety overhang. The way buildings were being thrown up and with the gold tunnels meandering beneath the town, he wouldn't be surprised if he pulled the entire building down, with the entire block falling after like a row of dominos.

With a deep breath, he pulled himself toward his friend. The mud sucked at his boots, threatening to draw them off with each step until he made it to the boardwalk. He fell to his back, catching his breath as Dan laughed.

"Shut up, big guy. It could be you next."

Dan adjusted his string tie and straightened his immaculate blue, brocade vest. "Hey, don't you have the stagecoach to meet?"

King stood and wiped his filthy clothes. His boots were full of mud and water, his pockets drenched, his beard encrusted with who knows what, and the brim of his hat turned down, nearly covering his eyes.

"You'd better get cleaned up before Mrs. Woods arrives." His friend tapped a finger against his smirking lip. "If the stage is almost here, you won't have time to clean up proper." Dan's smile suggested only one thing. "You know what you have to do, don't you?"

Knock his friend into the street? "Yes." Ignoring stares, he clomped toward the nearest horse trough. He removed his boots and poured the goo onto the street. With a grimace, he tossed them into the water, then, taking off his hat, climbed in. After dunking his head several times, he crawled out, stepped back onto the boardwalk, and shook himself like a dog.

A shout came from up the street. Darn. The stagecoach was here. He tugged his boots over his feet, slapped on his hat, and limped toward the stopping place. Someone's hand halted him.

"You should let me escort Mrs. Woods," Dan said, stepping in front of his friend. "You look like someone who spent a week hunting game for his restaurant and then rolled around in the mud. If there are any other women on the stage, you can help them."

Even though they'd probably be women for the whorehouses in the Badlands, he supposed it was better than nothing. The ratio of women to men was skewed toward men. Any new women in town were a welcome sight.

The stagecoach turned the last corner into town. Charlie pulled back on the reins. The driver strained back on the brake. The coach slowed. A shout came from a tavern to King's left. The doors creaked open. He caught a blur from the corner of his eye. A blur becoming a brick wall as it hit King in the side. A blur tossing him over the side of the boardwalk and back into the mud.

***Suzanna clutched her bonnet, the perspiration in her hands wrinkling the fabric. The driver had taken them down the winding, twisting mountainside at breakneck speed, sending her fellow passengers bobbing, weaving, and bouncing against each other. The small lunch they'd had hours ago was creeping its way up her throat.

Saliva pooled in her mouth. She swallowed deeply and patted her damp face with her handkerchief. The breeze from the open windows wasn't helping. Even Mrs. Woods looked a little green around the gills. A lady like her doesn't throw up, does she?

With one last turn, the horses slowed. A massive sigh of relief filled the inside of the coach as the driver urged the horses on. Taking a deep, cleansing breath, Suzanna peered around her sister and out the window at the passing scenery.

This was Deadwood? Where were the fancy houses? The cobblestone streets? The society ladies shopping? The paved sidewalks?

This was . . . She bit her bottom lip and gripped the small bag containing her meager coins. This was chaos. People, mostly men dressed in clothes that had seen better days, milled around on the raised wooden sidewalks. Scraggly beards, worn-out boots, cigars left dangling between their lips, and wearing hats that looked as if they'd been dragged by oxen.

The buildings they passed weren't much better. Had anyone measured before slapping them up in a haphazard way? At least most of the towns they'd traveled through had some type of order to their main streets. These buildings weren't in a straight row, and some of the boards used in construction still had tree bark on them. Signs of various sizes and shapes hung haphazardly, as if a drunk had put them up.

Julia grabbed her hand. "Oh, my. I believe there are Chinese people here. Look at their strange clothes."

Chinese? In Deadwood? Several children dressed in pants and tunics stopped to stare beneath a sign reading, *Hong Fee, Washing, Ironing.*

Before the coach came to a complete stop, Mr. Silverstone opened his door and stepped into the mud. He reached into the coach. "Here, Miss, give me your hand."

Suzanna peered down her nose at his dirty nails. No way was she going to touch him. The other door opened, and a wide plank board was placed between the coach and the wooden steps leading to a boardwalk. At least they wouldn't have to slog through the mud.

A handsome man, dressed in a crisp white shirt beneath a blue brocade vest, stepped onto the board and held out his hand. Was he rich?

"Mrs. Woods, I presume? I'm Dan Iverson. I can take you to your husband."

Mrs. Woods tittered. *Women her age tittered?* But she didn't blame the woman as she felt like giggling herself. Oh, my, he was good looking. Holding her hand in the crook of his arm, Mr. Iverson guided Mrs. Woods down the platform.

She and Julia waited for him to return. He would, wouldn't he? No gentleman would allow two single women to leave the stagecoach unescorted. After a minute, Julia stepped through the door.

"What are you doing?" Suzanna grabbed her arm.

"I'm not going to sit here and wait for some man to help us. We traveled here on our own, we can find lodging for the night on our own."

Her sister was probably right. The sooner they found a place to stay, freshen up and rest, the better. Tomorrow she'd meet with the people who hired her. Making a good impression was vital.

Julia was already on the boardwalk when someone reached inside. "Miss? If you'll give me your hand, I'll help you down the ramp."

The man's deep, raspy voice sent shivers down her spine. Not scary or creepy shivers like Mr. Silverstone produced. But something new and delicious, like heading into a new adventure. Holding her bonnet in one hand, she placed the other in his. Tingles spread up her arm. Her face flushed. Was she getting sick? That was all she needed in an unfamiliar town.

Lifting her skirt daintily like Mrs. Woods, she stepped from the coach, expecting someone handsome and gentlemanly. Instead, her eyes beheld the dirtiest, muddiest, most disreputable person she'd ever seen. The sides of his hat, which he hadn't bothered to remove, dripped water. With the amount of mud or whatever covering him, it was difficult to tell the color of his shoulder-length hair. The ends of a scruffy beard were matted together, while any skin not covered in facial hair looked as if he'd taken a bath in the middle of the street. His clothes didn't look or smell any better.

She yanked her fingers from his.

"Miss?"

"Thank you, but I believe I can walk on my own." With her nose in the air, she stepped past the man. As she reached the end of the plank, a cat ran past, followed by a mangy dog. The dog rubbed against her skirt. She tottered backward on her heeled boots. Her bonnet flew from her hand. She flailed her arms like a windmill.

"Miss!" the man yelled, grabbing her arm as two more dogs, barking as if they'd treed a raccoon, charged past.

The first one rammed into her legs, the second into the man. She clutched his arm to regain her balance. He grasped her other arm. Her heels teetered on the wooden edge.

"Hold—" The man's words were lost as they tumbled over the side.

The mud, as she landed on her back, was soft. Squishy, wet, and soft. Not like the man who landed on top of her, pushing her farther into the goo. Someone laughed. She opened one eye and, through muddy eyelashes, peered over the man's shoulder.

Several people gathered on the boardwalk, pointing and snickering. More townspeople followed, including children she'd probably be teaching. Soon, what she was sure was the entire crowd, was laughing. Tears pooled in her eyes.

"Get off me, you big oaf." She pushed against his broad chest. "People are staring."

The man raised up on his hands and looked down at her with bright, blue eyes, like the sky on a clear summer's day. Her heart skipped a beat and her stomach fluttered. She was definitely getting sick. Nothing else could explain it.

She closed her eyes and opened them again. Mud gathered in the creases in his forehead. "Get up. You're embarrassing me." Pushing against him was like trying to move a boulder the size of a house. "Please."

The man blinked, then, shoving against the ground, stood, extending his hand. "I'm so sorry this happened. Those d—" He cleared his throat. "I mean it's the darn dogs' fault."

Getting herself up was going to be a problem. Ignoring his mud-encrusted hand, she pressed her palms behind her and pushed upward, only to have her hands slip. She could do this.

"Show's over folks." Mr. Iverson, without a speck of dirt on him, shooed the gawkers away until only her sister and an older gentleman were left.

After the third attempt at extracting herself, the big oaf leaned down and put his hands on either side of her waist. She slapped his hands. "What are you doing, you lout? Get your hands off me."

"Miss, I'm only trying to help you out of this mess."

Before she had another chance to smack his hands away, he drew her up, the mud slurping and sucking at her clothes. As if she weighed nothing more than a mouse, he lifted her onto the boardwalk, his large hands spanning her waist. Her hair came loose from its bun, the long strands clinging to her blouse. She wiped at a muddy strand stuck to her face. Mr. Iverson, Julia, and the older man took a step back when she shook out her skirt.

The disreputable lug plopped his disreputable hat on his head. Maybe if she knew the man, which she positively did not want to, she would laugh at his grubby appearance.

"Are you all right?" Julia asked, holding shaking fingers to her mouth.

Was her sister hiding a smile? She'd better not be. Suzanna narrowed her eyes and fisted her hands at her waist. This was a disaster. Could things get any worse?

The elderly gentleman stepped forward. "Miss Suzanna Lindstrom?"

Suzanna raised her chin. How could this man possibly know her name? "Yes."

"Oliver Ogden at your service." He clicked his heels and gave a small bow like he was greeting royalty rather than a schoolteacher covered from head to toe in muck.

Suzanna took a step backward. Oh. No. It couldn't be. But it was. It was the man who had written and offered her a job. Probably witnessed the entire fiasco created by the imbecile standing beside her. Could the ground just swallow her up now? Wait, it almost did. She struck out her hand, then pulled it back, wiping her fingers on her skirt, which was ridiculous. Mud wiping on mud only created more mud.

"I'm, uh, pleased to meet you."

Mr. Ogden perused her from head to toe. "I believe I'll allow you to freshen up a bit. I'll see you in the morning in front of King's Restaurant." With that, he tipped his hat and strode down the sidewalk.

KING CLOSED HIS EYES. Where was a tunnel cave-in when you needed one? With so many tunnels snaking beneath the town's buildings and streets, why couldn't one swallow him up now? Of all the people he could dump in the mucky street, it had to be the new schoolmarm.

He'd only gotten a brief look at her before their tumble. Pretty. Young. Seventeen or eighteen at the most. Almost too young to be teaching the rough and tumble youth of Deadwood. What had Oliver been thinking? Probably no other well-educated woman would want to set foot in town. He took Suzanna by the elbow.

"We should get you and your companion to the hotel so you can," he took in Miss Lindstrom's bedraggled state, "freshen up."

The muddy young woman yanked her arm from his grip, and pointed her pert nose down at him, which was amazing as he had at least six inches on her.

"I don't need your help, *sir*." The last word sounded like he was some kind of marauder. "Kindly leave us and go back to," she sniffed, "whatever hole you dragged yourself from." She swished her skirt away from him and pivoted in a circle.

"Don't know where you're going, do you?" He tried to keep the sarcasm from creeping into his voice, but her haughtiness set him on edge. She was as prickly as she was muddy. Could he blame her? To be tossed into the mud in front of a good share of the town was embarrassing.

"I'm sure Julia and I can find our way perfectly well." She picked up her small suitcase and a large fabric bag and headed, surprisingly, in the right direction.

Dan ran a finger over his mustache and smirked. "That was quite a way to endear yourself to the new schoolmarm. Will she ask you to tea?"

"Shut up." With his friend at his side, King stomped toward his hotel, keeping his eyes on the swaying hips of the women a few steps in front of them.

Leaving Dan at his law office, he went around to the back of the hotel to rinse off before heading to his room.

He stopped at the well, toed off his boots, peeled off his socks, and dropped his hat on the ground. Even though he wanted to, removing his clothes would harm the sensibilities of the good women in town.

The bucket fell until splashing water echoed up the well walls. He cranked the wooden handle to bring the full bucket back to the top.

King poured the icy water over his head and shivered. The growing pool of water at his feet turned brown. He'd continue the process until it ran clear. Arms tired after the fifth bucket, he raised it over his head and lost his grip. The water splashed somewhere behind his head.

"You mindless baboon," a female screamed behind him.

Please, oh, please, don't let it be the schoolteacher. He turned. Miss Lindstrom's hands were fisted at her sides. Her hair, less muddy than before, hung over her face like the branches of a willow tree.

"You!" She wiped the hair off her face. "Why am I not surprised? Are all the men in town as clumsy as you? Because of you, I'm not allowed to enter the hotel and now I'm doused with ice-cold water." Without waiting for his response, she went on. "And why are you behind the hotel? Does the owner know you're here? Shouldn't you be off mucking out horse stalls?"

King dropped the bucket back down the well. So, the lady didn't realize he was the owner of the hotel and restaurant. Thought she was better than him. Thought he was a lowly manure mucker. He bit back a laugh. Who cared what the little spitfire thought?

Once the full bucket was at the top, he rested it on the edge. "You know what, lady? I've had enough of your complaints. If you don't like me being here, take it up with the owner."

"I'll do just that. Now give me the bucket so I can wash off after you leave."

Oh, he'd give it to her all right. "You have to come closer. The rope isn't long enough."

With a few tentative steps, she came closer. Close enough to . . .

SUZANNA DRAPED HER wet clothes over a chair and accepted a clean, fluffy towel from Julia. Accustomed to the thin, graying towels she'd shared with her siblings, this little bit of luxury made her feel like a queen. "Oooh, I can't believe he did that."

Julia sat on the double bed they were to share for the night. "Were you acting in your usual uppity way?"

"What do you mean?" She wasn't uppity. Merely wanted better things for herself, and a dirty, smelly, clumsy man like— gee, what was his name—was not one of them.

"Since we left the farm, you've had your nose in the air." Julia slipped out of her skirt and unbuttoned her blouse. "You know nothing about this man, yet you've pegged him as a down-and-out nobody. Why, he could own this place for all you know."

Suzanna snorted as she dropped a nightgown over her head. Instead of changing into their regular clothes and eating in the dining room, Julia had brought up a tray. "I doubt it. And besides, he didn't have to dump the bucket of water over my head. I'll admit the first one was an accident, but the second one was done on purpose. The lout."

"You need to keep an open mind. This town may not look like much now, but I bet my bottom dollar it'll become great in the future."

"That may be." She pulled back a thick quilt and fresh, clean, white sheets. "But from what I could tell, except for a few, the men in this town are like the buffoon. Unkempt, uneducated, and uncouth." She slid under the covers, keeping her feet from Julia's usually freezing ones.

Julia rolled away, turned down the lantern, and punched her pillow. "Just don't forget where we came from. Poor dirt farmers, not unlike the hardworking men in this town."

Chapter Two

A good night's sleep did wonders for Suzanna's outlook. Refreshed and wearing clean clothes, she was ready to tackle her new life. Today was the day she'd see the schoolhouse and small lodgings the town provided as part of her salary. While she taught the young of the city, Julia would sew for the rich ladies.

Once downstairs, they followed the directions of the desk clerk and entered the dining room. Yesterday, she hadn't had time or inclination to notice the expensive trimmings of the hotel. Thick burgundy carpet covered the floors of the lobby. She ran her fingers over a wall, enjoying the texture of the embossed rose and gold wallpaper. The couches and chairs were richly upholstered.

The restaurant's round tables, covered with lacy white cloths, were nearly full. Elaborate oil lamps and chandeliers gave the room a cheery atmosphere. Whoever the owner was, he must be rich.

After being shown to their table, she put a red-and-white checkered napkin across her lap and perused the menu. It was lucky they were moving to their new quarters today. Their coins were rapidly dwindling.

The coffee was delicious, not bitter like her mother's. The eggs, ham, and potatoes were done to perfection, and the toast light brown. She could get used to this kind of food, especially when she didn't have to fight her brothers and sisters for her share of it.

A shadow crossed their table. "Good morning, ladies. I'm Kingston Winson, proprietor of this fine establishment."

Suzanna took in his creased, pin-stripe pants, and moved up to a crisp white shirt beneath a finely stitched deep purple vest and string tie. A mustache, not unlike the one she'd seen on Wild Bill Hickok, drooped down to a square, chiseled jaw. The man's light-brown hair curled at his collar.

She turned her gaze farther up to his face. He was more handsome than the man from yesterday. With his good looks and money, he would make an ideal husband. Her eyes met his. She gasped. Those eyes. Those brilliant blue eyes. Eyes popping into her dreams during the night.

"You... You're..."

He snapped his heels together and gave a bow. "Yes, ma'am. I'm the lout, baboon, oaf. I wanted to make sure you were all right after yesterday."

Where were the words she needed? Julia raised an eyebrow and smirked at her. After acting like a shrew yesterday, she supposed she deserved it.

"I'm... I'm fine, Mr. Winson." Could she bury her heated face into her reticule? How did one extract one's self from an embarrassing situation? Retreat was the best option. She gathered her belongings. "Are you ready, Julia? We're supposed to meet Mr. Ogden outside."

Julia wiped her mouth on her napkin and rose. "How much do we owe, Mr. Winson?"

"Thirty cents apiece," he said, keeping his eyes on Suzanna.

Suzanna dug into her bag, set the money on the table, along with a few pennies for a tip and, turning her back on the man, sauntered from the room. The quicker she removed herself from his presence and the way he made her jittery and flustered, the better.

KING SCOOPED UP THE change and followed the women to the lobby. Without glancing backward, they left the building. He swept back the long, lacy curtains covering the tall windows facing the boardwalk.

The sisters stood side-by-side waiting for Oliver. Standing to the side of the window to get a better view, he watched the threesome walk down the boardwalk.

Suzanna Lindstrom intrigued him. She was feisty, mouthy, and with her blue eyes and blonde hair, about the prettiest thing he'd ever seen. As if she sensed his interest, she glanced over her shoulder. His heart skipped a beat. He let the curtain drop.

He returned to the dining room and rubbed his hands together. This was the first time since coming to Deadwood three years ago he held hope for his future, one he hoped would include Miss Suzanna Lindstrom.

HOW DARE THE MAN MAKE her look like a fool. Barely paying any attention to the short, stocky school board member strutting beside her, she seethed. Owner of the restaurant and hotel, indeed. Her cheeks were hot enough to cook eggs on. A tear rolled down her cheek. The audacity. The impudence. The rudeness. The least he could have done was tell her he was the owner of the hotel before dousing her with ice-cold water last night.

"Miss Lindstrom?" Mr. Ogden broke into her thoughts. "You need to be careful crossing the streets. We had a rainy spring and, with the snow melt from the hills, the mud is quite bad."

Hmph. After yesterday, as if he, and probably the entire town, didn't know. However, she was raised to mind her p's and q's and to respect her elders. "Thank you, Mr. Ogden. I appreciate your consideration." It wasn't quite what she was thinking but getting on the wrong side of a school board member wouldn't be a good idea.

Was that a chuckle coming from behind her? Was Julia laughing at her? Probably. They generally got along, but her older sister by one year grew more and more bossy the closer they got to Deadwood. And calling her uppity like Julia had last night? Well . . . she straightened her spine a bit more. It was simply preposterous.

Was it wrong of her to not want people to find out about their hardscrabble farm in Iowa, where her parents still lived with their remaining eight children? Was it wrong to want more than becoming attached to some man and work and slave from dawn until dusk and have a child nearly every year? Not that her parents weren't in love, they were. But why was a woman supposed to do all the household chores, plus help in the barn, when the man only had to take care of the outdoor work?

The men tipping their hats at her and Julia certainly weren't the type she'd want to set her cap on. Rugged, dirty, smelly, and dressed in worn-out clothes. Suzanna kept her eyes away from them. If she didn't acknowledge them, they wouldn't get any ideas. Would they? Besides, she had a year's teaching contract to fulfill. Part of it specified she couldn't marry or spend unaccompanied time with a man. A vision of the surprisingly handsome Mr. Winson flashed through her mind. Handsome or not, he certainly wasn't in her future plans.

"We're nearly at the school," Mr. Ogden said, removing his hat and wiping perspiration from his forehead with a red handkerchief. "It certainly warmed up this morning, didn't it?"

"C'mon, Julia," Suzanna called over her shoulder, "we're almost there." Excitement filled her. Her first real teaching position was almost at hand. Having her own schoolhouse had been a dream ever since she began teaching her younger siblings their numbers and letters. The proudest moment of her life had been when she earned her teaching certificate. Julia had hers, too, but didn't have the passion or patience to work with children. Her sister would rather be sewing.

"Well, Miss Lindstrom, what do you think?" Mr. Ogden said, taking her elbow to stop her from walking headlong into a clapboard building.

Suzanna raised shaking fingers to her mouth. "My goodness." Two stories tall, the yellow school building stood in a grove of trees on a small knoll, more than likely to keep it from flooding. Lush, green grass provided a safe play area for recesses. Either the building was brand new, or someone had given it a fresh coat of paint. A long rope hanging from the bell tower swayed in the morning breeze, the clapper's tone nothing more than a soft ping.

The double doors stood wide as if greeting her with welcoming arms. Sheer curtains flapped through the open windows. A set of wooden stairs rose on the outside of the building, leading to the second level. This was nothing like their small school back home in Iowa.

"Oh, my." Suzanna said, her heart racing. What had she gotten herself into? "Two stories? Am I expected to teach children on two different levels?"

Ogden shook his head and grinned. "No, Miss Lindstrom. The way this town is growing, the businessmen who cared to become involved decided we should look ahead to the future. We built a school to accommodate the future children. The upper story will be for older students. For now, you'll be using only the first floor. As there are more students, we'll add another teacher."

Suzanna let out a breath. How horrible it would be having to run up and down the stairs to teach different grade levels. Chaos would certainly ensue if she left the children alone for any amount of time on either floor.

"Shall we go inside?" Mr. Ogden swept a hand toward the entrance. "Be careful to not brush up against the walls. We've been trying to get the paint to dry." He gestured toward a set of three stairs. "Some idiot thought he needed to thicken the paint because he didn't think it would cover in one coat. Now it is taking forever to dry."

"Suz," Julia said from the bottom step, "you can investigate by yourself. I'll wait out here. After all, it's your domain."

It was considerate of Julia to stay out of the way, but she'd better not investigate their new home without her. Instead of taking the stairs two at a time into the building like she wanted, she followed Mr. Ogden at a sedate, teacherly manner.

A long, narrow hallway would serve as the cloakroom. Rows of hooks, some high, some low, lined the wall on either side of the door. Shelves above the hooks made a place for the children's lunch pails. She'd make sure the boys used one side and the girls the other. Hopefully the students had better lunches than the lard sandwiches she and her siblings had to stave off hunger during the long day at school.

Another set of doors led into the classroom which was every bit as big as it appeared from the outside. Three rows of double desks with an aisle between ran from the back of the room to the front, making room for at least thirty students.

Suzanna ran a finger over each, progressively smaller, desk as she strolled down the aisle to the front where an oak desk stood on a platform. Someone had polished the top of the desk until it gleamed like a new copper penny. If she were to sit on it, she'd probably slide right off and land in a lump on the solid floor.

Rows of bookshelves, filled with primers, lined the outside walls. Above the bookshelves was a picture of George Washington, with the American flag with its thirty-eight stars hanging beside it. A large, wooden cross and a map of the United States and its territories were tacked to the opposite wall. A gleaming potbelly stove stood sentinel in a corner, its stovepipe reaching into the ceiling.

Suzanna picked up a piece of chalk, stood before the blackboard behind her desk, took a deep breath, then printed her name, and repeated it in cursive. Unable to keep in a smile, she grinned and pulled the wooden chair from under the desk, sat down and opened drawers. A couple had quill pens, more chalk, chalk erasers, paper, and additional slates inside. She closed the drawers and folded her hands on the top of the desk.

"When will school start, Mr. Ogden?" Suzanna's words echoed over the rows of wooden desks holding individual slates.

"The students have been without a teacher for several months, and we're hoping to start as soon as possible, but we'd like you and your sister to get settled in. Today is Thursday. We're aiming for Monday, if you can be ready by then."

"I certainly will be." She'd be ready if she had to stay up all day and night between now and then. She couldn't wait to use her skills and knowledge to help the young of Deadwood learn.

Mr. Ogden had no idea there wasn't much to settle. Even though their mother had made sure they had nice clothes, there wasn't much of anything else. With only a carpetbag each, settling would take approximately fifteen minutes each, if that.

Mr. Ogden checked his timepiece. "Are you ready to see your new home?"

Instead of going through the front door, Mr. Ogden surprised her by walking down the aisle between the desks, past her desk, and out a door in the back of the room she hadn't noticed.

"This is a shortcut to your house," he added, steering her down a wooden, tree-lined path.

Julia stood under a large maple tree. Wouldn't it be wonderful to have classes beneath it while the weather was warm? "C'mon, Julia," she said taking her sister's elbow and squeezing it against her side, "we're going to see the house now. Isn't this exciting? You did wait for us, didn't you?"

"Of course, I did," Julia said, a bit of irritation in her voice. "I said I would, didn't I?"

Mr. Ogden stopped and pointed to four buildings off to the side of the walkway. One was a stable for students who arrived by horseback. A smaller building to its right held a small stack of wood. It would more than likely be filled by the time winter set in. One of the jobs of being a teacher was getting the stove fired-up in the morning. She'd assign older boys to keep it going during the day.

Set back from the stable and woodshed were two buildings, each with a half-moon carved into the doors. The necessaries. One had a girl with pigtails painted on it and one with a boy holding a slingshot. Would she and Julia have to use the girls or have their own closer to the house?

"Let's move on, ladies. I have an important meeting to attend in half an hour."

Suzanna gasped when the small house, painted the same color as the schoolhouse, appeared in a grove of trees. But unlike the schoolhouse, the trim was green. A front door, the same color as the trim, stood between two tall windows. White lacy curtains fluttered through open windows.

She'd expected a house similar to the sod structure they grew up in where twelve people had been crammed to the rafters, where the glass windows were so distorted everything looked wavy and misshapen. This house was as close to a soddy as a dictionary was to a primer. She squeezed Julia's arm. "Is this really ours?" she whispered. It had to be the home of a banker or lawyer or someone rich.

Julia blinked away the tears in her eyes. "I sure hope so," she whispered back. "If this is a joke, Mr. Ogden is going to get a piece of my mind."

"Shhh, Julia. He'll hear you."

"Welcome home, Misses Lindstrom," he said, bowing at the waist. "The parents of your students along with the school board hope you'll be comfortable here. I'll leave you to settle in." Slapping his hat onto his bald pate, he strode down the sidewalk toward town.

Suzanna opened the door and stood in the doorway, her fingers at her lips. "Oh, my, Julia. This is a palace."

Julia followed her into the house and stood behind her.

"Can you believe this?" Suzanna whispered, as if someone might overhear her excitement. "After seeing the awful streets and haphazard buildings in town, I expected to be living in a soddy." Giggling, arms stretched wide, she spun in a circle then stopped to get a better look at their new home.

The front door led to a large, fully furnished room. Two dark green, high-backed, padded chairs book ended a sofa in the same color and fabric. A rocking chair sat in a corner near a tall window. A black stove with shining metal trim stood in the corner, a ribbed, black bucket of coal beside it. A multi-colored braided rug, probably made from leftover material, covered the center of the room, edged by gray painted wooden floors.

Three doors led from the main room. The open door to the right revealed a large bed covered in a patchwork quilt. Another door to the left exposed a bed with a similar quilt. Two bedrooms? She and Julia wouldn't have to share a bed? She pressed her fingers to her lips. For as long as she could remember, they'd slept in the same bed, fighting for territory and covers. It was worse when one of their younger sisters joined them. It was difficult to recall a time when she didn't have to cling to the edge of the bed to keep from falling to the floor or having to push their younger sister's feet from their faces when she started sleeping with her head at the wrong end of the bed.

A swinging door, closest to the front door, called to her. "Julia, I'm going to check out the kitchen," she said, leaving her sister standing in the middle of the living room, silent, probably in shock at not having to share a bedroom.

Chapter Three

Anxious to find out what the Lindstrom sisters thought of the school and their new home, King raced around the men loitering around downtown. Had Miss Suzanna given Mr. Ogden a hard time or was she all sweet and nice beneath her snippy demeanor? He didn't blame her for being upset with him, but yesterday's incident wasn't his fault.

What kind of teacher would she be? Ill- or sweet-tempered? A taskmistress or easygoing? Strong or wimpy? Would she be able to handle the older boys, who were bigger and stronger? Another question was whether she'd last longer than the previous teachers.

King ignored the men taunting the man known as The Bottle Fiend. Why people were so mean to the man was beyond him. Yes, his clothes were nothing but rags, and he smelled like an animal who had died weeks before. Once he'd given the man money for a bath and clean clothes, but for some reason he preferred his smelly, disreputable ways. But, in his opinion, the man did a service to Deadwood by picking up the bottles and cigar butts men tossed carelessly into the streets.

The one time he'd accompanied Daniel to The Bottle Fiend's hovel, the odor had hit them square in the face a good block away, making their eyes water. The building was surrounded by the thousands of bottles he stored in barrels. King had stayed outside, letting Daniel talk to the man. The scent had lingered on his friend for several minutes on their walk back to town.

King tipped his hat to two ladies passing him on the boardwalk. Because of the piles of old rags, codfish boxes, clothes, and gunnysacks inside, Daniel hadn't made it past the doorway. How the ramshackle walls were able to hold up the roof covered with hundreds of rusty kerosene cans, was beyond him.

Colin Haywood came from his store and clapped King on the back. "Hey, King. What's your hurry?"

"I'm heading to Dan's to see if he's heard how the new schoolmarm and her sister like their place." King didn't miss Colin's grin. "What?"

"Just recalling you and the little lady falling into the street yesterday."

"Wasn't funny."

Colin rocked back on his heels. "That's your opinion. Personally, I thought it was hilarious. Will the little filly stick around for a year, or did you scare her off?"

King clenched his fists. All he needed now was for the sisters to leave town and have the folks blame him. Hell, what the town needed to do was round up the roaming dogs. After all, it was their fault. "For the sake of the children, I hope she sticks out her year. I'd hate to see all the time and money we spent enticing a teacher to come here go to waste." He gave his friend a dirty look. "I gotta go." He took two steps, turned back, and pointed a finger at Colin. "And if she leaves, it won't be my fault."

He wasn't kidding about hoping the teacher stayed. It had taken more than a large amount of reasoning with the men to convince them Deadwood could afford to pay the woman to travel to an unknown, still rather lawless town, plus provide housing for her and her sister. They finally agreed with the stipulation she had to teach for one year.

He couldn't blame the school board for being nervous. After all, the last three teachers hadn't worked out. The first teacher hadn't taught one day before disappearing, probably to seek his fortune in gold. A year ago, the next teacher, the wife of a miner, Minnie Callison, was found murdered in her bed. It was doubtful, but he hoped the new teacher wouldn't hear about the unsolved murder. The last teacher made the mistake of using pocket novels to teach. After being dismissed, she soon found a husband to support her. Supposedly it was love at first sight.

While he wasn't a fan the idea of falling in love simply by seeing a woman, he couldn't deny the jolt to his heart at a spruced-up Suzanna. Amazing what a bit of water had done to clean her up. Her eyes, a light blue, sparked with anger when she'd realized he was the man she'd called all sorts of names and dumped water over her. King chuckled out loud, drawing the attention of a few men loitering outside Al Swearingen's Gem Theater.

"Going crazy?" one man yelled.

"Talking to himself was how The Bottle Fiend started out. First sign of turning into an idiot," Al called out, slapping a nearby man on the back, nearly sending him toppling into the street.

If they wanted a fight, they were going to be disappointed. He had no time for men who did nothing but drink and whore around. After crossing the street, he opened the street-level door to Daniel's office located above the bank. He took the stairs two at a time, and, without knocking, entered Daniel's small office.

Daniel sat behind his desk, his feet propped on the desk, hands behind his head. Ogden was standing, his black, derby hat in his hands.

"I'd best be getting back to . . ." Ogden was saying.

Ogden was leaving already? Were they done discussing the sisters? "Off to where?" King asked, interrupting Ogden.

"The wife is whining about coming to town. She claims the bottoms of two of her cooking pots are ready to drop off. I promised her I'd take her to the tinsmith to see if they can be repaired. If not, I'll have to take her to Jensen and Bliss' Hardware to get new ones. If'n I don't do it today, she says I'll be eating my supper raw."

Daniel rose, tugged down the edges of his dark blue brocade vest, slipped on a black dress jacket, and plopped his hat on his head. He followed Ogden to the door and turned the handle. "Damn doorknob."

"When the hell is your landlord going to fix that thing?" King asked. Daniel had lived above the bank for nearly three years and the doorknob hadn't worked right the entire time.

"I don't know," Daniel said, turning the loose knob left then right. "I've asked him about a dozen times to repair it. I offered to do it myself, but he won't let me."

When Daniel finally finagled the doorknob and opened the door, Ogden stopped and slapped the doorframe. "Jumpin' Jeehosofat. I'll be losin' my mind if I'm not careful. Mary said to tell everyone about the party at the schoolhouse Saturday to welcome the new teacher. The women are making food and such. Starts at five o'clock. Clyde is bringing his fiddle, George his guitar, and Zeb the washboard."

"Sounds fun. Has anyone told the Lindstrom sisters about it?" Daniel asked.

Ogden scratched his head. "I didn't, but someone should." Ogden followed his friends down the stairs.

"Where're you headed, Dan?" King asked, nearly falling over as he reversed directions to trail after Dan when he left the building.

"Ogden took the new schoolmarm and her sister to the school and their house but didn't bother to tell them where to buy supplies." Daniel stopped at the edge of the boardwalk waiting for a wagon pulled by two oxen to pass, their heads down as they forced their legs through the mud. "I thought I'd stop by and escort the ladies to Haywood's Dry Goods and tell them about the dance. Why don't you come along?"

King hesitated before stepping into the mud to cross the street. He'd already crossed the streets a few times this morning, but each time he was reminded of yesterday's fiasco. "Um, sure."

"You're not afraid to see the new schoolmarm again, are you?"

King chuckled. "She sure is a feisty one."

"Which one? The teacher or her sister?"

They stepped to the side then tipped their hats to the banker, J.W. Woods, a man King despised, and his wife, Bertha. Deep down he knew the pompous jackass was a crook. But because a man believing people should bow and kiss his boots because he owned a bank, didn't mean he was doing anything illegal. It was only a sense he had. And with them vying for land, there was no love lost between them. When King had purchased land outside of town that Woods coveted, the tension had grown.

"Heard about your little encounter with the new teacher, King," Woods rolled back on his heels and smirked. "Poor woman. But then what could we expect from our illustrious hotel owner? Good thing you didn't drown her."

As if she were a coquette thirty years younger, Mrs. Woods flicked her fan wide, waved it in front of her face, and giggled. "I want to thank you again, Mr. Iverson, for escorting me to my husband's bank. J.W. appreciates it, too, don't you, James?"

J.W. ran a hand over his face. "Uh, yeah, sure, dumplin'."

King clenched his fists at his sides. It must bother Woods having to thank someone for helping him out. He strutted down the boardwalks as if he was better than everyone, tipping his hats to the ladies, acting like a gentleman. But on more than one occasion he'd seen the man going upstairs to visit the prostitutes. Would his carousing change with his wife in town? He ground his teeth together. How he'd love to toss the arrogant bastard into the street and watch him try to get his fat ass out. He held back a chuckle at the thought of Woods rolling around like a pig trying to gain purchase to stand.

Mrs. Woods tugged on her husband's arm. "James, you promised to take me to lunch. I'm famished."

King bit back a grin. "Going to my place?"

Woods tugged at his lapel and puffed out his chest. "Not likely. I wouldn't want my precious to be poisoned."

Once again Daniel held King back. "He's not worth it, King," he whispered to his friend. "Let him go to Oyster Bay." He turned to the couple. "Have a good lunch. Ma'am, Woods." With a tug on King's arm, they headed down the boardwalk, their boots thudding on the worn wood.

"Watch out for mud puddles and dogs, King," Woods called out behind them.

King's clenched his teeth. "Bastard."

"You got that right, but don't give him the satisfaction of seeing you angry. The only thing he cares about is himself."

After tipping their hats to a couple of ladies, King stood beside Daniel, then hesitated before stepping into another muddy street, an action Daniel unfortunately didn't ignore. He had a feeling his friend would tease him about it until they were so old neither could cross a street without a cane.

He chuckled, slapping his friend on the back. "Afraid?"

"Hell. Wouldn't you be?" Nothing more was said while they maneuvered through the muck. "Do you realize how many buckets of ice-cold water it took to clean myself off?" he asked when they safely reached the other side.

They walked past wooden buildings looking that looked as though one-eyed drunks had constructed them. "Why didn't you order a hot bath in your room?"

"Are you kidding? Leona would have shot me if I'd tracked mud into her—I mean my hotel. You know how particular she is about the place."

Even though Leona was his younger sister by one year, she'd let herself become a spinster and cracked the whip to make sure King's Inn was the best-kept establishment in Deadwood. When she'd first arrived to help King, Daniel had talked about courting her. He had to admit she was attractive—until she opened her mouth to give orders, expecting everyone to jump at her words. He wished she'd act more like their docile mother who'd given up on her daughter ever marrying and giving her grandchildren. Hell, there probably wasn't a man in the entire territory who'd put up with her strong personality.

Daniel picked up speed. King stopped at the edge of the school property. What was his friend's hurry?

"What the hell are you dragging your heels for?" Daniel asked when the buildings came into view. "You're not afraid the little filly will call you names again, are you?" He faced King, tipped his head to the side, and raised an eyebrow. "You reckon where those women stayed last night?"

King stomped from foot to foot shucking away the mud from his boots. "I . . . Um . . ."

"Spit it out man, the day's not getting any longer, you know."

"They stayed at my hotel."

"So, why does that have your spurs rubbing your ass?"

There was nothing to do but explain what happened, especially when Miss Lindstrom would probably string him up by the fingernails when she saw him. "Well . . . Um . . . Remember those buckets of water I said it took to wash away the mud?"

"Yeah?"

"Well, I might have accidentally on purpose dumped a bucket over the teacher's head."

Daniel's widened his eyes and gaped. "You what? Why the hell would you do that?" He held up a hand. "Wait, I don't want to know."

"Thanks. But she got her comeuppance this morning." Anyway, he thought it was comeuppance.

"What did you do?"

"I didn't do anything except show up at their table and introduce myself as the owner." King's grinned. "She barely said a word before scurrying out the door to meet Ogden."

Daniel shook his head. "Hopefully I won't have to pick up what's left of you when she cuts you to pieces this morning." Daniel grinned. "Well, let's get going so we can get them to the store before lunch."

King sighed and tipped his hat back on his head. "When you suggested it, I thought coming along would be a good idea. Now, I'm not so sure."

"You're a big, brave man." Daniel slapped King on the back. "Hell, you've been known to wrestle with a bear. I'm sure you can handle one tiny schoolteacher. Can't you?"

He sure as hell hoped so.

Chapter Four

Suzanna stood in the kitchen, eyeing the array of goods on the wooden table centered in the middle of the room. "What are we going to eat?" she yelled to Julia. "There are a lot of cakes and loaves of bread probably left by parents, but I don't see anything else."

"How much money do we have?" Julia called back.

Suzanna came through the kitchen door, carrying her pale-yellow purse. Julia had made their pouches from leftover blouse material. Hers was a pale yellow, while Julia's was a light blue. As a seamstress, her sister was handy with a needle and economical when it came to using every scrap of material she could get her hands on. Suzanna knelt on the floor beside Julia's legs and dumped out her purse.

"I have a grand total of fifteen dollars and . . . thirty cents." Suzanna said, resting back on her legs. "How much do you have?"

Julia sighed. "A bit more. Remember how I patched clothes and made a quilt for old Mr. Robinson back home? He was so happy, he paid me extra, so I have twenty-two dollars and eleven cents."

"That gives us thirty-seven dollars and forty-one cents." Suzanna bit her bottom lip. "Will it be enough? I don't get paid for an entire month." In the short time since leaving home, she had begun to understand her parents' worry about money. With so many children to feed, it must have worn on them something fierce, but she'd never heard them complain.

"Except for food, nearly anything else we'll need to cook is in the kitchen. I believe the parents want me to stay."

"We have sheets, pillows, blankets, coal, and more furniture than we've had our entire lives." Julia returned her money to her purse. "That means we'll only have to purchase food."

"Can we buy some material? When we stopped at the way stations, I noticed how outdated and backcountry our clothes are."

Julia pulled the purse strings tight. "You saw that, too? We'll have to see what the stores in town have for fabric. I want to dress up a bit more, too, to impress women like Mrs. Woods. I imagine she has influence in this town and could help me get work."

Suzanna ran a hand down her dark blue skirt. Would a town filled with ill-kempt, dirty men have any type of material Julia could use? Surely the few ladies in town needed to buy fabric somewhere. "I'm sure my skirts and blouses will be fine for teaching, but we need clothes a bit more special for church and social functions. If we tell the women you made the clothes you should get some orders."

"Let's come up with a shopping list." Julia stood and brushed out her skirt. "We don't want to buy what we don't need. Did you happen to see a general store when we came into town?"

Suzanna shuddered. "No. I was too busy trying to keep Mr. Silverstone's hands off me and observing the riffraff roaming around." After seeing buildings looking as if they had been built by drunks, grimy men, and the women hanging from second-floor balconies, she wondered if they had made a mistake in coming to Deadwood? Should she have taken a teaching position somewhere more civilized? But then, the civilized towns already had teachers.

"Not to mention taking a spill in the mud."

"Please, don't remind me." Suzanna wrinkled her nose. "If I ever see the brute again, it'll be too soon."

"Just remember he owns a hotel and eatery."

"That doesn't make him a gentleman," Suzanna said, sniffing. "Is there anything to write with?"

Julia stood and pointed to a small desk in one corner of the room. "Maybe there's something on this desk."

On the top were paper and an item resembling a pen, but without the quill. A tan cork stood out on a familiar bottle of black ink. Back home, they were still using quills.

"What's this?" Julia asked.

"Oh, that's one of those fountain pens. I saw one in the store in Drakesville when I went to town with Pa."

"How does it work?" Julia asked, fingering the black pen with a pointed tip.

After showing her sister how to draw ink into the pen, Julia took it and tapped the end to her lips. Suzanna could almost hear the wheels turning in her head.

"Let's see. What do we need?"

"Flour, sugar, eggs, milk, spices, lard, beans, rice," Suzanna suggested.

"And saleratus to make bread and rolls." Again, Julia tapped the pen against her lips. "Bacon, beef, and chicken. Cheese."

"Vegetables, fruit."

"If they have them."

"I wonder if we'll have time to plant a garden for food for the winter." Suzanna held her breath. It wasn't a secret her sister hated gardening—from planting the seeds, to weeding, and then harvesting and preparing food for the winter. She, on the other hand, enjoyed the menial tasks, especially if they took her away from helping with the younger kids.

That wasn't to say she didn't like children. She did. It was why she'd become a teacher. But, in her opinion, her siblings were little terrors. And there always was a baby or one on the way. There was no way she was going to fall for a man and become a slave to housework and children. A picture of Mr. Winson came to mind. Especially not a slave to some disreputable, low-down skunk.

Julia sighed. "I'll put seeds on my list."

Suzanna rose, pulled aside the sheer curtains, and peered out the window. "We'll have to ask, but it looks as if there is enough space in the yard to put in a garden. Maybe a few flowers, too." She dropped the curtain and settled onto the other chair. "How are we going to get to the store?" She frowned. "I don't relish the idea of trudging through the mud again, nor coming into contact with those degenerates. Who knows what they'd do to us?"

"I can't imagine anyone accosting us in broad daylight."

She huffed a breath. They'd traveled in the daylight, but it hadn't stopped Mr. Silverstone from trying to take advantage of her. Not to mention the encounter with Mr. Winson—even if it probably was an accident on his part. "After yesterday, I'm not so sure."

"The biggest question is how we'd get our purchases back here. It's quite a list."

"Will they deliver?" She couldn't imagine having to carry their purchases from town back to their house.

"I don't know, but it would be nice." Julia folded the list and put it in her coin bag. "It's not like we're miles from town. But we still have to get to the stores and have no idea which one is the best."

Suzanna checked a clock sitting on the desk. "It's nearly lunchtime. Maybe we should venture out. If we have enough coin left, we could stop somewhere and eat."

"At King's? Hoping to run into the owner again?"

"Certainly not!" Suzanna's cheeks heated at the sound of her own screech. "If I ever see the clod again, it'll be too soon."

"The lady doth protest too much, methinks."

Suzanna stomped to the kitchen. "Oh, hush up." Someone rapped on the front door. She hesitated in the doorway, then continued into the room. Who could be coming to visit? They hadn't met anyone. Had Mr. Ogden returned to tell them this house was simply a joke? Did they have to move? In the short time they'd been in the house, she'd already come to love it, and she hadn't even seen her bedroom yet.

Wait. Maybe it was a parent. Should she answer the door in case it was? Nah. Julia could. If it was a parent, she should freshen up a bit to make a good impression.

She stopped pumping water into a pan. What if it was someone who knew there were two young women living alone. What if they intended to rob them—or worse? Ma and Pa had warned them about men with nefarious intentions. She'd better make sure there were sturdy locks on the front and back doors and the windows.

Another knock reverberated through the room.

"Why don't you answer the door?" Suzanna asked, wiping her hands on a towel as she came from the kitchen.

"Um . . . because . . ."

"Oh, for heaven's sake." Suzanna pursed her lips. What was Julia's problem? "Answer the door. What if it's Mrs. Woods or one of the other important ladies from town coming to meet me?" Without giving Julia a chance to speak, Suzanna opened the door then immediately slammed it shut. "It's . . . it's . . ." She pointed a shaking finger at the door. "That man. The oaf. The defiler of women."

Julia rolled her eyes. "He didn't defile you any more than he did me. And he was a perfect gentleman this morning."

Suzanna crossed her arms over her chest. "I don't care. Don't you dare open the door."

"Since you've already opened it, it would be rude to leave the man standing on our front step." Julia took a deep breath. "Mr. Winson. What a nice surprise."

"Obviously, your sister doesn't think so." He glanced over Julia's shoulder at Suzanna, his eyes twinkling with laughter.

Before Suzanna could protest the man's presence, Julia pulled the door wider and swept a hand to the living room. "Please come in. We were discussing what we need from the general store." She closed the door and stood beside Suzanna.

Something akin to a butterfly's wings fluttered in her chest. Heat rose to her face. How dare he show his face here? He wore the same clothes as he had this morning. His mustache wiggled as if he were trying to keep from laughing at her. He'd removed his black cowboy hat and twisted the brim in his hands. He was as handsome as he was this morning. She held back a snort. What did she expect—that he'd turned into an ogre in the past few hours?

A vision of him throwing the ice-cold bucket of water at her last night flew threw her brain, snapping her from the idea Mr. Winson being handsome. She turned her attention from his sparkling eyes to the man beside him.

He was as tall and slim as Mr. Winson. Maybe his shoulders weren't as broad, or chest as powerful looking. Maybe his clothing or dark, wavy hair weren't as impeccable as the cad's. Unlike the defiler's perfect nose, this man's nose was crooked, as if he'd been in a brawl or two. His smile revealed twin dimples. She didn't care for dimples on a man, thought they made them look too feminine. There was nothing feminine about Mr. Winson. Like his friend, he held his cowboy hat and turned the brim over and over in his hands. Did men do that when they were nervous?

The man kept his sight on Julia, who in turn seemed mesmerized by him. The man's face was nearly as red as Julia's. Men blushed? She bet her bottom dollar Mr. Winson didn't blush. He was too strong. Too virile. She toyed with a ribbon at her throat. What was wrong with her? Why was her stomach jumping as if it was filled with frogs?

"Misses Lindstrom." Mr. Winson finally said, breaking what was becoming an uncomfortable silence. "You may remember me from this morning." His lips twitched as if he were trying not to smile. "And this is my good friend, Daniel Iverson. We came to escort you to town."

Mr. Iverson bowed as if he were in the presence of royalty, and not a schoolteacher and her sister.

Julia tipped her head at the men. "Mr. Iverson. Mr. Winson."

Mr. Winson kept his eyes on Suzanna, making the unexpected fluttering speed up. Was she getting ill? The man was a rake. A scalawag. A . . . He probably made women feel sick on a daily basis.

"Please, call me King. We don't hold with Eastern society rules out here in the West."

"And call me Daniel," Mr. Iverson said.

"I'm Julia and this is my sister, Suzanna. Thank you for your offer but I'm sure you have other things to do. We can manage ourselves."

"Excuse me, Julia," Mr. Iverson said. "But you're new here to Deadwood and . . ."

He paused and stared at Julia as if he'd forgotten how to speak. Did they have to worry they were in the presence of a man not quite right in the head? Should she make a dash for the kitchen and get a knife for protection?

"And what?" Julia asked before Suzanna had a chance to make a run for it.

"Um." He slapped his hat against his leg. "You aren't aware of the riffraff in town."

"Based on what we saw yesterday coming through town, I believe we have a good idea of what Deadwood is like," Julia said.

King rolled back on his heels as if he were bestowing his manly knowledge on two brainless women. All he needed to do to complete the picture of his pomposity in her head was to hold his lapels with his hands and strut like some preening peacock.

"Seeing is different than experiencing Deadwood," he said. "Yesterday, you barely had a chance to take in the, uh . . ." He licked his lips. "Uh, scenery before you were escorted to the hotel. While Deadwood is settling down and this side of town is quiet, no woman walking alone downtown is completely safe."

"Ladies, I agree with King." Daniel's chest heaved as he took a deep breath. "Please allow us escort you. We can either carry your purchases back here or help secure delivery."

"I don't want to go with them," she whispered to Julia, who squeezed her fingers. What was it about King that rattled her? And it wasn't the incident from yesterday. How could one man go from looking like the lowest, most downtrodden cad, making her so mad she could spit, to cleaning up into a handsome cad, making her insides tremble?

King bowed his head. "I assure you we only have your best interests at heart. We want to make sure you get to the store and home safely. We'll also," he winked at her, "make sure you navigate our muddy streets undamaged."

They probably would be safer with escorts, but why did it have to be Mr. Winson?

Julia took Suzanna's arm and tugged her to the other side of the room. "I think we should accept their offer."

"Are you crazy? I don't want to have anything to do with Mr. Winson."

"So you've said a million times. But remember Mr. Silverstone from the stage? What if he accosts you? Remember the drunks we saw yesterday and the noises coming from the saloons on the way to the hotel? What if someone hurts us? We'd be better off with these men than wandering around on our own."

Suzanna glanced over her shoulder and tapped a finger against her lips. "I suppose you're right, but you're walking with Mr. Winson."

"Why don't we walk side-by-side and let the gentlemen walk behind us?" Julia suggested. "That way we wouldn't have to walk with either of them."

"Or talk to them. Or look at them."

"Ladies." Daniel pulled out his pocket watch. "If we hurry along, you can shop, take lunch at King's restaurant, and we'd have plenty of time to escort you back home."

Julia nodded. "All right, gentlemen. Let us gather our bonnets and purses and you may show us the way to the store."

Biting her bottom lip, Suzanna tied her yellow bonnet and slipped her purse string over her wrist. They'd better not be making a mistake.

King slapped on his hat. "Ladies." He held the door and gave her a quick wink.

The butterflies in her stomach increased twofold. Yeah. This might be a big mistake.

Chapter Five

"So, what do you think?" King whispered to Daniel as they followed the two sisters down the boardwalk. Except for subtle differences, the women looked so much alike, they could be twins. The older sister was a shade taller than the schoolteacher and her hair a touch lighter. Now that they were in the sun and she wasn't covered in mud, evidence of red highlights from the curls peeking from her bonnet were apparent. They both walked ramrod straight as if they were afraid to relax.

Suzanna was a bit young, and as pretty as she was, having problems with a few of the older schoolboys could be an issue. A wave of protectiveness washed over him. He'd make darn sure they didn't give her any trouble.

Daniel nearly tripped on a loose board. "About what?"

"The women, that's what."

"Other than the fact the teacher cleaned up nicely, I haven't thought anything."

King slapped him on the arm. "Are you kidding me? Are you blind? They're pretty and have nice figures. The teacher seems a bit prickly, but I believe I'm in love."

Daniel stopped, making King change directions again. "Have you lost your mind? You only met the woman yesterday and, may I remind you, under rather unfavorable conditions."

"Yeah, well. There's something about her that," King placed a hand over his heart and batted his eyelashes like he'd seen flirty women do, "sets my heart on fire."

With a grunt, Daniel double-stepped to catch up to the women. "*Sets your heart on fire?* Jeez. Have you been reading Lord Byron again?" Shaking his head, he strode beside the women. "Ladies, we're getting closer to downtown. It would be safer if we were to walk beside you, so the men in town understand you're with us."

Julia stuck her nose in the air. "We'll be fine, Mr. Iverson," she said, hooking her arm through her sister's.

Before she'd taken a few steps, Daniel took Julia by the arm and spun her around to face him.

Was his friend crazy? While he agreed with Daniel about keeping the women safe, he had a feeling Miss Julia had a spark of fire in her. She would probably give Daniel a piece of her mind, or worse.

Julia flared her nostrils. "Mr. Iverson, unhand me this instant."

"As much as I want to, I'll not release you until you and your sister listen to me."

King stood behind Suzanna, folded his arms over his chest, and grinned. It was going to be interesting to see how Daniel was going to manage to extricate himself from this one. His friend was braver than he was.

"Mr. Iverson, if you don't let go of my arm, I'm going to scream so loud and so long, some gentleman in this town will surely come to our rescue."

"And I'll join her," Suzanna added, slapping her hands at her waist.

King tipped his hat back on his head. While he didn't mind a strong-willed woman— hell his mother and sisters were— these two were acting plain stupid. But as he valued his life, he wasn't going to say so. Let Daniel explain how dangerous certain men, and women, could be.

Hell, if Al Swearingen, the dance hall owner of the Gem Theater, were to set his sights on the sisters, they'd be gone in a flash, spending their time on their backs, servicing as many men as Swearingen could get through their rooms in one night. The man had no morals. Didn't care that he lied to women when he went on one of his recruiting trips back east. Thinking they were being hired as waitresses and might find a husband in the predominantly male population, they jumped at the chance at an adventure. Whether the women wanted their help or not, it was his and Daniel's duty to keep them safe.

Daniel sighed and pointed a finger at Julia. "Both of you listen to me. Life back in Iowa is significantly more civilized than here. There are men in this town who don't care that you're genteel women. With so many more men than women, there are those who will see you for only one thing. How can I make you understand you're not safe on the streets alone or together?"

Beside him, Suzanna huffed in a breath and her sister's face turned pale. Had they *finally* understood they weren't safe on their own? Suzanna hugged her purse to her chest.

"Is what he's saying true?" she asked in a soft voice. "Is it truly that bad in Deadwood?"

"Daniel doesn't lie, Miss Lindstrom," King said. "Unfortunately, he's hit the nail on the head. Unless escorted, women simply aren't safe." He didn't quite hear what her reply was, but it sounded like *what have I gotten myself into* before Suzanna took her sister's arm. Hopefully they'd scared the women enough to listen to them, but not enough to make the teacher decide to leave before school was in session.

Daniel removed his hat and raked his fingers through his hair. "Miss Julia."

"Oh, for heaven's sake, Mr. Iverson. Let's go so we can get our shopping done. My sister has a lot of work to do to get ready for the children on Monday." She glanced over her shoulder at him. "You do want her to be prepared, don't you?"

King nudged Daniel in the side. "Let them have their way, or we'll never get to Haywood's. We can only hope no one accosts them."

"I hate to say this, but maybe it would be a good thing if someone did. Teach the teacher and her sister a lesson."

"Maybe." King shrugged and swept his hand toward the sisters. "Ladies, lead on."

DIVIDING HIS ATTENTION between watching over Suzanna and the men loitering on the streets made King's eyes hurt. At least he knew Daniel would guard Julia, so his attention wasn't split one more time. They passed several men giving out wolf whistles. King clenched his fists at his sides to keep from knocking them out.

Suzanna's skirt swept against his pant legs. King held in a moan. Getting this excited about a woman he'd knocked into the mud and barely spoke to this morning was ridiculous. What the heck was wrong with him? And had he really told Daniel he was in love? What an idiot.

As they approached the "Badlands" of Deadwood, the number of men milling around in front of buildings, mostly saloons, increased. From its humble beginning, it hadn't taken long for tens of thousands of men to appear in Deadwood Gulch. Whenever he'd spent time at his ranch and came back to town, the population had doubled.

From the tents and shanties put up by the first arrivals, to hastily constructed wooden saloons, brothels, and businesses, the area was a mix of Chinamen, Negroes, Irish, and men from every walk of life. Deadwood was a melting pot of people hoping to strike it rich.

Although one couldn't tell by the mud-filled streets and buildings thrown up as if men, after a night of carousing, had a hand in building them, the town was actually becoming a bit civilized. As more women joined the throng, they brought with them a sense of settling. There were still killings, rowdy drunks, houses of ill repute, and men out to make a quick buck, but the more affluent businessmen were banding together to organize the town and have building codes. In his mind, the only way to organize anything in this place would be to raze it to the ground and start over.

King stepped closer to Julia as they crossed Wall Street, the imaginary line between the "good" and "bad" sides of Deadwood. It was too bad they had to enter the "Badlands" to get to Haywood's Dry Goods or John Wallace Groceries. He hoped Daniel was planning on going to Haywood's. Besides being friends with Colin and Sadie, they ran a clean, respectable place. Wallace couldn't be trusted any further than he could spit.

The noise increased when they crossed into the Badlands. Nothing shut down. Brothels, dance halls, and saloons ran all day and night. Even though it was before lunchtime, the raucous calls of the prostitutes mixed with the tinny pounding of pianos, and men arguing or laughing. The scent of cigars, liquor, and unwashed bodies made his nose burn.

Four men lounged outside the Gem Theater doors, their rolled cigarettes tipping from the corner of their mouths.

"Well, look what we have here." One of the men pushed away from the wall and staggered toward them. "Two new ladies coming to work at ol' Ed's. I've a hanker'n for some fresh meat."

Daniel clenched his hands when one of the men tipped his hat at them. "Joe, you're drunk. These ladies are not what you think."

King put himself between the other men and Suzanna, while Daniel tugged Julia to his side. Suzanna clutched the side of his coat.

"Let me do the talking," Daniel said. "Now Joe, you and your buddies go back into the Gem." He reached into his vest pocket and pulled out a small coin. "I'll spring for a round of drinks."

Behind Daniel, Julia screamed. "Let go of me, you brute."

King held back Suzanna when she took a step toward her sister. "Let Daniel handle this."

Damn. Somehow, while he was dealing with Joe, Mingus Thoreson had snuck up and made a grab for her. "C'mon, sweetheart. How's about a little kiss?"

Daniel pulled out his gun. Keeping it trained on Joe and his buddies, he glanced over his shoulder, ready to come to her rescue. "Thoreson, remove your hands from the lady."

Before Daniel had a chance to react, Mingus grunted, clutched his crotch, fell to his knees and then to his side, rolling into a ball like an armadillo. Tears streaming down his face, he rocked from side to side. "I'll. Get. You. For. This. Bitch."

"Don't you dare ever touch me again, you brute." Julia faced her attacker, fingers clenched in fists, arms held in a boxer's pose.

Even though he had a good idea what happened, he had to ask. "What did she do?"

"What our mother taught us to do." Suzanna answered. "Kicked him where it'll hurt the worst."

Okay, so maybe he wasn't in love with this woman. If he wanted to get to know her better, he'd have to make sure to mind his manners and keep his hands to himself. The last thing he wanted was to be rolling around on the ground like old Mingus.

Giving each man a glare, Suzanna walked to her sister's side. "And that's not the only thing Ma and Pa taught us, so if you baboons get any more ideas about accosting us, you'd better think twice if you know what's good for you." She took Julia by the elbow. "C'mon, sister, let's go."

Daniel scrambled to catch up with them. "Ladies, wait. I'm impressed by what you did back there, but only a few men saw you in action, so you still need protection. It's one thing to be face-to-face with your attacker, but what if they came up from behind you? What would you do then?"

Julia narrowed her eyes. "Want me to demonstrate what I could do?"

King snickered when Daniel answered, "Uh. No."

"Thought so." She wove through a crowd of men, ignoring their catcalls and whistles.

After the noise outside, the relative quiet of the Haywood's Dry Goods Store was a welcome relief. The bell over the store's door had barely stopped ringing before the sisters went to the fabric piled in shelves along an inner wall.

King leaned against a table filled with mining equipment, ankles crossed, arms folded across his chest, and grinned. "I guess Julia gave you what-for, didn't she?"

"Shut up, King." Daniel copied King's stance. "And you shouldn't talk so smart. I don't see Suzanna treating you any better."

"That's true. But I'm not one to give up. The schoolteacher interests me. She cleans up right nice."

"I'd be careful if I were you. Remember the school board had her sign a year's contract. With the trouble we've had with teachers, I'd hate to see another one leave."

"Don't worry, I won't do anything to besmirch her reputation."

Suzanna held a piece of lavender fabric printed with pale yellow flowers to her sister's face. With their nearly identical coloring, the fabric would look as good on either one of them.

"Do you have any idea what Suzanna's sister is going to do?" King asked, taking a cigar from his breast pocket.

Tipping his hat at several women perusing the shelves, Daniel nudged his friend in the side. "Better not let Sadie see you with that thing. She'll go after you with a broom."

King slipped the cigar back into his pocket. "For a moment I forgot where we were."

"I don't know what Julia will do."

Suzanna put down the pretty fabric and picked up a piece resembling the mud in the streets.

"Lord, I hope they don't buy that dreadful material," King said.

"Me, either."

King chuckled. Guess they weren't going to get their wish. Sadie spread the sickly, brown material on the table, grabbed the scissors, then stopped. She said something to the sisters, then piled the ugly fabric on top of several others. What on Earth would they do with so much fabric? If he watched any longer, he might lose whatever he'd eaten for breakfast.

"Let's go see what Colin is up to," Daniel said as if he read King's mind, turning his back on the ladies and the god-awful fabric.

Chapter Six

The next day, Suzanna sat at her teacher's desk, tapping a small knife on the wooden top. She'd hoped the last teacher would have left a supply of sharpened quills behind, but she wasn't so lucky. A stack of duck feathers lay to her right. On her left was the piddly pile she'd already finished. She never knew why, but at her old school she'd been assigned this mindless task and hated it. When she'd first learned to trim the tips, she'd have a cut on nearly every finger. So far today, she only had one. She sucked on the cut and stood.

At least the teacher had left notes on each student, so Suzanna knew where they were in his or her studies. But with them being off school for so long, how much would they have retained? At home, her mother made sure they kept up on their sums and reading when school wasn't in session. It wasn't unheard of for them to recite sums, poems, and historical facts as they did their chores.

Suzanna stood by one of the tall windows facing toward town. After the time they'd spent with Mr. Winson and Mr. Iverson, she couldn't concentrate. The rest of the day rolled through her mind. She shivered recalling the encounter with those awful men. The best part of the day had been going to Sadie and Colin Haywood's store and meeting the nice couple. Hopefully, they'd spend more time with them. Picking out fabric for new clothes had been exciting. The lunch at King's restaurant was delicious. It had been too long since Julia and she had enjoyed such a wonderful meal.

Mr. Winson's sister, Leona, ran the restaurant and hotel for him. Somehow, she'd made green beans so delicious, even Julia ate them.

It had been tempting to lick her plate after emptying it of roast beef, mashed potatoes and gravy. And her pie rivaled their mother's. In spite of being Mr. Winson's relative, she seemed like she'd make a good friend to her and Julia.

Then there were the ladies of the evening who'd come into the restaurant and approached their table. My goodness, how could women give themselves to men for money? Unbelievably, they wanted Julia to sew for them. Imagine her sister doing work for soiled doves. Suzanna rubbed her arms as if a cool breeze blew over her. Why, their reputations would be ruined if anyone ever found out. Besides, Julia would never work for them.

Suzanna smiled to herself. Mr. Winson had whispered his apologies in her ear, sending delicious shivers skittering through her body. It wasn't so much his apology for dumping the bucket of water over her head, but his warm breath against her ear. Who knew his breath would send sparks across her skin? She closed her eyes, letting the vision of his handsome face appear in her mind's eye. His warmth had seeped through her clothes when he carried her across the muddy street. What had people thought seeing a man carrying the new schoolteacher in his arms? With the horrible, muddy streets, would they simply believe Mr. Winson was being chivalrous?

What would her parents think if they knew that, one day after arriving, Julia and she not only were escorted to town by two unfamiliar men, but had lunch with them, were carried in their arms, and had them in their house—unescorted. While it was all innocent, people could get the wrong idea. As the new schoolmarm, she had a reputation to uphold and a year's contract to abide by.

As she walked back to her desk to resume shaving feathers, a wave of homesickness washed over her. Unlike back home in Iowa, supper last night, with only her and Julia, had been quiet, with more than enough food to eat. No one was scrambling for every morsel, no little ones crying, older ones fighting, and her parents trying to get everyone settled down to a peaceful meal. After supper they had written letters home, making sure not to mention Mr. Winson and Mr. Iverson. Julia had written about their trip out here and their cozy, new house, while she wrote about the school and the up-coming dance. By the time the letter arrived at her childhood home, the dance would be over and the school in session for at least a month. What tales could she tell then?

"The heck with the feathers," she muttered, sucking her injured finger. She pulled a stack of slates from a bookshelf and spent an hour writing the name of a child on each one, using cursive for the older children and printing for the younger, along with a picture of an animal. She wasn't the best artist in the world. She stepped back and admired her work. Would the children be able tell the difference between a deer, a horse, a dog, or a cat? She couldn't claim to be an artist. She placed the slates on the desks so the children could find their seats on Monday.

"Darn it. I can't leave these out. What if it rains tomorrow and the dance is held inside the schoolhouse?" She picked them up and put them in a drawer of her desk. No sense in putting temptation in front of anyone to either erase or add anything to the slates. She'd have Sunday to put everything back to rights.

Simply thinking about the dance being held in her honor made her nerves spike. While it was easy for her to interact with children, adults were a different matter entirely. And to be the center of attention would be awful. Sleep had been elusive. Tonight probably wouldn't be any better.

King—Mr. Winson—had asked her to save him a dance or two. It would be nice having someone there she was acquainted with, even if it were a man. Leona and Sadie said they'd be coming, making a few more familiar faces.

The bell from the telephone in the front of the room rang. She jumped and slapped a hand over her chest. Goodness, who would be calling her at the school? Did she remember how to answer? Yesterday, when they'd returned to the house with Daniel and King, they'd shown Julia and her how to use the phone. It had been scary and exciting. To be able to speak with someone clear across town was amazing.

With shaking hands, she lifted the receiver and, remembering not to yell into the speaker, answered. "Hello? Miss Lindstrom speaking."

The deep voice at the other end, tugged at her heart and made her a bit woozy. What was wrong with her? It was only Mr. Winson.

"Hello, Miss Lindstrom. This is King Winson. How are you this fine day?"

"Um . . . Um . . ." You idiot. Answer the man. "I'm . . . I'm fine. And how are you?" Why was he calling her at the schoolhouse? Had she done something wrong? Had someone seen him carrying her across the street? Was he calling to say she was fired before the year had begun? Maybe . . .

"Are you there, Miss Lindstrom?"

Darn. She'd been worrying about why he was calling instead of listening to find out why. What an idiot. "I'm here, Mr. Winson. What's wrong?"

"Nothing." His confusion was clear. "Why would you think that?"

Even though he couldn't see her, she shrugged. "Why else would you be calling me?"

"Can't a man talk to a beautiful woman if he wants to?"

Beautiful? Her? "Mr. Winson, you shouldn't say things like that."

"Why not? It's the truth."

Really? Didn't people in the west follow any rules of polite society? "You don't know me, so it's improper."

His sigh came through the phone. "I'm sorry. You're right, of course."

"So, why are you calling me?"

"I wanted to say I enjoyed our time together yesterday and to see how things are shaping up at school. Do you need anything?"

"I'm almost ready for the students, but I'm afraid to put anything out in case tomorrow's party ends up inside."

"Good point." It was quiet at the other end of the line as if he was afraid of what to say next. "Speaking of tomorrow's dance," King finally went on, "I'd like to escort you, but since you live behind the school, I would like to share dinner with you."

Suzanna's heart skipped a beat. Of course, she'd like to spend her time with him, but . . . "Mr. Winson, you are aware of the contract I had to sign, aren't you?"

He sighed again. She pictured him running his hands through his hair like he'd done yesterday at the restaurant. "Yes, I'm aware. You can't be seen in the company of a man and had to sign a year's agreement upon accepting the teaching position. But certainly, eating a simple meal in the presence of other people shouldn't be a problem."

Suzanna agreed, but she couldn't afford to lose her job. They needed the money. Until her sister got her sewing business up and running, their funds were limited. Besides, those rules were made by men, men who did their best to break those rules if they were interested in a woman. It was as stupid as having to quit teaching when a woman married. She didn't understand what one had to do with the other, but again, rules made by men, for men's benefit.

Her mother had lamented about men and their ideas about what women should and shouldn't do. Especially when Pa was laid up with his broken leg and Ma went to the bank to get a loan to get them through until he was healed. The banker had nearly laughed her out of the building. She'd never seen her mother so angry but surprisingly her father had sided with his wife.

"I'll make sure we aren't alone," King said, interrupting her thoughts.

Maybe Julia could sit with them. "I . . . I guess it would be fine."

"And don't forget to save a dance for me."

"I will."

"Good. I need to go help Leona. I'll see you tomorrow afternoon."

Before she could respond, the line went dead. Goodness. Was she crazy agreeing to eat with him? Only two days ago she thought he was a vile, uncouth, unkempt, irritating man. But now? She placed a shaking hand over her heart. He was kind, good-looking, and owned a restaurant and a ranch. And he made her heart do funny things, like skipping beats or just plain skipping. She was in trouble, trouble with a capital T.

Suzanna turned back to the room. Time to get back to the blasted quills. She'd take them to the house and ask Julia to help, but her sister needed to get her new dress ready for tomorrow. It was important she look nice when she met her students and their parents. First impressions were important. Her stomach flipped. Why, oh, why did the school board decide to host a party for her? Unless she was with people she knew, her shyness overtook her. How was she supposed to talk intelligently with the men and women of Deadwood and make them believe they'd made the right decision in hiring her? After all, she was only nineteen and hadn't been beyond her hometown her entire life.

Julia was always admonishing her about acting above her station, but goodness, what was wrong with bettering one's self? And didn't Julia understand by looking and acting like society ladies, she'd get their dress business faster? She did have to admit to herself that for all her proper ways, Mrs. Woods was a pompous know-it-all. Why

Mrs. Woods thinks she's so much better, but she sweats as much as everyone else.

Another quill down, way too many more to go. She tossed it on the smaller pile of pens and shuddered at the mess she knew the younger students were going to make struggling to use the ink and pens. The smocks Julia was going to make out of the yards and yards of ugly brown fabric they brought home with them, would hopefully help keep the children clean.

Thinking they would have to pay for it out of their own money, they were delighted when Sadie Haywood had given the entire length of fabric to them for free, telling them Mr. Haywood had purchased the bolt without telling her. Sadie had no idea why he'd thought a woman would want to use the ugly, muddy brown material. Since it had been collecting dust for a year and a half, she was happy to get rid of it.

The question was whether or not she could get the older students to wear the brown smocks. Well, they'd have no choice. She was the teacher and the boss. Her stomach rolled. She'd only ever worked with her younger siblings and her parents made sure they toed the line with her. With twenty students, ranging in ages from five to fourteen, things might be a little more difficult.

What if she had a troublemaker or two? At five foot eight, she was tall for a woman, but when boys hit their growth spurt and became taller than their teacher, they tended to become full of themselves and could be difficult. What would she do? Putting them in the dunce chair, which she hated to do, or making them write on the board after school would be as effective as filling a holey bucket with water.

Yesterday at lunch she met one of her future students. A lovely girl named Lucy who was excited to be going back to school.

"See, Suzanna," King had said. "The students are anxious to get back to their book learning. Having a pretty teacher will keep the boys coming back."

Heat had risen to her face at his compliment, but she hoped the boys came to school to learn, not become enamored with their teacher. Making learning fun would go a long way to bringing them back day after day.

Ignoring the butterflies dancing in her stomach, she gathered her belongings and locked up the building before taking the short walk to her new home. Tomorrow was going to be a long day and night.

Chapter Seven

"Hey, watch what you're doing," Daniel yelled at King. "You nearly dropped the board on my foot. What the hell is wrong with you?"

"Sorry." King wished he knew. Keeping his attention away from the Lindstrom sisters' house as he and Dan hauled empty beer barrels and boards from wagons to use for makeshift tables for tonight's shindig was difficult. Once or twice the curtains in the windows fluttered as if one of the sisters was trying to watch without being seen. Was it Julia or Suzanna or both?

When they'd had lunch the other day, Suzanna had acted nervous at the idea of a party in her honor. In his experience, women liked to be the center of attention. Had she been acting or truly scared about meeting parents and their children? And why would she be? Didn't she have to stand up in front of a classroom full of students?

He mentally shrugged. He'd never understand the workings of a woman's mind. Hell, he couldn't understand himself. The past two nights he'd tossed and turned in his bed at the hotel. Keeping the vision of the pretty schoolteacher out of his mind and dreams was near to impossible.

What was it about her? She'd been prickly—no, darn-right nasty—to him after the mud incident. Hell, he didn't blame her. If he'd been knocked into the mud by a stranger, he'd probably would have drawn his gun on the person. But she didn't have to call him so many names, did she?

Oh, but the look on her face at breakfast when she realized who he was, had been priceless. And, yes, he had felt a bit guilty at the tears welling in her eyes, but not much. But after spending time with her and her sister had given him another view of her. She hadn't been as prickly, had accepted his apology, and hadn't slapped him in the face when he'd carried her across the street. Thankfully, he hadn't dropped her.

King set a board across two barrels and straightened. Now, wouldn't that have made her madder than a wet hen? Having been the cause of the teacher landing in the mud twice in less than twenty-four hours would have certainly put him in the category of the most evil man to walk the earth.

"Would you please pay attention?" Daniel yelled, sucking on a finger.

"What? What did I do?" As much as he wanted to, he kept his gaze away from the little yellow house.

"You dropped the damn board on my finger." Daniel stomped off to pull another board from a wagon. "If I have a broken hand or foot because of you and can't dance with Miss Julia, I'll . . . I'll . . ."

"What? Make me dance with Mrs. Woods?"

Daniel chuckled. "Now that would be pure punishment." He rested a hand on the end of the wagon. "So, what's up with you?"

"Nothing." King slid a board from the wagon and set the bottom edge on the ground.

"Nothing, my foot." Daniel tipped his chin toward the sisters' house. "You watching the sisters like a hawk hasn't escaped my notice. Hell, I have been, too."

"That obvious, huh?" King hoisted the board on his shoulder, missing his friend by inches.

"Hey, you idiot, watch it." He followed with a board over his own shoulder. "I get it. You're smitten with the schoolmarm. But you know damn well she signed the contract for only a year."

King placed the board next to the first one and waited for Daniel to place his, completing the first table. Once the ladies put their fancy tablecloths down, no one would ever see how rough the table was. "I know it as well as you do. It's a stupid rule, but I'm willing to abide by it. She's caught my attention." He narrowed his eyes at his friend. "Just as her sister has caught yours."

Side-by-side, they went back to the wagon. Twenty barrels remained. Where were the men who were going to help set up this afternoon? With only him and Daniel doing the work, there would barely be time for him to head back to his hotel, get cleaned up, and return before another young buck latched on to Suzanna. With the high ratio of men to women in Deadwood, it wouldn't take long.

Daniel tipped his worn brown cowboy hat back on his head. "Can't deny it, but I don't have to worry about my attentions toward a woman making the town lose yet another teacher."

"How are things going at the ranch?" Daniel asked, interrupting King's thoughts about one Suzanna Lindstrom.

King paused from removing another board and tipped back his hat. "I need to go back next week. Paddy says there's something odd going on."

"Like what?" Daniel leaned an elbow on the wagon's sideboard.

"He says the horses have been acting spooked, jittery, like an animal is scaring them."

"Four-legged or two?"

King dragged the board to another set of beer barrels. "Good question. No one has reported seeing any bears or wolves lately, but it doesn't mean there aren't any in the area."

"If you need an extra hand with a rifle, let me know."

"Nah, you have enough with trying to build your law practice." When the board was in place, King wiped a shirtsleeve across his forehead. "Can't believe how warm it is for June."

"Yeah, I think it's going to be a scorcher this summer. Let's get this done so I can clean up for tonight."

"Wanna look good for Miss Julia?"

Daniel grinned.

King pushed the edge of a board to make it even with the others. "Hey, what are your thoughts about those prostitutes coming into the restaurant to speak with Miss Julia?"

"It was bold of them, that's for sure." Daniel lifted the back gate of the wagon. "I couldn't tell what she was thinking, but I can't imagine ladies like the Lindstrom sisters rubbing elbows with any of them."

"That's what I thought. They seem a bit naïve." King chuckled. "Miss Julia sure knew how to handle Mingus Thoreson. I bet he still isn't walking right."

Daniel climbed onto the wagon's front bench. "I certainly hope he doesn't retaliate."

"Never can tell with that idiot." When King had climbed in beside Daniel, he gave one last look at the sisters' house before slapping the horse's rump with the reins and turning the wagon toward town.

WHEN THE WAGON WAS out of sight, Suzanna let the curtain drop.

"Will you please get over here so I can hem the skirt," Julia said, irritation filling her words. "What's the big attraction out there, anyway?"

Biting back a sigh, Suzanna stepped up on a wooden footstool to make it easier for her sister to pin up the hem. "Nothing."

"Nothing my eye. I saw Mr. Winson and Mr. Iverson come with the wagon. You're drooling over Mr. Winson, aren't you?"

Suzanna slapped her hands at her sides. "I don't drool over men. Besides, I caught you at the window a few times, so don't go chastising me."

"Turn," Julia ordered. "But I didn't sign a contract for one year. If you break the contract—especially over a man—what'll we do then? Go back home? Wouldn't Ma and Pa love that?"

"I know, I know. You don't have to keep reminding me." She turned again when Julia tugged on the skirt. "I won't do anything stupid. Anyway, it's stupid a teacher can't be seen with a man."

"I agree, but that's what the contract says."

"Does it say I can't be seen with a man if I'm with other people?"

Julia shrugged. "You'd have to read it again."

"I can see why women shouldn't be seen in saloons, but if a man wants to court a woman, it shouldn't be anyone else's business."

"Again, I agree." Julia set aside her pins. "I'm done, so you can take it off."

Suzanna removed the light-blue skirt and put on her serviceable brown one.

"What do you want me to say?" Julia asked. "Even though I agree with everything you've said, you can't go breaking a signed contract."

"Well, it's stupid." She plopped down on one of the chairs and kicked the hem of the skirt.

"You're pouting like Louisa does when she doesn't get her way."

"I am not pouting like a three-year-old." Suzanna folded her arms beneath her breasts and sighed. "Okay, I guess I am. Why do men make things so confining for women?"

"Do you want to be like those women we met Thursday at lunch?"

Suzanna sat up straight and shivered. "Goodness, no. I'd never want to end up having to take care of men like that."

"Well, then," Julia sat on the chair by the window and threaded a needle, "you'd best abide by the rules, or we'll be kicked out of this house and end up in a brothel."

She closed her eyes. A vision of the handsome Mr. Winson filled her mind's eye. To be escorted by such a manly man set her heart pounding in her ears. What would it be like to be kissed? She touched her fingers to her lips. Would his mustache tickle? Would his lips be warm against hers? She'd never been kissed before. A few of the boys back home had tried, but none of them interested her the way Mr. Winson did.

Another vision, this one not quite so happy, replaced the image of Mr. Winson. The awful man from the stagecoach, Mr. Silverstone. The way he'd tried to touch her with his elbow against her breast or put his hand on her knee when the coach wobbled too much. The way he'd whispered the nasty things he wanted to do to her, even giving her the name of the place where he'd be staying. Like she ever wanted to meet a man alone, especially at some place called The Gem Theater.

At first, she'd wondered why someone would be staying at a theater. When they'd been accosted the other day, she found out what type of place it was. There was no way she'd ever she be seen entering the building. She probably wouldn't last two minutes before being attacked and—she shuddered. The possibilities were too horrible to contemplate.

"Do we need to bring any food tonight?" Julia asked, interrupting thoughts that were becoming quite distressing.

"I believe Miss Winson said we didn't have to because the party is in my honor."

"I feel funny showing up empty handed." Julia bit off a piece of thread. "Maybe you can make lemonade to bring."

"We don't have enough lemons, but there's time to make up sugar cookies."

"Good idea, Suz. I'd hate to have people think we don't have any social skills."

SUZANNA GRASPED JULIA'S arm with shaking hands. "My nerves are about shot. I've met so many parents and their children. I don't remember a single name."

"I see Leona Winson," Julia answered, squeezing her sister's hand back. "At least she's someone we've met before."

"Well, Misses Lindstrom," Leona said. "What a pleasure to see you again."

"Please, call us Suzanna and Julia," Suzanna said.

"And you may call me Leona," Leona replied, placing pies on one of the tables.

"Are those your delicious pies?" Suzanna asked. They'd had a sample of her apple pie at lunch two days ago. Her mouth watered simply remembering.

Leona grinned. "Been baking since early this morning. Even managed to wrangle King to help, too."

Julia raised her eyebrows. "Your brother helped?"

"Sure. Our mother made sure us kids knew how to cook and bake. She said she didn't want any of her sons to starve if they never found a wife."

"Sounds like our mother," Suzanna said, a pang of homesickness bringing tears to her eyes. "She also taught us how to cook over a campfire in case we ended up someplace where we didn't have a stove."

"Smart woman." Leona stood back and eyed the tables. "I do hope there is enough for everyone."

Suzanna glanced at the people milling around the schoolyard. Many were dressed in what she figured were their Sunday finery, but there were plenty of men who looked as if they hadn't cleaned up in weeks. Women stood in groups talking. Children raced around adults in a game of tag.

The spread of food grew as people arrived. The boards stretching across empty beer barrels groaned beneath the weight. The aroma of roast beef, pork, and other delectable foods made her mouth water. It was a good thing she'd eaten a couple of cookies before coming to the school, or her stomach would growl louder than the men tuning up their instruments.

Julia swept her hand at the over-stocked tables. "If anyone brings anymore food, the tables will break."

Leona laughed. "Don't worry, as soon as suppertime is announced, the food will disappear faster than a fox chasing a rabbit."

While they were talking, the group of men who'd brought instruments struck up a lively tune. Before they could tap a toe, several men approached, asking them to dance. When were they ever going to eat?

Half an hour later, Suzanna grabbed Julia's arm as she left the grassy dance floor and pulled her over to a chair. "Heavens, my feet hurt. I'd love to take off these awful shoes."

"Looks like it's about time to eat." Julia kicked at the hem of her skirt.

"When are the musicians going to stop playing so we can get a break from dancing?" Suzanna tapped at her damp face with her handkerchief. "I'm not an expert, but the only ones who can dance are married, and they're only dancing with their wives."

"You must be reading my mind," Julia said, laughing. "I've never been swung in so many different directions or had my feet stomped on so much in my life. Even big ol' Johann Swenson back home was lighter on his feet, and they were huge."

"All these people here can't have children in school, can they?" Suzanna asked. "I've met quite of few of the families, but I danced with men who don't seem to be attached to women or children."

Suzanna bumped her shoulder against Julia. "By the way, my dress turned out lovely and I've received several compliments." Hopefully the women who'd made those comments to her would want Julia to sew for them. Unfortunately, Mrs. Woods, the banker's wife, stuck her nose up at her when she was introduced by one of the mothers. Hadn't they spent several days being bounced and jostled in the stagecoach? Why was the woman now acting like they hadn't met? A banker's wife must be several steps above a lowly teacher in the social hierarchy of Deadwood.

"Mrs. Woods didn't say a thing about it."

"I wouldn't worry about Mrs. Woods, Suz. I have a feeling her importance in Deadwood is all in her head. I don't see anyone going up and talking with her."

Sometimes her sister knew the right thing to say, just as she knew what colors were right for a person's hair and complexion. Take her dress for instance. Due to the warm June weather, they'd decided to make the top short sleeved. The neckline, edged in cream lace matching the trim on the hem of the skirt, dipped to Suzanna's collarbone. The way the men lined up to dance with her, they must have noticed. She'd put her hair in a low chignon, leaving tendrils curling down her cheeks. Everyone had always said she and Julia looked so much alike, so hopefully she was as attractive as her oldest sibling.

"Well, you look lovely." Julia said.

"Thanks, but if I am, it's your dress making me so." Suzanna's stomach gave an unladylike growl. "Heavens, are we ever going to eat? I'm so hungry I may make a fool of myself in front of my students by shoveling food into my mouth like a ravenous pig and licking my plate clean."

Julia turned her attention from her sister to the two men who'd recently shown up and headed their way.

Suzanna glanced over shoulder to see who'd distracted Julia. "And I have to say, you look lovely yourself, sister. You weren't able to make anything new, but the skirt and blouse you sewed before we left Iowa is rather attractive."

"I have to agree with you, Miss Suzanna," Daniel said, standing before them with King at his side.

King grinned. "You ladies look mighty fetching."

"I was wondering if you were going to come tonight," Julia said, keeping her attention on Daniel.

"We were here earlier setting up tables and chairs," Daniel tipped his head to the dimming sky, "and worrying about the weather. Then I had to clean up and a meeting to attend."

"And I had to help Leona get pies ready." King smiled. "I'm not very adept in the kitchen, so after changing clothes from helping here, I had to change again."

"Why? Did you fall in the mud again?" Was she being too bold egging Mr. Winson on?

King slapped a hand over his heart. "You wound me. It was flour this time."

The music stopped. Colin stood in front of the musicians. "Can I have your attention, please," he called out in a booming voice, halting conversations. "My wife has informed me the food is ready."

A cheer rose from the gathering.

"She also tells me our guest of honor and her sister will start the line."

Suzanna clasped Julia's hand. Her face turned red. "I can't walk in front of everyone."

"You'll be fine," King assured her.

"But... but... It's different when it's a bunch of kids, but there's at least forty adults
here."

King took her hand and pulled her to her feet. "Will it help if I go with you?"

"Yes, but don't get too close or people will get the wrong idea about us."

"Nothing could be further from my mind." He swept a hand forward allowing Suzanna to precede him. "Heck, are we allowed to have a dance? Surely you've been asked a dozen times to dance already."

"Goodness. Where do I begin?" she said, taking in the array of hot and cold dishes. It would almost put an Iowan gathering to shame.

King handed her a cloth napkin. "I suggest you take a bit of everything, so you won't offend anyone."

"How will I ever know who to thank for this?"

"It'll probably be easier to put a thank you in one of the papers."

Suzanna progressed to the table with the meat on it and glanced at her nearly overflowing plate. Where was she going to put a chicken leg? "Which paper?"

King shrugged and forked a large piece of beef onto his plate. "Doesn't matter. We don't have any idea when one of the papers will come out. Sometimes it's once a week. Sometimes twice a day. Newspaper shops come and go with regularity."

With her plate in one hand and fork and knife in the other, she searched the schoolyard for a place to sit.

With his plate, King pointed to a patchwork quilt spread out beneath an elm tree. "Leona set it out for us."

How was she supposed to sit on the quilt? With her hands full, she was either going to spill everything off her plate or fall over trying to get to the ground. Either way, this could prove to be embarrassing.

As if he realized her dilemma, King dropped his utensils on the quilt, then took her plate. Even without her hands full, gracefully arranging herself on the ground while being watched by at least forty people wasn't easy. If only they'd quit staring at her. Once she was settled with her legs tucked to her side and her skirt covering her ankles, she reached up for her plate.

"I'll get us some lemonade," King said, handing her his plate as well.

With Daniel and Julia settled on the quilt, there wasn't much room for King when he returned. Their close proximity would surely be noticed by everyone.

"What do you think of the party so far?" King asked, sitting next to Suzanna then taking his plate from her.

His leg bumped hers. She swore his heat seared through to her skin. She hissed in a breath.

"Are you all right?" King asked.

What should she say? That he set her heart pounding with his close proximity? That she hadn't been able to get him off her mind since Thursday. That he made her panicky and excited at the same time? Nerves. That's what she could use as an excuse. "I'm just a bit nervous. I didn't realize so many people would show up," Suzanna answered. "They don't all have children, do they?"

Daniel laughed. "Not hardly, but when men from the mines hear there's going to be a shindig, they'll come for free food and dancing, especially when word gets out there are a couple of new females in town."

Julia rubbed the toe of her boot. "I can attest that most can't dance."

"Or get so excited about kicking up their heels, they forget how," King added.

"Will you dance with me later?" Daniel asked Julia, stabbing a piece of pork.

"Of course, but please don't tromp on my feet. My poor toes can't take any more."

"I promise I've never tromped on any woman's feet."

Why was Julia giggling as if she didn't have a brain in her head? What was wrong with her? Besides her parents, her sister was one of the smartest people she knew. And she was smiling at Mr. Iverson as if he'd hung the moon only for her. She dropped her gaze to her plate rather than watching Julia act like a simpering idiot. It would also help keep her from gagging at her sister's antics.

"So, Miss Suzanna," King said, "Do you have the schoolhouse ready for the children? It wasn't going to rain, so we didn't bother going inside to see what you've done."

"I'm as ready as I'll ever be, I guess. Tomorrow I'll put back the things I'd stored away in case the building would be used."

A young girl, carrying a pitcher, approached them. "Would anyone like more lemonade?"

"Why, hello, Lucy. It's good to see you again." At least this was one student's name she'd remember on Monday morning.

Lucy blushed. "Hello, Miss Lindstrom. I couldn't help overhearing you talk about the school. If there is anything you need help with, let me know."

"Thank you. I'll remember that on Monday. I'm sure I'll need a hand then."

"See, you already have a helper." King held out his glass for a refill. "And I have to tell you, Lucy is a hard and responsible worker."

"Thank you, Mr. Winson." With a shy smile and quick curtsy, she left.

If half her students were like Lucy, teaching would be a breeze. She could only be so lucky. The silence as they ate made her nervous. She didn't like keeping quiet, which drove her parents and siblings crazy. Maybe that's why teaching served her well. She could talk as much as she wanted, and the students *had* to listen. Didn't they?

"So, what do people in Iowa do for fun?" King asked, his deep voice raising goosebumps on her arms.

Suzanna had to stop and take her mind from his voice. "I guess we do the same things as people do everywhere. We hold dances. Play cards. Julia and I were raised on a farm, so most of our time was spent doing chores and helping with our younger siblings."

"Are you the oldest?"

She shook her head. "No. Julia is. There are eight younger than me."

King set down his plate and picked up a fallen twig, breaking it into pieces. "Wow. That's a lot of kids. How do your parents handle so many?"

"They get a lot of help from the older ones." She placed her empty plate on top of King's. If she ate like this every day, she'd look like Mrs. O'Brien back home, who had to weigh three hundred pounds. "How about your family? Where are you from?"

King hesitated. Didn't he want to talk about his family? He had at least one sister.

"Leona and I were raised in northern Wisconsin. Our parents are still there in a small town called Bloomer."

"Is it a farming area?" If they'd both grown up on farms, they'd have that in common.

"There is a bit of farming, but there's a lot of logging, too." King said. "Northern Wisconsin is mostly woods."

Since most Iowans farmed on cleared land, she couldn't imagine what it was like. "Did you cut down trees?"

King shook his head. "My dad worked the woods during the winter, while my mom and us four kids kept up the farm. After the snow melted and the woods were too muddy, he came back home and worked the farm with us." He picked up another twig and tossed it off the quilt. "I thought going into the woods so interesting, when I turned sixteen, I talked Pa into letting me go with him for the winter."

"And was it interesting?"

King snorted. "I absolutely hated it. Mucking out barn stalls was infinitely more fun than slogging through snow sometimes hip deep, fighting with a two man saw to cut down trees so large two men's arms couldn't reach around it, and using chains to stack the logs on sleighs, while praying the logs wouldn't slip and crush you. The logs were dumped onto frozen ponds and when they thawed, you had to scramble over the logs in the water and, using log pikes send them down the river."

"Sounds like a dangerous job."

"It is. After one winter, I never again complained about milking cows, slaughtering pigs, or walking behind the oxen to plow fields."

Suzanna handed her plate to one of the children. "And now you own a restaurant and hotel."

"And a ranch."

"Couldn't get away from farming, huh?"

King smiled. "It's more like it's cheaper to raise my own animals, than have beef, eggs, and other goods shipped in. I also get to fulfill my desire to cut down trees by supplying wood to many of the people in Deadwood."

"The school, too?"

"Yep. So, you'll see me around in the fall, filling up the woodshed."

She'd enjoy watching him. With his broad shoulders, he probably was quite muscular beneath his shirt. Too bad she'd be too busy teaching to spend her time gawking at him from the school windows.

"What brought you out west?"

"Like every other person living in Deadwood, it was the lure of gold. But like my friend, Daniel, I quickly realized standing in ice-cold water and panning for gold wasn't for me. When I first came here in seventy-seven, there wasn't much here for food and lodging. I realized there was more money to be made having a decent establishment with decent food. Not everyone who comes here is looking to stay in a brothel." He jerked his head back. "I'm sorry, I shouldn't have brought it up in proper company."

So, he was a gentleman. "After lunch the other day, Julia and I talked about them. We feel sorry for those women."

King raised an eyebrow. "You do?"

"Women don't have very many choices in life. Other than being a teacher, our choices are to be a wife and mother, seamstress, or milliner." Would he think she was crazy for getting on her soapbox about women's rights? Too bad for him if he was one of those men who thought women had only one place in life. "Then when we do become teachers, we are so restricted, one wrong move, and we're fired. Heaven forbid we find a man we like, let alone get married. It's as if getting married, which is about the only thing we can do, penalizes us."

"I hadn't thought about it that way."

She took a deep breath. She might as well keep going. "And then if a woman doesn't find a man to take care of her, she could end up in a brothel, taking care of men's needs. I saw the way people treated those women, especially the men."

"I can't disagree with that."

Good. Maybe it meant he wasn't one of those men. Her estimation of him rose another notch. A man walking between dancers caught her attention. She hitched a breath. What was Mr. Silverstone doing here?

King glanced over his shoulder. Fiddlesticks. Other than Julia, she didn't want anyone to realize she knew the reprobate. Unfortunately, King zeroed in on Silverstone, who'd stopped and stared at her.

"Do you know him?" King narrowed his eyes. His voice was sharp.

"He was on the stagecoach with us."

"Stay away from him."

While she hadn't had any plans to search him out or spend time with him, King's authoritarian tone rubbed her the wrong way, but she wasn't about to tell him that. "Since a teacher can't be seen alone in the presence of a man, it won't be a problem." Huh, let him ponder on that one a bit.

King frowned then stood and held out his hand to her. "May I have the pleasure of this dance?"

Had what she said satisfied Mr. Winson? Would he question her again about Mr. Silverstone? A bad feeling crept over her, one that made her determined to keep an eye out for the octopus man.

Chapter Eight

Even at a proper societal distance holding Suzanna in his arms, and dancing the waltz was heaven. The music was too loud to carry on a conversation. Suzanna was an amazing dancer and followed his lead flawlessly, but his mind drifted since the music was too loud to carry on a conversation.

The panic in her eyes and the way her face had gone white when she'd seen Silverstone made him wonder how well she knew him. Did she recognize him from Iowa? Had something happened on the trip to Deadwood? Had the man taken unwanted advances?

"You're squeezing my hand, Mr. Winson," Suzanna said, interrupting his angry thoughts about someone harming her.

"I'm sorry, Miss Lindstrom." He eased his grip and twirled her around the grassy dance floor. He needed to keep his attention on her but catching sight of Silverstone leaning against a tree watching them, sent his hackles up. He thoroughly disliked the man, and since he had spent time with Suzanna, his dislike had grown deeper.

He'd had dealings with Silverstone twice, and the man set his teeth on edge. On the surface he acted like an upstanding businessman, looking to make a deal on King's horses. But he'd seen him talking with Woods, and anyone who associated with the banker couldn't be trusted. If they were in cahoots, there was bound to be trouble brewing.

Sure enough, there was Woods walking toward Silverstone. Pressing his hand on Suzanna's back, King turned her so he could keep an eye on the men as they disappeared behind the schoolhouse.

"Are you all right?" Suzanna asked. "Don't you want to dance with me?"

Suzanna's words brought him back to the present. "I'm sorry. My mind wandered to a business matter. It has nothing to do with you."

She relaxed in his arms. "Good. I'm a bit nervous with all these strangers here."

"It is hard leaving home, isn't it?" He knew the feeling well. Leaving his brother, sisters, and parents three years ago had been difficult, but there wasn't enough land for everyone to farm. Besides, his love went more toward horses than cows.

The music stopped and, before he could ask for the next dance, another man stepped in. Daniel was still dancing with Julia, the lucky guy. Why couldn't he have been interested in the sister, who was free to do as she pleased? He thought about Suzanna's earlier words. Anyway, as well as a woman could.

He didn't know what to believe. For someone from rural Iowa, Suzanna certainly had enlightened ideas. Ones he agreed with. His own mother and sisters used to complain about how women had no rights. And if she didn't marry, she had few choices.

And Suzanna's openness in voicing her opinion about the prostitutes was surprising. He'd seen plenty of men using the tunnels beneath Main Street to get to a brothel one night and the next day treat those same women as if they were the scum of the earth. A bunch of hypocrites.

If—he watched Suzanna laugh as her partner twirled her to the polka—no, when he married, he'd make sure his wife had equal say in decisions made for them and their children. And if he had daughters, he'd make damn sure their husbands felt the same way.

Woods and Silverstone came back to the party, shook hands, and went their separate ways. Fortunately, Woods went to his wife's side. Unfortunately, Silverstone headed his way.

"Winson." Silverstone smirked before stopping beside him.

"Silverstone," he answered between clenched teeth.

Silverstone tugged down his bright red brocade vest and rocked back on his heels. "Saw you dancing with the little filly. Nice body, wouldn't you say?"

King clenched his fists and stuck his hands in his pockets. "I don't talk about innocent women that way."

"What makes you think she's innocent?" Silverstone's grin didn't reach his eyes.

Suzanna and her dance partner passed in front of them. Her cheeks were rosy. Strands of her blonde hair had slipped from her bun. She smiled at him, making his heart jump. She was beautiful and as pure as the day was long. Silverstone was bluffing. He'd bank his ranch on that.

"What makes you think she's not?" King faced Silverstone. "What did you do on the stage? If I find out you hurt or harassed Miss Lindstrom or her sister, I'll hunt you down and make sure you don't ever harm another woman."

Silverstone raised his hands in surrender. "Don't worry, Winson. Nothing happened." He winked. "I had the pleasure of sitting next to her. You know how it is when people are crammed into those damn coaches together. Hard not to get a few touches in."

King stabbed a finger in the bastard's chest. "You stay away from her. She's here to teach, not become any man's paramour—especially yours."

"I've seen the way you've been watching her. Practice what you preach." Silverstone smirked and poked King's chest.

"Don't even ask about buying any of my horses, Silverstone." His jaw ached from clenching his teeth. "My ranch and horses are off-limits to you."

Silverstone's grin would make a devil look sweet. "Don't worry. I wouldn't go near any of your horses." With a tip of his hat, he stomped off into the night.

King doubted every word the man said. And nothing good could come out of Silverstone and Woods being together. He stared at his boots and shook his head to get rid of the image of Silverstone touching Suzanna. He wasn't kidding when he said he'd bring harm to the asshole if he came anywhere near the sisters.

Skirting the dancers kicking up their heels, King wandered over to a group of men who headed the annual horse races on the outskirts of Deadwood. He planned on entering a couple of his three-year-olds and hoped to sell a few others to these gentlemen. It was easier to sell locally than to ranchers in California.

AN HOUR LATER THE FOOD was nearly gone. Empty dishes and unclean plates were packed into baskets then placed onto wagons parked haphazardly around the property. Suzanna gathered the children for games of blind-man's bluff and follow the leader. It was a good way to get to meet the children she'd start teaching on Monday. Maybe she should be helping clean off the tables, but with Julia's help, the job was quickly nearing a finish. She tried not to admire Mr. Winson's muscles as he helped Mr. Iverson lift a wooden keg of beer onto one of the empty food tables. Lucy and several other young girls carried jugs of lemonade to the tables before skipping off to join their friends.

With children laughing, men grouped together talking about whatever men talked about, and women bouncing babies and spreading rumors, it was as if she was back in Iowa. A female voice yelled out. Julia? Leaving the children to their own devices, she picked up her skirt and raced to where a man was talking with her sister. Except it didn't look as if he was talking, but more like accosting her. It was the man Julia kicked between the legs the other day, Mingus or something like that. This couldn't be good.

Before she could step in to help, Julia slapped the man on his ears. From previous experience when she bad-mouthed her mother once, she knew getting smacked in the ears with open palms hurt like the dickens. The man dropped the ground.

Mr. Iverson pushed his way through the crowd Julia with King, Suzanna, and the sheriff following. "What happened?"

"He wouldn't take no for an answer, so I . . ."

"Gave him the ear whack?" Suzanna finished for her.

"Ear whack?" King asked, helping the sheriff pull Mingus to his feet. "What's that?"

Suzanna stood next to her. "To stop someone, you slap them on the ears with open palms. Hurts like crazy."

"Stupid bitch," Mingus swore still holding his head. "I'll get you for that. You'll be sorry you turned me down."

Sheriff Winkman yanked Mingus' arms behind his back and snapped on a pair of handcuffs. "How many times do I have to tell you to leave a lady alone when she says no? If you want a woman, you go to the saloons." He pushed him forward. "And I have no idea why you thought it would be a good idea to show up here. These are decent folk, not for the likes of you."

Julia took a deep breath and wiped damp, shaking hands down her skirt. "I didn't see him until it was too late."

Daniel placed his hands on her shoulders. "Did he hurt you?"

She blinked away tears. "Other than touching me on my backside and nearly knocking me out with his horrid smell, no."

King raised his arms to the gathering. "Everything's fine, folks. Let's get back to the party." He nodded to the men holding their instruments. "Gentlemen."

After a brief tune-up, the group struck up 'Ol' Dan Tucker,' a song Suzanna loved to dance to. As couples formed squares, Daniel took Julia's hand.

"C'mon, let's join in." Daniel said. "The four of us can make a square."

Half an hour later, King leaned against the side of the schoolhouse, ignoring the beer in his hand. The balmy night air had turned the drink lukewarm, so he might as well pour it out. Most of the younger children's energy had wound down like a top at the end of its spin and were spread out on blankets, hay bales, or wherever they'd dropped, leaving their mothers free to dance up a storm. The sheriff and his deputies patrolled the edges, watching for drunks causing trouble and teenagers sneaking off to do what young people were wont to do. A few of the older ladies kept an eye on the beer to make sure the young bucks didn't sneak a sip or two.

King shook his head. Had he been as dumb when he was a teenager? Probably. There had been more than a few times when his father hauled him to the woodshed with a switch in his hand. A good wallop on his backside usually brought him to his senses—at least until he came up with the next hare-brained idea.

Daniel strolled to his side, his eyebrows nearly touching his nose. "Quit scowling." King said. "You look as if you're going to bite someone's head off."

"Hmph." He crossed his arms over his chest. "Why aren't you dancing with Suzanna?"

"If you'd take your eyes off Julia and her partner long enough, you'll see she's dancing with someone else."

Daniel curled his fingers into fists. "Doesn't it bother you?"

"Sort of, but as much as I enjoy her company, as a teacher who hasn't spent one day with her students in the classroom, she certainly can't favor one man over another."

"Julia doesn't have the same problem." Daniel drained his glass of lemonade. "I was wondering how Suzanna went from hating you for getting her muddy, then dumping water on her, to being so chummy."

"She's smart enough to recognize an intelligent, handsome, charming man when she sees him in his cleaned-up form."

Daniel snorted, keeping his attention on the couple moving as if they'd been born to dance together. "Oh, brother. You do have quite an ego, don't you?"

"Someone has to." King pointed to Julia and Mr. Hotchkiss. "I couldn't help overhearing her say his name. How does she know him?"

"I have no idea, unless she danced with him before we got here, and if Hotchkiss holds her any closer, I'm going to have to knock the guy out right in front of God and everyone else."

"You look as if you're ready to pick a fight with someone," King said, nudging Daniel in the side. "Doing so won't endear you to Julia."

"I know. I know." The music thankfully stopped, but before Julia left the dance floor giving him a chance to step in for his turn, another man took her hand, leading her into a polka. "I'm not sure what the hell is going on with me. Ever since I set eyes on the woman, I can't concentrate on anything else. Hell, I nearly ran Mrs. Woods over yesterday while walking down the sidewalk."

"You falling in love?"

Daniel sniffed as if the one word reeked like a dead skunk. "Not hardly. How can a person fall in love with someone he's only spent a few hours with?"

Rocking back on his heels, King shoved his hands into his pockets. "Damned if I know, but I've heard of it happening before."

"Well, not to me, it hasn't. Besides, I have no intention of letting a woman latch on to me simply to have someone to take care of her."

Even though Suzanna had piqued his interest, he wasn't about to admit it to his friend. Besides, after knowing Daniel for three years, it would be a joy watching Julia bring him to his knees. "We'll see, my friend, we'll see."

Chapter Nine

"Josiah Joshua Johnson." Suzanna took a deep breath and counted to ten. This boy was going to be the life of her. "Pick up the burr from Magdalene's chair before she comes back from the necessary." Ducking his head, he did as asked. "Now bring it here." She held out her hand and ignored his trembling chin. If there was anything she'd learned in the first month of school, it was that beneath Josiah's angelic eyes and sweet, innocent smile lay a mind as cunning as when Julia was when trying to get out of eating her beans.

The boy handed her the burr and, without her saying a word, went to the chalkboard and took a piece of chalk from the tray. This time she wasn't going make him write *I will behave* a hundred times. The only thing it did was make the other kids laugh when he'd make faces behind her back. As if she didn't know what he was doing, but every time she glanced at him, he was busy writing on the board.

What she was going to do next was probably mean, but then so were the tricks he was always pulling. Yanking the girls' braids. Locking them in the necessary. Throwing the younger boys' hoops in the trees. Loosening the cinches on saddles. It was time he learned a lesson of his own.

"Not so fast, Josiah. Come here."

With a smirk, he replaced the chalk on the tray and stood in front of her. She held the burr in her hand. "Put this on your seat."

Josiah opened his eyes wide. "What? Why?"

"Just do as I say," she said then pointed to the burred seat. "Now sit down."

THE SCHOOL MARM

"I can't sit on a burr. It'll hurt." Josiah folded his arms over his chest and pouted.

"You can and you will. It's about time you learn how your antics hurt others."

"Can't I write on the board like I always do?"

Suzanna shook her head. "Remember the Bible verse we learned last week? *Do unto others as you would have them do unto you?*"

Josiah didn't do anything, but the other children nodded. A few, who had suffered at his hands, grinned. Maybe making him suffer at his own hands wasn't such a good idea. Would it make the other children believe retaliation was acceptable? But Josiah had to learn there were consequences to his so-called jokes.

"Now, put the burr on your seat and sit." She tried to keep her voice level, but it was hard when she was shaking. Hurting children was not part of her nature. Even when her younger brothers pulled tricks on her, she'd laughed it off. But if she didn't take control, the other children might believe they could get away with bad behavior.

A tear rolled down Josiah's cheek as he set the burr down and eased himself onto the chair. If she knew for sure he was genuinely sorry, she'd have made him stop, but if she gave in . . . well, she didn't want to think about what would happen.

"Ouch. Miss Lindstrom, it hurts."

"Five minutes, young man. You'll sit on the burr for five minutes and think about how it feels. From now on, whenever you harm one of the other children in this school, it will be done to you."

Josiah folded his arms over his chest and pouted. "I'm telling my father about this and you'll be sorry."

She probably would be sorry. "Go ahead and tell your father, and I'll tell him how you've been treating your classmates." She glanced at the wall clock. "Four and a half minutes." She left Josiah and stood before her desk. "Now, children, here's what I want you to do . . ."

After setting the older children working with the younger ones on their sums, she took the burr from Josiah and had him work on writing out the multiplication table on the board. Then she took the middle-grade students and helped them with memorizing and reciting *The Midnight Ride of Paul Revere*. The older students had already learned it and once the others had, she planned on having them put on a play for their parents.

The rest of the day went smoothly. It was as if the children finally realized she wasn't going to put up with any of their shenanigans. However, by the time the children left for home, she was exhausted. Handling twenty-five children ranging in age from five to fourteen was tiring. Keeping them all on task at the same time made her brain hurt. As the year went on, hopefully she'd get used to it.

After the children were gone, she spent the next hour and a half checking their work, straightening the room, and getting ready for the next day. The heavenly scent of cooking chicken wafted through the windows. Supper must nearly be ready. Her mouth watered. It was nice not having to help cook every meal, but it was only fair she helped to clean up. Julia was home all day, yet her sewing jobs had picked up. Anyway, there was more money in their coffers. Her sister never spoke about who she was sewing for, and Suzanna never asked. As long as they had money for food, she was content.

She put on her bonnet and walked down the aisle to make sure the front door was locked. She'd leave by the back door. As she reached out to set the lock, the front door flew open, slamming against the inner wall. She jumped back, the door barely missing her outstretched hand.

The silhouette of a man filled the doorway. He took a step toward her. She took a step back.

"Wh . . . what do you want?" she whispered, clutching the top of her blouse. "School is done for the day."

"I know that, little lady. I have a bone to pick with you." He took another step toward her. At least three inches taller with forearms the dimension of tree trunks, his size alone intimidated her, not to mention his deep, booming voice. He didn't remove his wide-brimmed hat, which meant he was either angry or not a gentleman, or both. Everyone knew a man should take off his hat in church, school, or before a lady. His blue pants and shirt were filthy and smelled as if he'd been rolling around in horse dung.

She retreated until the coat hooks poked her in the back. "Who are you?"

The man stabbed a finger at his broad chest. "I'm Asa Johnson, Josiah's father."

Oh, boy. Josiah hadn't wasted any time tattling to his father. "Yes, sir." Keeping the tremors from her voice was difficult. She looked up at him. "What can I do for you?"

He poked a finger in her face. "Well, little missy. You can start out by telling me why you had my son sit on a burr."

The man might be taller and his upper arms as big as her thighs, but she wasn't about to be intimidated by him. She gulped. At least she was going to try. She crossed her arms over her chest. "What did Josiah tell you?"

"You made him sit on a burr."

"Nothing else?"

Asa glared. "What else could he have said? My Josiah is a good boy."

Suzanna refrained from crossing her eyes and snorting. Either the man was blind to his son's antics or he truly believed what he said. "Mr. Johnson, from the day school started Josiah has been a little troublemaker."

"I don't believe it." Asa leaned closer. "Do you have proof?"

"Proof?" How on Earth was she supposed to provide proof? "Other than what the other children have said and seeing him put the burr on Magdalene's chair this morning, I don't have concrete proof."

"Just as I thought. The other kids are out to make trouble for my son."

"Why would they do that?"

"Because . . . Because . . ." Asa's face turned red. "Well . . . because he's smarter than the other children and they're jealous."

Telling a parent his son was certainly not smarter than the other children would probably not be wise. Most parents thought their children were geniuses. But reality was difficult for parents to swallow. What should she say to the man?

"Mr. Johnson, Josiah certainly has a sharp mind." Which she sincerely wished he'd use for better things than antagonizing the classroom. "But he is no smarter than any of the other children in school."

It didn't seem possible, but his face turned a deeper shade of red.

"My son is certainly smarter than the other brats in this building, and if you had any brains of your own, you'd see that, missy." With his upper lip curled in a snarl, he looked her up and down. "How the school board ever had the idea to hire someone like you, is beyond me."

Hold you temper, Suzanna, hold your temper! She took a deep breath. "Someone like me? What does that mean?"

He poked a finger into her chest. "It means you come here all high and mighty with your education and high and mighty ideas, that's what. You and your fancy clothes and fancy ways. Why, I bet you've never so much as pulled a weed in your entire life."

This time she couldn't hold back a laugh. "Really? You think I'm too good for the people in Deadwood? You're an . . ." Heck, calling him an idiot wouldn't serve any purpose. She slapped his hand away. "I'll have you know, Mr. Johnson . . ."

"What's going on here?" A familiar voice filled the entry. "Johnson, what're you doing here? You're supposed to be breaking those horses."

Asa glanced at King, then Suzanna. "I'm here to talk sense into this woman. She thinks my Josiah is a troublemaker. She made him sit on a burr today."

Was King snorting? Was this funny to him?

King raised an eyebrow. "Really, Miss Lindstrom?"

"Yes, but . . ."

King stepped into the room. "Johnson, it's time you leave, or I'll call the sheriff. I'll speak with Miss Lindstrom." When Asa hesitated, King pointed to the door. "Now, Johnson. And I don't ever want to hear you've come to upset the teacher again."

Asa glared at her. "Fine. But she hasn't heard the end of this. No one, and I mean no one, harms my child."

Suzanna released a breath when Asa charged from the building. Was she going to have to worry if the man would return when she least expected it? What if he showed up during the day and harmed the children? He didn't have a gun, but it didn't mean he couldn't return with one at a later date. Was she going to have to hide a gun in her desk for protection?

"Are you all right?"

"Yes." She straightened her shoulders. "I'm grateful you showed up when you did, but I was able to handle Mr. Johnson myself."

King crossed his arms over his chest. "Really? You always let strange men poke you in the chest?"

Even though King was gentlemanly enough to keep his eyes on her face, heat crept up her neck and warmed her cheeks. It was a word people didn't use in mixed company. "Of course, I don't, but I've handled big men like him before. Men who believe they can make a woman cower. And if I can't make parents comprehend that

I have control over my classroom, they'll feel they can come here and tell me how to do my job."

"I hadn't thought about it that way. My father taught me it's a man's job to protect women." He raised an eyebrow. "And who did you have to protect yourself from?"

Suzanna flapped a hand at him and turned to the classroom. "Only a couple of guys back home who thought they deserved a kiss or two from a girl simply because she danced with him."

King followed her into the room. "That's right. Would you have treated Asa like Julia did to Mingus Thoreson when he bothered her?"

"Probably. At least it would get across the idea I don't put up with anything." She tapped the edges of the papers on the desk, straightening them out into a neat pile.

"So, did you really make Josiah sit on a burr?" he asked leaning against the edge of her desk.

Suzanna drew her eyes away from King's powerful thighs. His presence was making her nervous or at least making her nerves jump. "Yes."

"Why?"

She held the papers to her chest and explained the situation.

King chuckled. "I know the boy. He probably likes writing on the board so he can get out of classes."

Suzanna nodded. "You have that right."

"Can't you take recesses away from him?"

"You're kidding, right? I have to be outside with the other children. Can you imagine the trouble he'd get into if left to his own devices?" She shuddered.

"Yeah, I guess that's not such a good idea." He rested his hands on his knees. "Asa has this over-inflated idea about his son, but now I wonder if the things happening at the ranch aren't tricks he's pulling."

"You're having trouble out there?"

"Nothing I can't handle."

Obviously, he wasn't going to share. "By the way, what brings you to the schoolhouse?" She raised an eyebrow at him. "Need tutoring?"

King laughed. "You're cute."

"You shouldn't say such a thing."

"Why not? It's true."

She pressed the papers closer to her chest. "You simply want to embarrass me."

His dimples deepened. "Maybe." King slapped his knees and stood. "Mr. Ogden and the school board wanted someone to come out and see how things were going. I volunteered."

Suzanna's cheeks grew warmer. It wouldn't be long before her skin would melt right off her face. "That was kind of you."

"Well, it was an excuse to see you again."

She stomped her foot. "Mr. Winson, you must not say things like that." She turned her back on him and walked toward the back door.

King sighed. "I've asked you to call me King."

"That's not proper."

"C'mon, Suzanna. Like I've said before, we don't hold with strict Eastern etiquette out here." He followed her. "Besides, I always tell the truth. And the truth is, I'm attracted to you."

Suzanna spun on her heel to face him, nearly crashing into his broad chest. "Remember the contract?" She imagined an old spinster had written those rules. An old, ugly spinster who couldn't get a man if he were the last one on Earth. "I can't afford to break the contract."

"I know." He raked his fingers through his hair. "It's a stupid rule. I can see a teacher not drinking or going into a saloon. Hell—" He flinched. "I'm sorry. Heck, no proper woman should be seen in a saloon." He walked to the front of the school. "I'll leave now. Make sure to lock up after me," he called over his shoulder, then paused.

"By the way, members of the school board and a few parents will be stopping by now and again to see how things are going and to make sure the older boys don't give you any problems."

Suzanna followed him to lock the door. "It's not the older boys giving me grief. They want to learn something more than mining for gold. It's Josiah who is the problem."

King slapped his hat on his head. "I doubt it will do any good, but I'll talk to his father about the boy." He tipped the corner of his hat.

"Good afternoon, Miss Suzanna. Until we meet again."

Chapter Ten

King nudged the flanks of his Appaloosa. "C'mon Chester. I want to get to home before it gets dark."

While the horse was one of his favorites, there were days when the gelding was more interested in eating every leaf and tuft of grass, nibbling every branch, and smelling every rock and flower to see if it might taste good from the hotel to the ranch. Today was one of those days. With woods on either side of the trail, there was too much temptation. He pulled the reins guiding the horse back to the path.

He cracked a yawn. After visiting with Suzanna yesterday afternoon, he'd had a hard time falling asleep. Not only did her beauty fill his mind but seeing Johnson at the schoolhouse yelling at her made him even more protective of her. After seeing the Lindstrom girls in action against certain men, he didn't have any doubt she could take care of herself, but it was a man's job to protect a woman. No matter if she was a prostitute, a teacher, or a snooty muckety-muck like the banker's wife.

Thoughts of the banker raised his hackles. He and Silverstone had to be up to no good. He and Woods had never been on good terms. Woods thought because he was a banker, he had the right to buy up land in the Deadwood area before anyone else. King had yet to figure out how the banker knew when land was coming up for sale.

But when several lots on Main Street had become available and King had beaten him in buying them up, Woods had set out to make his life miserable. Telling people the food at the restaurant was spoiled. The beds had bedbugs, and his horses weren't worth the price of a horseshoe. He could handle those slanderous things, but when word spread like wildfire that Leona was servicing men in her upstairs room, he was ready to do battle.

The problem was, he couldn't prove it was Woods spreading rumor. Luckily most people in town knew what type of man Woods was and didn't pay any attention. Besides, when it came to the food, especially the pies Leona made, people couldn't resist eating at his establishment. And anyone who thought his sweet sister was a whore, didn't need to put down their coin for her food anyway.

Thankfully, there were several banks in town, and he didn't have to deal with Woods. But why was he talking with Silverstone? He gave Chester another nudge and slapped the reins on his neck. After seeing the two men talking at the dance, he couldn't shake the feeling something was up. Especially with the odd things going on at the ranch.

Even his housekeeper, Hilda, had reported clean clothes from the clothesline vanishing, a freshly baked pie disappearing, no eggs in the chicken coop in the morning, and a hunk of ham gone from the smokehouse.

Water had been thrown on a stack of hay. Before he'd noticed, the hay was already turning moldy in the heat. Tools and feed had gone missing and a wagon wheel from a brand-new wagon had snapped off while some of his employees were hauling wood.

A few of the smaller incidents King believed could be associated with Josiah. Toads found in a drawer in the kitchen scaring Bertha half to death. She wasn't scared of toads, but no one would expect to have one jump out at you from a silverware drawer. The men had learned to check beneath saddle blankets before putting saddles on the horses.

King shook his head. Why was the kid so engrossed with burrs? He didn't blame Suzanna one bit for making the brat sit on one. One of these days, he was going to tell his men if they found a burr under a blanket, to remove it, but not let the kid know. Then tell Josiah he had to ride the horse, just to see his reaction. He didn't want to harm one of his horses, but the temptation was strong. Seeing the young man flying through the air when the horse started bucking would serve the kid right.

After fifteen minutes of prodding the horse on, the roof of his barn came into view. Pride filled his chest. He'd worked darn hard to build his ranch. With most men looking for gold, there were few ranches or farms in the vicinity. In fact, he only knew of one north of Deadwood near Fort Meade.

As he rounded a bend in the trail, the rest of the ranch was visible. While he'd love to have the barn painted red like in Wisconsin, the color was virtually non-existent out here. He'd used the trees from the surrounding eighty acres of woods for lumber, leaving the wood to weather to a gray color. Four other buildings—a small one for chickens, a smokehouse, an icehouse, and one for his pigs— were whitewashed like the two-story main house. Whitewash was easy to come by as it was cheap and easy to make, but he hadn't been able to bring himself to have a white barn.

King entered the main yard, swung down from Chester, looped the reins over the hitching post in front of the house, and removed a package from the saddlebag. When he brought her a gift, it was usually spices or other useful kitchen items, but this time he'd bought flowered, light blue fabric. Her husband, Paddy, had hinted—no, told King—of Hilda's desire to make a new dress for herself to wear to church.

The front door was open. He imagined the back was, too, letting in a cross breeze through the house. The stout figure of his housekeeper filled the entrance.

"Hello, King. Whatcha bring me this time?" While her words were stern, a smile lit up her eyes.

Hilda might act fierce, but on the inside, she was soft as a kitten's fur. She and Paddy had been with him ever since he'd arrived in Deadwood. Originally, Paddy had been like the other men—crazy for gold. While her husband was drowning his feet in icy water, Hilda had helped King start the restaurant and hotel. When he'd decided it was in his best interests to start a ranch to supply the business with meat and vegetables, he'd asked Hilda to join him. Hilda was tired of her husband never finding gold and being gone all the time, so she practically grabbed the man by the ear and hauled him out to the land.

Paddy had been a carpenter before heading west, so his construction knowledge was invaluable. They'd been with him for two years and, in his opinion, were more like his parents than his employees. If it weren't for them, he was sure he wouldn't have made a go of the ranch.

Keeping the brown-papered package behind his back, King took the two steps to the covered porch in one step. "Why, Miss Hilda, what makes you believe I brought you anything?"

Hilda shook a finger at him. "Because, young man, you always do." She wiggled her fingers as a sign to hand it over. "I'm sure it's something I can use in the kitchen. So, give it to me so I can get lunch started."

King hid a grin. Wasn't she going to be surprised? "First, sit down."

"Now, why should I sit down?" she asked, folding her arms over her ample breasts.

"Because you work too hard." With the package still behind his back, he took her hand and guided her to one of the four rocking chairs on the front porch.

She sat down and set the chair in motion. "This is ridiculous, King. Hand it over."

With as much flourish as he could manage, King swept his arm from behind his back and placed the package on her lap. "For you, my gracious lady."

"Oh, go on. I'm no more gracious than those pigs over there."

King sat in a chair beside her. "You are, and no one can tell me any different. I don't tell you often enough how much I appreciate you." He pointed to her lap. "Now, unwrap your gift."

She ran her hands over the wrapping. "Gift? It's not for the kitchen?"

"Open it," King said sighing. Women, he'd never understand them.

Paddy joined them and leaned against a porch column and winked at King. "Welcome back. I see you brought my beautiful wife a present."

Hilda pressed a hand to her chest. "Oh, you two. You're crazy. First, he calls me gracious then you say I'm beautiful."

"You are," the men said in unison.

"Open up the package, Hilda, before whatever is in there falls apart. King didn't buy you a gift so you could sit there and stare at it."

Hilda untied the knot and let the strings slide to her lap. As if the package was a piece of precious glass, she turned it over and slipped a finger beneath the fold. King tapped a foot on the floor. If she didn't go any faster, he'd tear the wrapping off for her. Keeping packages wrapped was not one of his virtues. Ever since he was a kid, he'd always wanted to see what was hidden.

Finally, Hilda spread the paper. "Oh, my." She ran a hand over the fabric. "Oh, my." A tear ran down her cheek. "Oh, my."

"Can't you say anything else, woman?" Paddy asked, a hint of humor in his voice.

"I don't know what to say." She held the material to her chest and peered at King. Without another word, Hilda sniffed, jumped up from her chair, and raced into the house.

"What?" King raised a brow at Paddy. "She's crying. What did I do wrong?"

The older man laughed. "Nothing. She's happy."

"Happy? Then why the hell is she crying?"

"That's what women do when they're happy."

King stood, passed Paddy on the stairs, and released Chester's reins. "If I lived a million years, I'd still never understand women."

"I've been married to Hilda for twenty-five years, and I still have trouble figuring her out." With the horse between them, they walked to the barn. "If you ever find a woman you can understand, let me know, and I'll tell you you're lying." They entered the dim barn. "While you take care of your horse, I'll fill you in on what's been going on in the last week."

WITH HIS ARMS FOLDED beneath his head, King lay on a pile of hay. Sated with the supper of roast pork, fried potatoes, pickled red beets, and apple pie, he followed a falling star as it disappeared into the horizon. After spending a week in noisy, rowdy, smelly Deadwood, the peace and quiet of the ranch soothed him. Above him stars twinkled. He spotted the Big and Little Dippers and Orion's Belt.

Unlike Wisconsin, where it would have been impossible to lay outside without constantly swatting at pesky mosquitos, there were surprisingly few bugs and no blood-sucking insects here. As a child and young adult, he'd never imagined leaving his home state, but in the past two years, he'd grown to love the west. Yes, things were wild, but the challenges of creating a life of his own overcame the disadvantages of living in an untamed town.

Hilda had been mostly quiet during supper eaten around the wooden kitchen table Paddy had made, but she sniffled every time she glanced at him. If he'd known the material would make her cry, he'd have bought her a new potato masher.

As usual, Suzanna came to mind. He smiled to himself then grimaced. What was it that made her stick in his mind? Other than a childhood crush on the neighbor girl, there hadn't ever been a woman who'd caught his attention like this. Yes, she was pretty. She seemed to have a kind heart. She was strong enough to handle twenty-five children of various ages. Hell, she probably wasn't much older than the older students.

His stomach clenched at the memory of Asa yelling at her. Whether she believed it or not, Suzanna needed protection. While going to the store that first day, and as stubborn as the sisters had been, he highly doubted she'd accept his help. In his twenty-six years, with the exception of shielding his youngest brother from a bully at school, he'd never had this urge to hit someone on behalf of another person.

An owl's evening hoot was answered by another. Maybe its partner? Did owls partner for life? Most animals didn't. He let out a deep sigh. He was lonely. The restaurant and ranch kept him busy, but it didn't fulfill a need burning inside him. Watching the way Hilda and Paddy interacted with each other like two spring chickens—hugging, kissing, and teasing each other—he understood having a partner made life easier, brighter, happier. He knew the couple had spats now and again, but more than once he'd caught them in an embrace. The first time, he'd spun on his heels so fast, he'd left a gouge in the dirt. Now it didn't bother him, simply made him lonely.

It was more than his body's need for release. Hell, if that was what it was, he could go to any of the brothels and pay for a woman. He shuddered. No way. Those women were bad. He was Christian enough to realize they'd been put in terrible situations with usually no way out except death. In his opinion, men like Al Swearingen who brought women out here on false pretenses should be strung up by—He shut the idea down.

Another shooting star dropped from the sky. Why were there so many tonight? Damn. His mind was jumping around like a jackrabbit. What he needed to worry about was who the thieves were.

Something rustled in the brush. King held his breath and eased his hand to the gun lying beside him. It wasn't safe going around without a means of defense, whether it be against four- or two-legged varmints. A few seconds later, the pungent scent of skunk wafted through the air, growing stronger by the second. Time to hightail it to the house. If a family of skunks was passing through and saw him, he wouldn't be good to be around for days. Besides, it was getting late and he'd have a busy day tomorrow working with the horses to decide which to sell to the Army and which to keep for racing or working on the ranch.

He was halfway to the two-story house when he paused and cocked his ear toward the woods. A cough? There it was again. He pulled his gun from its holster.

"Who's there?" The night was silent. Even the crickets had stopped chirping. "If you know what's good for you, you'll come out right now." He cocked the gun when a figure appeared at the edge of the woods. "Stop," he called, aiming the gun at the person's chest and pulling back the hammer.

"It's me, Mr. King. Josiah."

He let out his breath and released the hammer. "What the hell are you doing in the woods at this time of the night?" Besides the scent of skunk making his eyes water, a sniffle filled the air.

"I was . . . I was . . ." More sniffling.

"Come out here and tell me what you're doing out here."

Reeking of skunk, the young boy shuffled closer. Tears ran down his scratched and muddy face, creating white stripes like those on a skunk's back. "I . . . I was looking for toads."

King slipped the gun back into the holster and covered his nose with a blue handkerchief. "Why?" Josiah took a step closer. King held out a hand to the boy. "Stop. Don't come any closer."

Josiah wiped a sleeve under his nose. "I wanted to take one to school to show the other kids."

Holding back a chuckle, King put a frown on his face. More than likely the boy wanted a toad to scare Suzanna or one of the other girls. "Really?" he said, keeping his tone skeptical. "I bet every kid in the school has seen or held a toad, including the girls."

"It's the truth, Mr. King. I swear."

Like he would believe the scamp. "Well, I'm going to go get your father. He can deal with your smell."

"Please, Mr. King. Don't tell my dad."

King did chuckle this time. "How do you think you're going to keep being sprayed by a skunk a secret? And if I find out you lied to either of us about why you were in the woods, I'll make sure to find as many chores as I possibly can to keep you busy from now until you're old enough to marry."

With that, he left the boy sniffling, strode to the Johnson's small house, and pounded on the door. "Asa, wake up."

After a few seconds, Johnson's sleepy-eyed face appeared in the crack of the door. "Whatcha want, King? We're sleeping in here."

"Not all of you."

"Whatcha mean?" Johnson opened the door wider.

"Where's Josiah?"

"Whatcha want my boy for?" He stuck his head out the door. "Holy month of Sundays," he said, pulling the collar of his nightshirt over his nose. "Who the hell got sprayed by a skunk?"

"Get your pants on and see for yourself. He's standing at the edge of the woods between the haystack and my house." Without waiting for his ranch hand, King headed for his house.

"Hey, aren't you comin' with me?"

"Nope," King called over his shoulder. "You can handle this one on your own." And maybe, just maybe, Johnson would learn his son wasn't such a good boy after all.

The next morning, King stood on the front porch, took a deep breath, and coughed. The air was still filled with the distinct odor of skunk. He pulled his red bandana over his nose and walked to the barn, passing one of the several horse troughs located throughout the ranch.

"Mornin'." Asa said beneath the white cloth covering his nose and mouth. He pushed a screaming Josiah under the water. "Mighty fine day, isn't it?"

Josiah sputtered and spit when he pulled him back up. "Pa, you're drownin' me."

He grinned at King and set the soapy scrub brush to Josiah's hair. "I do believe it will be a sunny day," he said ignoring his son's yells. "A great day for cleaning, wouldn't you say?"

"I do believe you're right, Asa," King laughed at the boy's flailing arms and kicking feet. "For sure you'll have to change clothes when you're done scrubbing your son clean." He hoped he left at least some skin on the boy.

"Yep. And I might use Hilda's clothesline to hang him out to dry, too."

With a light step, King entered the wide barn doors. One of his other hands, Ross O'Mara, was filling each horse's feeding trough with hay, a job Josiah usually did before leaving for school. "Morning, O'Mara."

The man didn't answer but tipped his hat and went to the next stall. O'Mara hadn't been with him long and was the quiet sort. Before he'd shown up at the ranch a month ago looking for work, saying he'd had enough of mining. He said his back hurt, his hands were arthritic, and he had nothing to show for his work. For a man who looked to be in his mid-thirties, he did move slowly, so King was inclined to believe his story. O'Mara did his chores without complaint, didn't swear, spit his chewing tobacco in the container placed in the barn, and had a way with horses.

Without another word, King passed the man. While not the largest barn King had ever seen, it was big enough for eight stalls, four on each side of the wide straw-covered aisle. The doors at the opposite end of the barn were opened to let the not-so-fresh air flow from one end to the other. When he and Paddy had built the barn, they'd put in a tack room at the front of it and, across the aisle, a small office for Paddy. King entered the office. Paddy sat at the desk. "Morning."

"Mornin', King. Looks like Asa's angel got himself into a heap of trouble last night," he said. "If we're lucky we'll get a good rain to wash away the smell."

"According to Asa, it's going to be a beautiful day."

"Damn." Paddy tossed down the paper he was looking over and leaned back in his chair. "So did the little brat say why he'd been in the woods?"

King dropped onto a white chair, its paint peeling and flaking to the floor. It had been his first attempt at making a piece of furniture. While not the best-looking and, with one leg a might shorter than the others, it at least held his weight. "He said he was looking for a toad to take to school."

"Hmph." Paddy hooked his fingers behind his head and eyed King. "Hilda said there was another chunk of ham missing from the smokehouse and there were only five eggs this morning."

"Did Josiah steal them?"

Paddy shrugged. "Could be. But why? Food is plenty. There's no reason for the boy to want more."

"I remember always being hungry when I was his age."

"Me too, but he only has to ask Hilda for food. She wouldn't deny him."

King rubbed the back of his neck. "If he is stealing, there has to be more to it."

"Was his pa with him last night?"

"No. I woke him up to take care of the kid. I wasn't going to touch the boy."

"Can't say as I blame ya." Paddy shook his head. "I can't figure out why he'd be in the woods after dark. I sure as hell wouldn't be."

"Maybe we need to keep an eye out when the sun sets."

"I'll talk to one of the hands." Paddy stood.

"Wait." King grabbed Paddy's arm. "It could be any one of the men who's stealing from us. I'll do it myself."

"What about when you're not here? Between hunting and being at the hotel, you're only here every other week."

"Damn. I hadn't thought of that." King jammed his hands in his pockets. "I'll come up with something. The big thing is to keep an eye on the horses' feed and hay. I can't afford to have them getting sick from spoiled food. If you can do that for me when I'm gone, that'll help. We can always replace food, but replacing a horse is too costly." He stood in the doorway. "It's almost as if someone is trying to ruin me."

"Ya. I thought of that, too. But who?"

King slapped the doorframe. "That's the million-dollar question, isn't it?"

Chapter Eleven

Late July 1879

Suzanna sat beside Julia, who sat beside Daniel on the wagon he'd rented. Excitement, along with nervousness, flowed through her. They were on their way to King's ranch to spend two days. Because she hadn't been on a farm since leaving Iowa, she was anxious to see what type of farming King did.

She'd had a hard time not giggling at Daniel's yellow eye. The last time she'd seen him on a picnic with the Haywood's two weeks ago, it was a horrible shade of purple and blue. Why they called it a black eye was a mystery to her. She'd never seen anyone whose eye was actually black after being socked.

Of course, Julia had oohed and aahed over his injured eye when he picked them up, as if he were a child in need of comfort. It wasn't as if she hadn't been with him after the picnic, where, among other incidents, she accidently popped him one in the eye. The entire episode was hilarious, but, thankfully, it had happened to Julia and Daniel and not her and King.

As Daniel discussed how the town's bigshots were talking about laying out and making Deadwood official, Suzanna kept an eye out for any unusual trees, flowers, or bugs she might use in her classes.

While being judiciously chaperoned by Colin and Sadie, King had helped her gather items for the classroom. Unlike Julia and Daniel, who they'd left napping, the storekeepers didn't let her and King out of their sight. A few times, King had managed to sneak them behind some bushes pretending to find nuts, but it wasn't long enough for King to do more than brush his fingers over her cheeks.

Suzanna's body tingled at the memory. She thought for sure he'd kiss her, but the darn Haywood's' were too quick for them. She mentally sighed. It was for the best anyway. She needed this job too badly to chance losing it by simply kissing a man, even though he was a dashing, well-built, funny, smart . . .

"Are you listening to us?" Julia said.

"What?" She turned her thoughts from King to her sister. "I'm sorry. I was thinking about a lesson I want to do with the children next week."

"Likely story," Julia whispered. "I see how you're blushing. You're thinking about King, aren't you? You know darn well you can't—"

"Oh, for Pete's sake, Julia. Quit reminding me. I've heard just about enough about the stupid contract."

Daniel leaned forward and rested his elbows on his knees, slapping the reins gently on the horse's rump. "Something wrong, ladies?"

"No, Daniel." Julia's voice went from snotty to sweet as maple syrup. "We're discussing a class Suzanna wants to teach next week."

"Anything interesting?"

Suzanna shrugged. "I hope so. I want the children to learn the various types of plants and flowers growing around us."

"King can help with that. He's a wiz at what grows around Deadwood." Daniel guided the horse around a bend in the trail. "You know, a lot of the kids in Deadwood haven't ever been on a ranch. I wonder if he, and the parents, would allow you to bring the children out here for a day."

"That's a wonderful idea, Daniel." Julia acted as if he were the most intelligent man in the world.

She had to admit, it was a good idea. "I could use some help, though. There's no way I'd bring so many children out here on my own and be able to keep track of them."

"I'll talk to King about it and see what his thoughts are."

"Thank you, Daniel." It truly was a wonderful idea. "It would be fun to show the children what it's like in the country." She folded her hands in her lap. "What is King's ranch like? Is it like a farm?"

"Didn't he tell you about it at the picnic?"

"No. I was busy collecting things for the classroom, and then you, two..." She giggled.

Julia slapped Suzanna's arm. "It wasn't funny."

"No, it wasn't funny. It was hilarious."

"Glad you find the misadventures of others so hysterical. Why, I could have been attacked by the mama bear."

Suzanna sucked in a breath to keep from laughing. Sometimes it was fun to see her older sister taken down a peg or two. Julia always thought Suzanna acted above her station as a poor farm kid, but sometimes her acting like the all-knowing older sibling was irritating. After all, they were only a year apart in age.

"Girls, let's not bicker," Daniel said. "Except for my eye and our egos, no one got hurt."

"Don't forget your tongue." Suzanna couldn't help reminding him of Julia accidentally hitting him in the jaw, making him bite his tongue.

Daniel shook his head. "Okay, so let's get back to what King's ranch is like. I don't get out here often, but when I do, I'm greeted by his housekeeper, Hilda, like I'm her long-lost son. You'll love her and she'll take you under her wing like you're her daughters. She and her husband, Paddy, never had any children of their own, so King is like one of theirs. I believe she spoils him when he's home."

"What type of animals does he have?" Suzanna asked.

"I'd say the usual farm animals. Cows, pigs, chickens, ducks, a couple of sheep. Hilda has a large garden where she grows fresh vegetables for the restaurant."

The roof of a building came into view. "Anything else?"

"Horses. He has a lot of horses."

"Why?" Julia asked.

"He breeds some for racing, sells others to people in California, and raises sturdier ones for the Army at Fort Meade and for his farm."

As they drew closer, the roof became part of an unpainted barn. Daniel slowed the horse and pulled up in front of a white, two-story house with a covered porch running the length of the front.

"I need to warn you a bit about Hilda," Daniel said, peering around Julia at the house. "On the outside, she acts like a she-bear, but on the inside she's soft as cotton. I already said how she loves King. But I swear the woman has eyes in the back of her head. Somehow, she sees everything happening on the ranch. She'll keep an eye on you ladies to make sure King, myself, or any of the ranch hands don't pull any shenanigans. If she can't she'll sic Paddy on us. And, believe me, Paddy is built like an ox and none of us want to have to deal with him when he's angry."

A SHORT, ROTUND WOMAN with her hair in a Dutch braid came through the front door. "Daniel, my boy. It's about time ya got here." Her German accent was strong as if she'd only recently came from the old country. She folded her arms beneath her ample bosom and tapped her foot on the wooden floor.

Suzanna swallowed around the lump in her throat. The woman looked formidable. Maybe it hadn't been such a good idea for them to come out here for the weekend. Maybe they should tell Daniel to turn the wagon around and take them back home.

Before she could utter a word, King approached the wagon and, removing his dusty gloves, helped her from the wagon. His appearance surprised her. She'd always seen him dressed in nice pants, a white shirt and tie, and a coat. Today he wore dungarees, a plaid shirt rolled up to his elbows, a pair of work boots, and a hat that may have spent time with the pigs. Daniel hopped down and assisted Julia, who came around the front of the wagon and stood beside her.

"I'm not so sure about this," Julia said under her breath. "She looks rather scary."

"I agree."

In the next moment, Hilda's demeanor changed. Her wide grin exposed dimples in her plump cheeks. She ran down the front steps and approached with arms opened wide.

"My dears." Her German accent deepened. "So nice to have women on the ranch. Ya. Such pretty ladies, too." She gave each man a speculative look and slapped her hands on her ample waist. "Who are these lovely ladies?"

Daniel grinned. "Hilda, this is Julia Lindstrom and her sister, Suzanna, who is Deadwood's new schoolteacher. Ladies, this is Hilda Kearney, King's housekeeper."

Hilda took the women by their elbows and led them to the front porch. "Come join me for coffee and my special apple strudel." Before they entered the house, she yelled over her shoulder, "King, bring da bags in for dese ladies."

They had no choice but to follow the housekeeper into the house. "Here, let me take your bonnets. No need for such fripperies inside da house."

While not large, the interior was like a mansion compared to their small soddy back home. They immediately stepped into a long hallway. A staircase, its banister polished and shining like a new penny, rose to the second story. A door to her left revealed a living room with a large fireplace gracing the outside wall.

Before Suzanna had a chance to poke her head into the living room, Hilda pointed to a door situated at the base of the staircase.

"On this side is King's office." The housekeeper moved down the hallway. "On the left is the parlor, although why we have one is beyond me. Mr. King has yet to show any interest in bringing a woman to live here." She pointedly looked between the sisters.

Oh, boy. Hilda must believe King brought us here to find a wife. Wonder which one of us she has pegged for him. A cursory glance showed a room devoid of furniture, with the exception of a small secretary made in oak.

"King made it himself. Of course, Paddy helped because King didn't know the difference between an awl and nail."

"It's lovely, but a bit empty," Julia said.

"Ja. I keep tellin' King he should decorate it, but he says it can wait." She eyed the women again. "Personally, I think he's waiting for a wife to make it her own."

Yep, she was definitely wondering which one of us will be decorating the room. Julia smirked at her. If Hilda hadn't been watching, she would have stuck her tongue out at her sister.

Hilda pointed to a room across the hall. "This is the dining room. I don't know why King had to have one. After all, we take our meals in the kitchen."

"That's what we do, too," Julia said.

"Our current house doesn't have a dining room," Suzanna added. "And there wasn't room for one in our soddy at home."

"You lived in a soddy?" Hilda raised an eyebrow.

"Yes, we did. Our family has a farm in Iowa. We have eight siblings who are still at home."

"So, you both have worked on a farm? Fed animals? Gathered eggs? Cooked?"

"Yes." She didn't want Hilda to get the wrong idea, so she wasn't about to add they knew how to take care of babies, too, because there was always one being born.

Hilda clapped her hands and smiled, her dimples deepening. "Why, dat's wonderful."

When Hilda walked down the hallway, Julia nudged Suzanna in the side.

"What?"

Julia grinned. "She's thinking you'll make a good wife for King," she whispered.

"And why is it me she's pegged for King?" Suzanna nudged Julia back and smirked at Julia's wide eyes. "It could be you." Put that in your pipe and smoke it. Without a backward glance, she followed Hilda into a kitchen that took up the entire back of the house.

If she were to walk straight through from the hallway, she could go out a back door. On the right side of the room were cupboards, above and below and counters filling the outside walls. Unlike their house in Deadwood, the cupboards had real doors, not curtains. A window above the sink with a pump handle revealed pine and what looked like apple trees. A large, sturdy, butcher-block table stood in the middle of the area. Surely it wasn't where everyone ate. There were no chairs.

"Over here is where we eat," Hilda said as if she'd read Suzanna's mind. "Ya, we aren't fancy here."

It was fancy to Suzanna. An oak table with eight chairs, three on each side and one on each end, surrounded the table. The outer walls were filled with windows, bringing outdoors inside the house. There was a closed door in a corner of the room. Probably a pantry, but wasn't it an odd place to put one? Wouldn't it have been better in the working part of the kitchen?

"Ya. King loves his windows. Says he can't stand dark rooms."

"I can see that," Julia said, awe filling her voice. "Our soddy only had two windows, so it was always dark inside, even on a sunny day."

Julia hadn't mentioned the two windows had been covered with greased paper, giving little light or protection from the cold winter winds and making the small house seem smaller.

"Ladies." Hilda clapped her hands to get their attention. "I'll show you the upstairs. There are four bedrooms. One is King's and one Daniel stays in when he visits. But with you ladies here this weekend, they'll stay in the bunkhouse."

Suzanna almost said it was ridiculous for King had to vacate his own bed simply because she and Julia were staying. But propriety was important, even out here where no one would know they shared the same floor of the house.

"Da boys should have your bags in your rooms by now. When you're done getting settled, I'll have a nice lunch ready for you."

Hilda opened the closed door. What was she doing? Why wasn't she going back down the hallway? The door revealed a wide set of stairs.

"King said his parents' house had a back stairway, so his mother could sneak downstairs in the morning without waking anyone up."

What a clever idea. It probably kept the children from running through the house while they entertained guests, too.

Like the downstairs, there were two doors on either side of the hallway. A window at the opposite end gave the only light, making it dim and dark. Four candle sconces hung on the walls, which must be used at night. Maybe if the bedroom doors weren't closed during the day, it would illuminate the hallway better.

Hilda opened a door. "This is your room, Miss Lindstrom," she said to Julia. "And this one is yours." Her room opposite of Julia's was a bright, cheerful room. Hilda left, her heavy footsteps echoing down the back stairwell.

Her bag hadn't arrived yet, so she walked past the patchwork quilt-covered bed with its metal head and footboard. She took in the scenery from the window. A breeze ruffled the sheer curtains pulled aside to let in the light.

She must be in the front of the house, as the porch roof hid her view of anything but distant trees and the barn. A movement in the woods caught her attention. It didn't look like an animal. It was too tall, but not tall enough to be a man. A young boy? Why would a boy be out in King's woods? Did he have a child he hadn't told her about? It wasn't any of her business if he did or not. But why would he hide a child?

The deep murmur of voices came up through the window distracting her from the woods. What was so important about King and Daniel's conversation that they hadn't brought up their bags? She'd love to get out of her traveling dress and into a skirt and blouse. Oh, well. She'd have to wait until they were done with their yammering.

KING GRINNED AT THE women disappearing into the house. He shook his head and handed a bag to his friend. "You get what Hilda's thinking, don't you?"

"'Fraid so." Daniel carried two of the bags. "How are we going to convince her we're not out to marry them?"

"Maybe you aren't, but I am," King said, coming to a halt at the porch stairs.

"Really?"

King frowned. "Is it so hard to tell I'm interested in her?"

"Well, no." Daniel followed his friend up the porch steps where King set his bag on the floor. Evidently this conversation wasn't over. "What about her teaching?"

"I'll be patient for the remainder of the year, which is actually ten months now. I don't want her to lose her reputation or her job." King raised an eyebrow. "And what about you and Julia? I've seen how you look at each other, so you can't tell me you don't have feelings for her."

King snorted at Daniel's red face. "You don't need to answer me. A blind man could see it. So, what are you going to do about it? She doesn't have the strictures of a teaching contract."

"I don't know." Daniel removed his hat and raked his fingers through his hair. "I know you're going to think I'm stupid, but I'm . . ."

"Falling in love with her?"

Daniel peered through the screen door. "Shh. Keep your voice down. How can a man tell if he's in love or not?"

"Beats the hell out of me." King ran a hand down his face. "If having a woman on your mind all the time, wanting to be with her every hour, and worrying about what the rest of your life would be like if she wasn't with you is love, then I'm head over heels with Suzanna."

"We're a lost cause, aren't we?"

"At least we're in good company."

"You gents coming in or not?" Hilda's strong voice came down the hallway. "The ladies would like to freshen up."

Daniel chuckled. "Better do as we're told, or Hilda will feed Julia and Suzanna, but not us."

"WOULD YOU LADIES LIKE a tour of the ranch?" King asked after a lunch of cold ham sandwiches, hot chicken soup, and warm lemonade.

"I'd love to," Suzanna said. "I'm curious about the difference between a ranch and farm."

"For one thing, it's the size of the property," King answered, pulling out her chair.

Suzanna found the bonnets Hilda had hung on hooks behind the front door. After handing one to her sister, Suzanna tied hers beneath her chin, and followed the other three out the door. How she wished she had the nerve to hook her hand in King's elbow as Julia had with Daniel and gaze up at him with adoring eyes. Well, okay, maybe not the adoring eyes part. Julia looked simply idiotic the way she was simpering over Daniel. Is that what happened when you kissed a man—your brain turned to mush?

Suzanna admired the large corral surrounded by white fencing. While the barn wasn't red like she was used to, it was certainly larger than the one back home. There weren't any cattle, only horses.

"How many acres do you have, King?" Suzanna asked when they reached the fence.

"Just shy of a thousand." King propped his foot on the bottom board of the fence. "With the woods, rocks, cliffs, rivers, and creeks on the property, I don't have nearly so much open ground to work, only enough to raise most of what we need at the restaurant and feed the hands here at the ranch."

That many acres were incomprehensible. "Oh, my. That's a lot of land, but I can see why you'd need so much. Back home we have only twenty acres, but it's mostly flat, so we can use it all for crops."

King stared across the corral. "Back in Wisconsin we had forty acres, but twenty was wooded, and we farmed the rest. Once I bought this land and decided to ranch, it was difficult getting used to finding ways to use the land. With so many trees, I cut them down, sell part of it in town, and donate some to the school."

"What about our house? How will Julia and I get wood?"

He tucked an errant strand of hair into Suzanna's bonnet. "Don't worry, we plan on making sure you have enough wood for the winter."

He pointed to a clearing to the right of the barn. Corn, nearly waist high, fluttered in the breeze. "As I cut the trees, Paddy and I cleared the stumps and turned the land into fields."

"Do you use the crops for the ranch?"

"Not all of it. I try to use as much as I can for the restaurant." He pointed into the woods. "Believe it or not, I have a large field out there where I raise steers. I use the beef, and whatever wild animals I can kill, for the restaurant and also sell to the Army."

"Do you have any cows?"

King grinned down at her. "Ah, a woman who knows the difference between cows and steers."

"I'd better or my father would skin me alive. Most people believe all cattle are called cows."

"Besides the two at the ranch, I have three cows in the barn behind the restaurant. I have a woman to milk them and churn butter. I sell the excess milk and butter to the other restaurants in town." He took her elbow and guided her toward the barn. "Hilda raises the chickens. Some are solely for eggs, others for butchering."

"I imagine it helps not having to buy food from others and having the income from selling your extra." The more she talked with King, the more impressed she was with his intelligence. Brains, brawn, and beauty wrapped up in one man. Although she had a feeling he wouldn't enjoy knowing she considered him a beautiful specimen of the male species.

They stood at the barn door letting their eyes adjust to the dim interior. The whinnying of horses told her there was more than one inside. At home they'd only had two plow horses, Dell and Dale. Tall and wide, she, Julia, and their younger brother, George would ride one or the other if their pa wasn't using them.

Behind her, Julia was telling Daniel about their team as they came up to the barn.

"Anyway, Dell and Dale were plow horses. Maybe seventeen hands. Big heads. Big back ends. Wide middles. If Pa wasn't using them, whenever we had a spare moment Suz, George, and I hauled blocks of wood to whichever horse was free and climbed on, one behind the other."

"No saddle?"

"Are you kidding? There wasn't a saddle big enough for either of the horses. We didn't use a bridle or reins, either. The person in front held on to the mane while the other two held on to the one in front of them."

Suzanna turned and grinned. "Oh, my gosh. Are you telling him about Dell and Dale?"

"Yes. I was maybe eight, Suzanna, seven, and George, six. We must have looked ridiculous on top of the horse, plodding around the yard, our dresses hiked up to our knees."

"The horse was so wide," Suzanna added, "and our legs so short, they stuck straight out from their sides, our muddy bare feet flapping in the breeze like Ma's sheets on the clothesline. We thought we were special riding miles from the ground."

Suzanna smiled at the memory. "Even though they were huge, they were gentle yet worked like . . . well, plow horses." The scent of horse dung brought on a flash of homesickness. Was George still giving the little ones rides? Was he now in front with Patsy and Timmy behind him, giggling like she and Julia had?

"Suzanna?" King said, bringing her back to the present, as he entered the barn. "You coming?"

"If you raise animals for food, why do you have horses?" They stopped at the first horse. Daniel had told them this already, but she wanted to listen to King's deep voice.

"I breed some for racing," King said, running his hand down the forehead of a pure-black horse poking his head over its door. "I also raise sturdier ones for miners and any farmers we have in the area, and for the Army at Fort Meade."

Daniel stood in front of the next pen scratching the ears of a brown horse with a white diamond on its forehead. "Hi there, Penny. How's my girl today?" He waved Julia over. "King raises the racers for a couple of men who own a racetrack in California. They come out here in the fall and spring to see what he has for sale. King has become well known for his fast horses."

Suzanna rubbed her hand against the horse's silky muzzle, accidentally touching King's fingers. Their warmth burned her skin. She caught her breath. Had King noticed? The way he jerked his hand back made her wonder if he had. What could she say to cover the awkward moment? "Aren't there racetracks around here?"

"Of course," King said, moving to the next stall where a handsome ginger-colored mare with a white star on her forehead, greeted him. "Besides racing the road between here and Lead, the Deadwood Driving Park Association has a track they take care of."

"Do you race your horses there?" Julia asked, standing beside Daniel, who was giving attention to a Palomino and nudging his pockets.

"Sorry, Trigger, no carrots today." He gestured to the ginger mare. "King usually races Star."

"Does she win?" Suzanna asked, following King down the straw-covered dirt floor.

King shrugged. "Sometimes. It depends on how many men enter." He took a water-filled bucket and lifted it over Star's door. "The entry fee can get as high as a thousand dollars. So, a man would have to be rich or hit the mother lode to enter."

Suzanna enjoyed the silky softness of Star's muzzle. "How much does the winner get?"

"Winner takes all," Daniel called from across the floor. "So, if ten men enter, the winner takes ten thousand dollars."

"Ten thous . . ." Her breath caught. "Men actually pay that much to race a horse?" At home, men raced simply for bragging rights. "How often do they have contests?"

King removed the empty bucket. "A few times a summer. More men have entered once we banned Nelson Armstrong from entering."

Julia stood by Suzanna. "Why?"

"No one trusted the veterinarian," Daniel said. "His horse, Gold Dust, was simply too fast, so we suspected Armstrong was doctoring the horse with a drug to make him faster."

"Do you enter, too, Daniel?" Julia asked a hint of worry in her voice.

Daniel laughed. "Are you kidding? Number one, I don't own a horse; number two, I don't have that kind of money; and number three, I'm not crazy enough to race a horse fast for fear of falling off. I leave it to brash and foolish men like King."

They reached the end of the barn, stopping to greet each horse. With four horses on each side, and with her and Julia taking the time to admire and pet each one, it was a bit before they walked out the open doors at the end of the barn. A fence started on the right side of the door, went out to the woods, and edged along the trees to the left forming a wide path.

"This would take us out to the corral." King took Suzanna's elbow and turned her back to the inside of the barn. "I don't want you lovely ladies to get your shoes dirty."

Suzanna nearly laughed out loud. Get their shoes dirty? Why, anyone walking in Deadwood had their shoes immediately covered in mud. As hard as she worked on keeping them clean, she hadn't had a neat pair since moving out here. And if it wasn't muddy, it was dusty. "I wouldn't worry about that, King. Remember, Julia and I were raised on a farm."

"Would you ladies like to go for a ride?" King asked.

On one of his racehorses? Suzanna gulped, but before she could say anything, Julia piped in.

"Um, if we're going to ride, do you have anything in the slower range? One who is old, lazy, and doesn't care if the rider has never used a saddle before?"

King laughed. "You, too, Suzanna?" When she nodded, he went on. "I'm sure I can find one for you. I'm afraid I don't have a side-saddle for you ladies."

"Plodding sounds good to me." She smiled at King. "We haven't used a regular saddle, let alone a side-saddle."

"Great," King said. "I'll get one of the hands to saddle up our horses while we change clothes and ask Hilda to pack us a snack."

They stood outside the barn doors while King talked to Paddy. From the corner of her eye, she once again spotted movement in the woods. This time the person was taller and slid behind a tree as if he didn't want to be seen. Why would someone be hiding at King's? Before she could ask, another man came from the barn and glared at her. Mr. Johnson? What was he doing here?

MOUNTING A HORSE WITHOUT showing her legs and riding a horse with a saddle, were things Suzanna had never counted on doing. Being the gentlemen they were, King and Daniel averted their eyes while she and Julia swung their legs over the horse then arranged their skirts to cover any bare skin showing. Personally, she wished for a pair of pants like they'd worn on the farm, making life easier. Someday, maybe women would be able to wear pants like men and not be looked down upon.

They were certainly warmer in the winter. No cold air blowing up skirts. No snow sliding into boots. And the freedom to run and play like her brothers and the boys at school. It would also keep disgusting boys like Jeremy Skitter from trying to lift her skirt to see what was beneath it. She shuddered.

"Cold?" King asked, bringing his horse alongside hers where the path widened enough to ride side-by-side.

"No." She gripped the reins, making her horse turn its head and try to move closer to King. Julia and Daniel rode behind them, their voices too low to hear the conversation.

"Lighten up on the reins a bit." When she did, he frowned. "What's wrong?"

"I'm not sure. I thought I saw someone in the woods from my bedroom window this morning. The person wasn't large, so it could have been a child." Was this the point where he tells her he has a son? "When we were waiting for you to come from the barn, I saw someone again, only this time it was an adult."

"The young one was probably Josiah."

"Josiah? What would he doing out here? I thought he lived in town."

"No. His father works for me and has a small house here."

"Oh. I was wondering why Mr. Johnson was in your barn. It was probably Josiah I saw then." Suzanna guided her horse around a tree stump in the middle of the trail.

King shook his head. "Damn kid will never learn."

"What do you mean?"

"He won't stay out of those woods. A few days ago, he was wandering out there in the dark and got sprayed by a skunk. You'd think it would keep him from exploring."

"Well, boys like to explore. Anyway, my brothers do, though we don't have much for them explore in." She bit her bottom lip. "But the person I saw this afternoon was an adult. When he saw me, he hid behind a tree."

KING DIDN'T LIKE THE sound of that. It wasn't the first time one of his hands had told him someone was skulking around, but as soon as they raced to find the person, he was gone. It had to be the person stealing from him. He and Paddy needed to set a trap to catch the culprit.

"I'm sure it's nothing," he said, not wanting to scare Suzanna while she was visiting. "That scamp, Josiah, said he was looking for toads to bring to school."

Suzanna laughed. "Sounds like something he'd do. I'm sure it wasn't for show and tell, either. I'll have to keep a better eye on him." She glanced over at him and frowned. "But why would he be looking for toads in the dark?"

King shrugged. "Beats me. What bothers me is even though being sprayed by a skunk after Asa was in bed, Asa still thinks the sun rises and sets on the boy. His wife died early last year. I believe he's afraid he'll lose his son, too, and it has made him overlook the boy's shenanigans." He'd been keeping an eye on Suzanna making sure the ride wasn't wearing on her. "Has Asa shown up at the school again?"

"No. I lock the door as soon I see the last student leave. I call Julia when I'm leaving school, and she watches for me until I'm safely at home. I hate having to look over my shoulder all the time."

"I'll have a talk with him again." He stopped his horse in a small, grassy area in the woods. It wouldn't be the first time he'd taken a break here. "We've been riding for an hour. Let's take a break." He didn't miss the look of relief on Suzanna's face. Would she be able to dismount without falling from the horse?

Daniel and Julia came up behind them. "Why're we stopping?" Daniel asked.

"The ladies aren't used to riding and we've been in the saddle for an hour. Now would be a good time to see what Hilda packed for us." King swung his leg over the saddle and hit the ground.

Daniel did the same and stood at Julia's side. "Need help?"

Julia released the reins. "Um, I've never dismounted from a saddle before. How do I do this?"

"Put your hands on the saddle horn and swing your right leg over the back of the horse. I'll be here to help you." Daniel held up his arms and when Julia swung her leg over the horse's rump, he took her by the waist and eased her to the ground. The smile she gave him said how much she appreciated the help.

King wrapped his horse's reins around a branch and stood by Suzanna's horse. Now what should he do? Daniel and Julia were dating, so his friend could get away with holding Julia by the waist. He was sure if they'd been alone, Daniel would have stolen a kiss or two. But he and Suzanna weren't dating. She was the schoolmarm, and according to the damn contract, couldn't be touched by a man. He curled his fingers into his palms and raised an eyebrow at Daniel, who grinned back.

Julia slapped her hands at her waist. "Oh, for heaven's sake. It's not as if you're going to molest her by helping her down. Besides, who's going to say anything?"

Who was blushing more, him or Suzanna? When she swung her leg over the back of the horse's rump, he put his shaking hands around her slim waist. As much as he would have liked to let her body slide down his, he stepped back and gently released her when her feet touched the ground. With a shaky breath, he turned on his heel and led her horse next to his, looped the reins around a branch, and willed his body to calm down. Hell, one year. No, make that ten months, two weeks, and six days until Suzanna was free.

Behind him, Daniel chortled. Ass. With his body under control he restrained from giving his friend the middle-finger salute. Instead, he removed the basket tied to his saddle horn and the blanket he'd attached to the back of his saddle. Without looking at her, he handed Suzanna the blanket. "Can you and Julia spread this out?"

Daniel slapped King on the back. "Year's a long time isn't it?" he whispered, his voice filled with laughter.

"Shut the hell up or I'll tell Julia about the time you got so drunk, you fell into a horse trough and nearly drowned. What'll she think of you then?" Without waiting for an answer, he joined the ladies, set the basket on the spread-out blanket, and knelt beside them. "I believe Hilda put lemonade and some of her famous sugar cookies in here."

He pulled out a jug of lemonade and four jelly jars to be used as glasses, all wrapped in towels to keep them from breaking. A bowl also wrapped in towels held enough cookies for ten people.

Julia took the bowl. "How much does she think we eat?" she asked, giggling.

King dug back into the basket. "She also put in apples and gingersnaps."

"Good ol' Hilda," Daniel said. "She never forgets anything."

Suzanna sat, tucked her legs to the side, and pulled her skirt over her shapely ankles, disappointing King when they disappeared. She poured lemonade into the glass jars and handed them out. "Daniel, Julia was telling me about the men getting sick in town. Has anyone figured out how or why they're getting ill?"

Daniel took a bite of cookie and shook his head. "No, a few of the saloon owners have hired me to try to learn what is going on." He glanced at King. "But I'm not the only one trying to solve a mystery. King's having problems of his own."

Smacking his friend wouldn't look good in front of the girls, but the temptation was strong.

Suzanna set her cookie on her lap. "Really? What's going on?"

"It's nothing serious." Why couldn't Daniel have kept his big mouth shut. "Only food disappearing."

"Food? Are you kidding me?" Daniel said, scowling at King. "What about someone watering down your hay, turning it so moldy you couldn't use it for the horses. What about two horses going missing? Or the cattle disappearing?"

Suzanna gasped. "King, is that true?"

"Yes, but it's nothing to concern yourself about."

"Does this have anything to do with Mr. Johnson?" she asked, propping her glass of lemonade against her leg.

Daniel brushed an ant from the blanket. "Why would you think Asa is involved?"

"I had a little incident with him at the school. Nothing serious."

"I still want an explanation, Suzanna."

King stepped in and told him what happened. "I took care of it. He can't be involved with the thefts around here."

"How can you be sure?" Daniel shook his head. "He does have a bit of a temper, and Josiah is just as bad. We can't have parents accosting our teachers simply because their kid pulled a stupid stunt and got in trouble for it."

Julia placed a hand on Daniel's. "Settle down. King said he handled it. The man works here, so he can keep an eye on him."

"All right, but I still don't like it. Maybe the kid is stealing food and selling it in town."

King shook his head. "I doubt it. It would be hard to hide food while riding a horse. He doesn't have anything to carry it in. And it would be a bit hard to bring horses into town without people asking where he got them." He took a swallow of lemonade. "Besides, this isn't your problem. You have enough to worry about with trying to solve the mystery of the men getting sick. Paddy and I will catch the thieves."

"That's true," Daniel said, taking his third cookie from the bowl.

A rustling from the woods caught King's attention. Had anyone else heard it? The noise stopped then started again.

"Did anyone else hear that?" Suzanna asked, a cookie an inch shy of her lips.

"I did." Julia glanced over her shoulder.

"Me, too," King and Daniel answered at the same time. "Could be a deer."

Julia went pale. "Or maybe a bear?"

"Don't anyone move," King whispered. "Let's let whatever it is go away on its own."

The wind whispered through the pines. A fly landed on the lip of Suzanna's jar. An ant crawled over his leg, picked up a cookie crumb and skittered away. They let out a collective sigh when the noise stopped, but as soon as King moved to stand, it started again. Thoughts of Josiah and the skunk flashed through his mind. That would be all he needed. Getting sprayed by a skunk would endear Suzanna to him about as much as them landing in the mud together.

"Look," Suzanna said, jutting her chin to the woods behind Daniel, "but do it slowly."

"Heavens," Julia whispered. "Daniel, don't move."

"Damn," King muttered under his breath. He'd apologize to the ladies later after the skunk coming out from under the brush left the area.

"What's happening?" Daniel asked, his voice barely above a whisper.

"A skunk," Suzanna shuddered. "Oh, lordy, it's a family of skunks, and they're headed this way."

The temptation to jump up and run was strong. "Don't. Anyone. Move." King said through his clenched teeth, as a large female, followed by five babies, ambled their way. One skunk was bad enough, but a mother with babies could be downright dangerous. It was rather humorous when Josiah was sprayed, but now he couldn't see any humor in the situation.

Because no one was moving, the bees took it as a sign to come in and enjoy their lemonade. Each one of their glasses had one or two flying in. One flew up and landed on Daniel's mustache. He twitched his mouth.

"Don't do that," King whispered. He wasn't sure if baby skunks' sprayers worked until they were older. But why take a chance they didn't activate as soon as they were born. Besides, if the mother sensed danger, a spray from her could be disastrous to them.

The skunks waddled closer, the babies more than a little bit curious about the food and people sitting like statues. He dared a glance at Suzanna. One particular inquisitive youngster was crawling onto her lap. Tears ran down her face, but she didn't flinch when the kit took a cookie from her hand and curled into a ball on her lap like it was a kitten settling in for a rest. Tonight, when they were safely in the ranch house, he was going to sketch Suzanna and the skunk and maybe they'd get a good laugh from the incident.

The mother and the other babies attacked the bowl of cookies. Their murmurs and grunts of delight as they chewed through the snack filled the air. King's eyes began to water and his nose itch from the slight scent of skunk. How many more cookies were in the bowl? Just once, why hadn't she packed enough for one each, instead of for an army—and not an army of skunks?

"I'm going to be sick," Julia whispered, barely moving her lips.

"Don't you dare," Suzanna whispered back. "Breath through your mouth."

The kit on Suzanna's lap, having finished her cookie, ambled off and joined its siblings. One of them hissed at the newcomer. Another one swatted at it with its paw. The mother growled. Two others tipped the bowl over near Daniel's feet. Suzanna's kit raced after the bowl, knocking one of its siblings onto its back. The mother drew back her lips and hissed again.

Would she spray her offspring? Would the offspring spray each other? His nose itched, eyes watered, and a cramp was building in his calf from sitting cross-legged for too long. The mother, obviously angry at the fighting, grabbed one of them in her teeth and dragged it kicking and screeching to the woods using skunk language to call her other babies. Leaving the empty bowl behind, the four siblings scampered off after their mother.

"Can you see them?" The bee continued cleaning his antennae, so Daniel barely moved his lips.

"Yes," King answered. "Don't move yet. With what seemed like an eternity, the sounds of the sextet moving through the brush dissipated. He let out a deep breath. "Okay. We're safe."

Julia huffed out a shaky breath. Suzanna flopped onto her back and threw an arm over her face. Daniel swore and swatted at the bee.

"Sorry, ladies for swearing."

Julia flipped a hand in the air. "Don't worry. If I was the swearing kind, I'd join you. This was worse than the bear at our last picnic."

King stood and chuckled. "We should reconsider ever going on another picnic again. I believe we're jinxed." He took Suzanna's outstretched hand and helped her up.

"I'm never going to get the scent of those critters out of my nose." She picked up the tipped-over glasses and placed them in the basket, tucking a towel in between them. "Can we go home now?"

"I wanted to show you my cattle, but we should head home. The skunks were heading in the direction I wanted to go, so it would be best if we hightail it out of here."

Julia picked up the bowl and wrapped a towel around it. "Sounds like a good plan to me."

King shook his head as he mounted. Mud, bears, men attacking, and now skunks. Time spent with Suzanna and Julia was never boring. Would they ever get a break?

When they had everything in the basket and the folded-up blanket tucked behind King's saddle, they mounted up and headed for the ranch, the trip back going considerably faster than the one going out.

Chapter Twelve

Monday morning, Suzanna unlocked the schoolhouse door. The children weren't due to arrive for an hour yet, so she had time to set out slates for the younger children and quills and ink for the older ones. She pulled up the blinds and raised the windows to refresh the stale weekend air. She paused at the window facing the woodshed and horse pen and drew in a breath.

There were two horses in the stall munching on hay. Two horses she was positive didn't belong to any of her students. School had been in session long enough she was familiar with each child's horse. She cracked open the front door to scan the playground then searched through the windows on the other side of the building. No children were playing or lounging about. Why were there horses at the school and where were the owners?

Suzanna lifted her skirts and raced between the desks to get a better look at the horses. Her skin prickled and a jolt of fear went down her spine. Instead of standing in front of the window, she peered around the corner and gasped.

The horses were gone. Had she imagined them? Heaven knew she was tired from the weekend, but not so tired she'd conjure up two horses that didn't exist. She checked to the left, then right. Nothing. Once again, she checked out the front door, but re-locked it. There was nothing out the back door, nor the other side windows. How could two horses have disappeared into thin air?

Shrugging, she sat down at her desk and tapped a quill against the wood. Should she add this to the mysteries Daniel and King had or ignore it? Should she call King? He had ridden back into town with them yesterday afternoon. But what would she say? There were horses in the horse shed who'd up and disappeared into thin air? He'd think she was crazy. Best to put it out of her mind and relive the pleasant weekend.

Except for the skunk incident, the weekend had been fun. There were more walks, but no picnics. They played checkers, cribbage, and even a couple of rounds of charades. King taught them a card game played in his home state of Wisconsin. Sheepshead was a rather unusual game where instead of the king being the high card, the queen was. It took them a while to learn it, but after ten or twenty hands, they got the hang of it.

Since she and Julia missed the farm so much, King allowed them to feed the horses, and, to give Hilda a break, the pigs and chickens and collected eggs. The eggs were washed and packed in cotton batting to take to the restaurant. Hilda had disapproved of guests helping with chores, but once they'd explained how much they missed doing them, she gave in. Of course, telling their parents in their weekly letters home how much they missed doing chores would be a mistake. For sure they'd laugh until their sides ached.

While King, Daniel, and Paddy were ensconced in King's office doing whatever men do when they get together, she and Julia helped Hilda make bread and more cookies. Working with the older woman was almost like being with their mother again. Hilda had a great sense of humor, making the chore of breadmaking more enjoyable. At home, she'd enjoyed baking bread about as much as Julia enjoyed weeding the gardens.

Hilda regaled them with stories of her long trek from her home country of Germany to London and the long voyage across the ocean to New York. How she helped nurse those who became seasick from the rolling waters. How, once she was able to take a break on the deck, she nearly slipped on the wet surface, only to be caught by a handsome man before she tumbled head-over-heels over the side of the ship, then tumbled head-over-heels in love.

The story pulled at Suzanna's romantic heartstrings. They'd gone their separate ways in New York, but hadn't forgotten each other. Paddy had worked the docks, while Hilda worked for a rich family north of the city. It took two years before they saw each other again, and, according to the housekeeper, she fell in love all over again and married him within a month.

Suzanna shook her head at the memory. She also recalled her mother saying how quickly she'd fallen for their father and they'd married within six months of meeting. Maybe it wasn't so unexpected that Daniel and Julia were serious already. More than once she'd caught them in an embrace and kissing. Neither acted embarrassed, and she had a strong hunch there would be wedding bells before Christmas.

The front door rattled. Suzanna jumped and slapped a hand over her heart.

"Miss Lindstrom," a boy she recognized as one of her older students called out. "How come the door's locked?"

Suzanna raced down the aisle and into the cloakroom hallway. "I'm sorry, Thomas. I was so busy it slipped my mind."

Thomas placed his lunch bucket on the shelf. The boy, almost fourteen was already taller than her. It could be intimidating having students bigger than her, but so far, the older boys were always polite and respectful.

"That's all right, Miss Lindstrom." He leaned against the doorframe. "Did someone use the stable over the weekend?"

"I don't think so, but I wasn't home." Her heart skipped a beat. "Why?"

He shrugged. "There's hay missing and water in the buckets. I always empty the buckets before the weekend, so the horses can have fresh water on Mondays."

So, she hadn't been mistaken. There had been two horses there this morning. But where did they go? Her stomach churned, but she didn't want to worry the boy. "Maybe a critter like deer helped themselves."

"Can't be. I make sure to put the ropes across the entrance after school so it doesn't happen, but the ropes are on the ground this morning."

"I didn't know you did that." She patted him on the arm. "I sure there's a logical explanation, but right now I need to ring the bell. Thank you, Thomas, for taking care of the stable and for telling me." First thing she was going to do after school was call King at the restaurant. For the time being, she'd put it out of her mind—or try to, anyway.

At recess, instead of playing a game of catch, Thomas and two of his friends, walked the edge of the woods while the rest of the children played tag or jumped rope.

Even though she had a good idea what they were up to, she had to ask. "What are you boys doing?"

"Billy is good at tracking," Thomas answered, "so we thought we'd try to figure out what was eating the hay this weekend."

"Did you find anything?"

Billy squatted down and pointed to an indentation in the dirt. "See here, Miss Lindstrom. You can see the tracks of two horses and two men. It looks as if they led them from the stable and through the woods." He tipped his hat back and peered up at her. "You sure you didn't see anything this weekend?"

Suzanna nearly laughed at how adult he sounded. Almost like King and Daniel when they talked about Daniel's case. "Like I told Thomas, I wasn't home this weekend, and I had no reason to come out here when my sister and I returned home." The boys would more than likely tell their parents about their findings and how she hadn't been home. Best to set the record straight she'd been gone with her sister. It wasn't any of her student's business but mentioning where they'd been was wise.

"Who would keep their horses in our stable?" Billy stood. "It's illegal."

Yes, the boy definitely sounded like an officer of the law or an investigator. "I believe it's illegal, too. I'll call one of the board members after school today and have them come take a look."

"You want us to stay after school?" Thomas fisted his hands and puffed out his chest. "A woman shouldn't be left alone when there's stealing going on 'round here. No telling what they might do."

Suzanna couldn't help smiling. What a sweet gesture. They were trying so hard to act like the men they were becoming. "Thank you. I appreciate it." She clapped her hands together. "Enough investigating. Let's get back to work. Make sure at the next recess none of the children come over here and destroy the evidence."

All three boys puffed out their chests. "We will." They bobbed their heads in unison.

Males.

The afternoon moved as slow as the sloths they were studying. Between eyeing the clock and walking down the aisle by the stable-side window, pretending to check on the student's work, the time inched along. Several times she had to tap the three boys' desks to bring their attention to their work and not what might or might not be happening outside. She couldn't blame them. A mystery to solve was right up young boys' alleys. Hopefully, it was simple and not dangerous.

And true to their word, during the afternoon recess, they kept the other students away from the area. Of course, the boys standing with their arms crossed over their chest as if they were protecting a chest of gold, only increased the attention of the children. More than once a ball *accidentally* rolled into the brush, only to be grabbed by

Thomas or Billy before the offending child could retrieve it themselves. The boys were doing a bang-up job.

Suzanna walked past the clock. Thank the heavens it was finally four o'clock. "All right, children. You may put away your work. Your assignment tonight is to read to your parents from the books I gave you today."

One of the older girls raised their hand. "Yes, Letty?"

"Is it all right if the younger ones read to an older sibling? My folks are always busy."

"That would be fine, as long as you help them with their words." With a family of twelve children, her parents were more than likely extremely busy. Back home, it took everyone, to handle their large family.

She stood by the front door greeting each child as they left for the day and waving to the parents who met their children and escorted them home. With the riffraff in Deadwood, she'd do the same thing. When everyone was gone, she closed the front door, set the lock, entered the main classroom, and jumped. Billy, Thomas, and John leaned against her desk hands jammed in their pockets. "Boys, you scared me. I thought you'd left."

"Sorry, Miss Lindstrom." Thomas stepped away from the desk. "We said we'd escort you home."

It took three boys to help her walk the short distance to her house? She hid a smile. "That's very thoughtful of you. Let me gather my things and we can leave through the back door."

Billy swept out a hand to let her go first. "And we'll be here first thing in the morning, too."

"You three are such gentlemen." Their grins made her words worth it. She was about to lock the back door, when a thought occurred to her. Teaching the boys to be men was part of her job. "Here, Thomas." She handed him the key. "If you would lock the door, I'd appreciate it."

If his chest stuck out any farther, he'd break a rib. True to their word, the boys followed her to the front door of her house. "Thank you, boys. You've been wonderful. Now, you'd better scoot home before your parents worry about where you are. I'll see you in the morning."

Suzanna placed her lunch bucket and books on the bench, sat down, and, using the boot hook, undid her shoes and toed them off. She wriggled her toes. Heavens, it felt good to get them off her feet. Walking stocking footed into the living room, she called out to Julia.

"I'm in the kitchen." Her sister was bent over a sheaf of papers.

"Working on your story?"

"Mmm, hmm," Julia mumbled without looking up.

"The children love your stories." Suzanna took a glass from a shelf and removed a jar of milk from the icebox. She loved how their milk was delivered to their doorstep every other day. No milking to get what they needed. The cool liquid was refreshing.

"Mmm, hmm."

"Someone kept their horses in the school's stable over the weekend."

"Mmm, hmm." Julia set down her pen. "What did you say?"

"I saw two horses in the stable this morning."

"Whose were they?" With her eyebrows turned down, Julia twisted in her chair.

"I don't know. They were gone before I could check, and I thought I'd imagined them. But Thomas, the boy who helps me in the morning, said an animal had eaten the hay."

Julia tapped the papers into a neat pile. "What did you do?"

Suzanna shrugged and rinsed out her glass at the hand pump. "What could I do? The children started arriving. Thomas and two of his friends did a search of the area during lunchtime and found hooves and two sets of footprints."

"Should you call the sheriff?"

"I'm going to call King first. He has an employee giving him problems, so I want to give him a chance to investigate himself. Besides, I don't really care for the sheriff."

Julia took the pile of papers into the living room and set them on the desk. "Does it have anything to do with the thefts at King's?"

"I don't know." She followed her sister into the next room. "I don't get why anyone would choose to leave their horses out here, anyway. It's not like it's on the way to anywhere." She picked up the receiver to the telephone on the wall. She'd never get used to the idea she could hear someone's voice through wires. The first time King had shown her how to use the telephone, she thought for sure she would hurt herself.

She cranked the handle and asked the operator to connect her with the restaurant. There weren't many telephones in the city. She only knew of a few, but they were the ones she would need to call; the sheriff, Daniel, King's Restaurant, Haywood's store.

Leona answered on the third ring. "King's Restaurant. Leona speaking."

"Leona, this is Suzanna Lindstrom. May I please speak with King?" Leona didn't respond. Suzanna held the receiver away from her ear. Had she hung up?

"Sure. Hang on a minute. He's in the back."

Suzanna twisted the short receiver cord around her finger. Too bad the cord wasn't longer so she could sit down and wait. Maybe she should have told Leona to have him call her back. Five minutes passed. What was he doing? A thought struck her making her blush. He *was out back* which at home meant someone was using the necessary. How embarrassing. If she hung up now, would he call her back.

"Suzanna? Are you there?" King's voice sounded rushed as if he'd run.

"I'm sorry to bother you."

"That's fine. I was out back hauling water into the laundry room for Leona." His deep breath came through the receiver. "What can I do for you?"

Thank goodness she could ban the idea of where she thought he'd been. "Something weird happened at the schoolhouse, and I'm a bit worried."

"What's going on? Did Asa come back to harass you again? I told him to leave you alone."

"No, he wasn't here, but . . ."

"I'll be right out there," he said after she gave him a brief description. "I'll bring Daniel, too."

The line went dead before she could say thank you.

"What did he say?" Julia pushed something beneath the couch. Her face was red.

"What's wrong?" Suzanna bent at the waist to see what her sister had hidden, but before she had a chance to see what it was, Julia sat on the couch and spread her skirt, hiding the floor.

"Nothing. Why do you ask?"

"You've been acting strangely lately. Between doing clothing repairs, keeping the house and garden, cooking and working on your stories, you're busy, but you also seem more tired than usual. What's going on?"

Julia wiped her hands on her skirt. "Nothing. Trying to figure out what my characters should do next. So, what did King say?"

Suzanna wasn't sure she believed her. Julia had never been good at lying, and she'd bet her next month's pay her sister was up to no good. She mentally shook her head. When Julia was tight lipped, she was tight lipped. Besides she had other things to worry about.

"King is coming out here with Daniel."

"Coming here?" Julia patted a few strands of hair loosened from her bun. "Oh, my I'd better change."

"Why? This isn't a date or anything. They're coming here to see what they can find at the stable."

"It doesn't matter. You should change, too." Julia stood and flipped her hands. "Now, shoo. Go make yourself presentable."

Suzanna went to her room. Before clicking the door shut, she peered through the crack. Julia bent over and picked up a piece of bright red fabric from the floor, cupped it in her hand, and went into her room. What on Earth was Julia doing with red material, and why did she feel the need to hide it?

She shrugged and closed her door and stood in front of the mirror over her dresser. Her birthday wasn't coming up anytime soon, so Julia couldn't be making a dress for her. Besides, there was no way she'd wear the color. The shade was too bold for her tastes.

Suzanna ran a brush through the sides of her hair and tucked a few stray strands in place. There was nothing to worry about. Julia wouldn't do anything illegal or sordid. Her sister simply wasn't the type.

A knock on the front door sent her flying from her room. The men had made good time. She opened the door as Julia came from her room, wearing a fresh blouse and skirt. Her cheeks were rosy, and her smile could have melted the sternest of men. Suzanna glanced between Daniel and her sister. And Daniel wasn't a stern man. Goodness. Their smiles were sweet enough to make her want to gag.

"Um." King took a step into the room. "Before these two get sappy, show me what you saw."

Suzanna followed King from the house and turned to the other couple. "C'mon you, two. Stop gawking at each other. Daniel is here to help King."

King stopped outside the school's back door. "Tell me again what happened."

"Where do you want me to start?"

"Where you first saw the horse."

Suzanna unlocked the back door and led them to the window facing the stable. She tugged up the shade. "I was pulling up the shades when I saw them. I thought maybe a couple of the children had come early, so I checked out the front door. When I didn't see anyone, I raised the rest of the shades and a window. I went back to the stable side," they followed her across the room, "to open the windows to get a cross breeze, when I noticed the horses were gone. It shook me a bit. I thought I was seeing things, so I let it go."

King opened the window and stuck his head out. "Then what?"

"Thomas arrived and told me an animal had eaten the hay and if I'd seen anything, which of course I hadn't because I was at your place."

"Let's go outside and take a look around." King pushed the window shut and pulled the shade down, darkening the room. "Makes me wonder if someone knew you and Julia would be gone for a few days."

Suzanna locked the back door behind her. "Thomas and his friends looked around during lunch recess and noticed some boot prints and hooves leading into the woods."

King and Daniel followed the trail into the woods. "What did these horses look like?" King called over his shoulder. "Did they have any special markings on them?"

"All I saw were their rumps, but they were both cinnamon-colored. One had a lighter-colored tail with a black tip at the end, and the other had white socks on each hind leg. Other than that, I couldn't say."

DAMN. HE AND DANIEL came back to the stable where they'd left the women. Too bad Suzanna couldn't give a better description of the horses, but he did have a horse he was saving for the Army with a black tip on its tail. It also had a diamond-shaped marking on its forehead, but because she hadn't seen their heads, he couldn't be sure the horses were his.

"The boys were right. There are two sets of boots leading the horses. They went through the brush." King took off his hat and raked his fingers through his hair. "They probably headed up into the hills. I'm not much of a tracker, and once they get into the rocky hills, they'll be hard to follow."

Suzanna touched his arm. "What now?"

"There's not much we can do." He gave Daniel a pointed look. Would he take the hint and not worry the girls? He was going to have to head back to the ranch tomorrow. It was too late to do anything today. The question was whether he should go to the ranch first or the racetrack and Fort Meade.

Julia frowned. "Don't you put your mark on your horses so people can tell they're yours?"

"I don't know. I didn't notice any yesterday, but I do keep several at another location. I have a barn halfway to Fort Meade where I keep horses I'm going to sell or ship to buyers. I couldn't sell them if I branded them. The new owners want to put on their own brand."

"Don't you have anyone guarding it?" Daniel took Julia's elbow and walked back to the house.

"Of course, I do." Was the person guarding his horses working against him? He hadn't been to Sturgis in a month or so.

They'd reached the girls' front door.

"Would you like to come in for refreshments?" Julia asked, giving Daniel a coy smile.

King tipped his hat. "I'm sorry. Not tonight. I have to get back to the restaurant. I'm sure Leona has a million things for me to do."

"And I need to get back to the office," Daniel added. "I have a case to solve."

Suzanna dropped her shoulders. "Oh."

Even though he was worried about the horses, he couldn't deny he was thrilled she was disappointed. "Daniel, let's get going. Ladies." He turned on his heel before he changed his mind. He strode down the lane, assuming his friend followed.

Chapter Thirteen

"Hey, wait up." Daniel let out a breath as he ran up to his side. "What's the hurry? You can't do anything tonight, anyway."

"I know, but this has me worried to no end." As they passed the school, he stopped and stared at the stable. "If those horses are mine, and I have a hunch they are, I could be losing a lot of money."

"Do you ever wonder if you're stretching yourself too thin?" Daniel matched King's long stride as they continued toward town. "I mean, you're running the restaurant and hotel."

"Actually, Leona is." King sidestepped a pile of dog droppings on the boardwalk. Something needed to be done about the refuse around the town—animal and human.

"I know, but you're still playing a big part in it." Daniel pushed aside a cat who refused to move. "You also run the ranch." He held up a hand. "I know, I know. Paddy runs it. Besides raising your own beef, chickens, and pigs and readying them for the restaurant, you hunt for wild game, raise race horses and working ones for Fort Meade, find potential buyers for them, make sure they get shipped properly, and . . ." he threw up his hands, "hell, I don't know what else."

King hadn't thought about it. Daniel hadn't mentioned the bookwork that came with everything. No wonder he was tired. They stopped in front of the restaurant. "Want to come in for supper? My treat."

"Can't say no to that, can I?"

Instead of sitting in the busy main dining room, King went into the kitchen where a table was set aside in a corner for employees to eat. He lifted lids, peered into pots, and opened the ovens. "Looks like there's an abundance of hash and beans." He raised an eyebrow at Daniel. "Not one of Leona's favorites to make, but I like it."

"Beggars can't be choosers." Daniel took his place at the table. "Got a beer?"

King removed two plates from a stack and, as if he'd done this his entire life, scooped up hash, slapped some on each plate, spooned on beans, grabbed utensils, and set the plates on the table all without spilling a drop. Hell, if he had, Leona would have been after him with a wooden spoon.

"Impressive." Daniel picked up his fork. "You could get a job as a cook or waiter to add to your list." He took a bite. "This is delicious. Why don't you sell more of this?"

"I think it's the name, hash. People have the idea it's made from the left-over parts of the beef the cooks on wagon trains or cattle drives make."

"Maybe you should come up with another name for it."

King took a bite and closed his eyes, enjoying the flavor rolling over his taste buds. "Like what?"

"I don't know. I'll give it some thought." Daniel dug into his beans.

Ignoring the bustling going on around them in the kitchen as Leona and her girls served up meals, brought in dirty dishes, and the cook slammed pots and pans, King closed his eyes and savored the hash and beans.

"I have a favor to ask." Daniel said, breaking their silence.

Oh, no. Daniel's needing help didn't always turn out well. He swiped a chunk of bread through the bean juices. "What?"

"I need help with this case. How and why are men getting sick? It has to be bad liquor, but I can't figure out where it's coming from. This weekend I want to spend time in the woods above the crossroads between from Lead and Deadwood. Someone is bringing booze into town and I need to figure out how so I can get paid."

"I'd enjoy that, but I have my own problems." A movement at the window over the sink caught his eye.

Daniel followed King's line of sight. "What?"

"I thought I saw Woods and Silverstone walking past." He tossed his napkin on the table, pushed back his chair, and went to the back door. He eased it open and looked up and down the alley. No one was there. He scratched his head and returned to the table. "I swore I saw them."

"Like Suzanna swore she saw those horses?"

"Oh, I believe she saw the horses, but I'm not sure I saw those two assholes."

"Those two are up to no good, I can feel it."

"Me, too." King drained his glass of beer. "I wish I could help you this weekend, but I can't. Why don't you ask Colin? He'd likely be glad to get out of town for a bit."

Daniel shrugged. "I don't know. It's not that I don't trust Colin, but except for you, I don't trust anyone. The fewer people who know what I'm going to do the better." He sopped up the rest of the food on his plate with a piece of bread. "Besides, you know he can't lie to Sadie or anyone else. What's he going to say to make her believe him?"

"I guess you're right. That means you'll have to go on your own."

They were silent for a minute, each intent on finishing their meal. Daniel wiped his fingers on his napkin and patted his stomach. "A delicious meal as usual. I don't see why a man doesn't scoop your sister up and marry her."

King stood and chuckled. "Can you imagine any man putting up with her harridan ways? She's too used to having her own way. A man wants a biddable wife."

"Like Suzanna?" Daniel rose and took his plates to the sink. "I think she's a lot like her sister, and biddable is not a word I'd bestow on Julia. That's why I . . ."

"Love her?" King raised an eyebrow and grinned at his friend. "You love Julia?"

Daniel paused and stared at King. "Yes. Yes, I do. I'm man enough to admit it. Are you?"

King laughed and slapped King on the back. "Well, I'm not in love with Julia, so I don't have to be man enough."

"That's not what I meant, and you know it." Daniel followed King toward the back door.

"You two had better wash your own dishes. I don't get paid enough to wait on non-paying customers." Leona leaned against the doorframe, hands at her hips, a grin playing at her lips.

His hand on the door handle, King paused. Busted. If he didn't love his sister so much, he'd fire her. Hell, even if he didn't love her, he couldn't fire her. Besides being an incredible cook, she took care of the hotel, made sure every room was spotless, and handled the guests as they came in the front door. He didn't understand how she did it, and if washing his plate, fork, and glass kept her happy, he'd do it a million times over.

King released a deep sigh and nudged Daniel in the side. "C'mon, let's get this over with or I'll never hear the end of it." He bowed to Leona. "Yes, ma'am. We'll do it right now."

Leona's grin meant trouble for him. She tipped her head toward a stack of dishes on the counter. "I'm short-handed today, so while you're at it and are eating for free, you can do the rest of the dishes, too. I'll be back to see how you're doing."

Daniel rolled up his sleeves. "See what I mean? She's an evil taskmistress. No man would want her." He held up a dishrag in one hand and a dishtowel in the other. "Wash or dry?"

Two hours later, after he and Daniel had washed not only the dishes, but also the pots and pans, the counters, and mopped the kitchen floor when the restaurant closed after the lunch hour, King was in his office located next to the front desk. He tapped a finger against his lips, leaned back in his chair, propped his feet on the desk, and contemplated his wrinkled hands. He didn't begrudge helping Leona, but he certainly didn't like his hands looking like he was a washerwoman.

He dropped his feet to the floor and paced. Where should he go first tomorrow? His stables near Fort Meade, or out to the ranch? Which would be more productive? He could possibly do both, but with them in opposite directions and, depending on what he found out, he could be gone for a few days. He raked his fingers through his hair and huffed out a breath.

If he got up early enough, it made more sense for him to go to Fort Meade first and check things out there, then head for the ranch. At least he'd have a place to sleep. Bunking in with his horses at the racetrack or sleeping under the stars wasn't quite as appealing as resting in his own, comfortable bed. Decision made, he left the room, located Leona showing a new girl how to dust properly, and told her he'd be leaving for a few days.

Leona would get upset if he raided her kitchen for supplies. She knew exactly, probably down to the last grain of salt, how much and what food she had. He wouldn't want to take anything from her cupboards, only to leave her short for the dinner hour. Plus, he needed to take supplies to Sorely, his racehorse manager. A trip to Colin and Sadie's store was in order.

"I'll be back in a bit," he called to Leona over his shoulder as he left the building.

As usual, the streets were bustling with men and a few women. He couldn't figure out how the men who'd come out here to look for gold could ever find any if they weren't mining but lounging around town or drinking and whoring in the brothels. While men had been getting sick, there had been fewer of them in the taverns, but there were always those who thought they were invincible.

Paying more attention to the interesting mix of miners, businessmen, and prostitutes hanging over the brothel balconies calling to prospective customers, he didn't see the man standing in the middle of the sidewalk.

"Well, well, well. If it isn't the high and mighty, King Winson."

King took a step back. Damn. He didn't need to deal with this man today. "Silverstone."

Silverstone grasped the edges of a newer-looking, yellow vest and rocked back on his heels. This was the first time King had seen the man dressed in anything other than a worn-out pair of brown pants, a grubby shirt, and ragged long coat. His hat looked new, and his nails were clean and short. Where had the man gotten the coin for new duds?

"I hear ya having problems out at your ranch."

Where and when would he have heard that? "Things are fine out there, Silverstone." Could he push the man out of the way and hope he fell into the nearby water trough? For all his clean clothes and outward appearance, his teeth were still yellowed, and his breath smelled like he'd eaten skunk for lunch.

King took another step back. "I'm not sure where you're getting your information, but my ranch is none of your business."

Silverstone smirked. "I wouldn't be so sure of that, Winson." He jabbed a finger at King. "You'd better watch out. Takin' you down a peg or two will be a pleasure." With a tip of his hat, he stomped past King and wove his way through the people until he was out of sight.

What the hell was that about? How did he know about the thefts—if that was what Silverstone was talking about. Was one of his employees talking about him and his business? Johnson maybe?

The man was still angry about being called to task about accosting Suzanna and learning his son wasn't the angel he thought he was.

Running his hand around the back of his neck, he continued walking to Haywood's store. If Colin wasn't in the building, gathering the necessary supplies would go quickly. If Colin was present, he'd be in for a jawing session lasting for an hour or so. Hoping his friend was out on deliveries, he entered the store.

Nearly two hours later he was laden down with food for several days, extra shotgun shells, a coffee pot, skillet, metal plate and cup, utensils and extra grub for his trainer at the racetrack. He'd left his bedroll at the ranch, so he slung two blankets over his shoulder.

Whenever he traveled to and from the ranch, he carried his shotgun, so at least he didn't have to spring for new one. With his gear in hand, he left the store, happy he'd only lost two hours with Colin. When the man got to gossiping, there was no stopping him. The subjects he struck on were never ending; the weather, the state of the United States, whether the Dakota Territory would join the union and when, how many men struck gold, how many more were coming to the area to try and strike it rich, who had been shot lately, his thoughts on the men getting sick, and whether the railroad should come through Deadwood or not.

The topic of women being allowed to vote was a hot one and a few men who'd come into the store joined in the discussion. Personally, King thought women were every bit as intelligent as men, in fact in many cases, more so. Why shouldn't they be allowed to vote? As the discussion grew heated and several of the men voiced their opinion about women not having the intelligence to make a proper decision without a man's help, Sadie's movements became louder. Slamming merchandise, stomping around the store, muttering under her breath. It was probably a good thing her husband was for women's rights, or Colin would be sleeping in the stable out back.

Ears still ringing, King widened his stride barely acknowledging the few women on the boardwalk. He still had plenty to do before bed if he was to get an early start in the morning.

King set his feet in the stirrups and guided Chester from the stable behind the restaurant and hotel to the alley. Fortunately, the mud had finally dried up, making it easier to traverse through the streets. Unfortunately, the streets and alleys were rutted from wagon wheels, horse hooves, and boots. Keeping his horse from breaking a leg was always a challenge, but once he got away from Deadwood, the road usually became a bit better, but he had his doubts.

Early morning was one of his favorite times of the day in Deadwood. The sun's red and golden rays made an appearance behind the hills. Most people hadn't risen yet and those men insisting on staying up all night carousing, drinking, and whoring, had finally given up their drunken posts and holed up somewhere. Even the dogs and pigs roaming the streets were still bedded down.

King tugged the reins guiding Chester around a hole large enough it had to have been made from one of the many tunnels beneath the streets. On more than one occasion, a portion of a street along with a building would disappear when the earth gave way. In his opinion, mining beneath the town should be outlawed.

Passing placer mines, their crooked, wooden sluices crisscrossing the creek, he waved to a few miners beginning to stir. Wisps of smoke from campfires dotted the edges of the creek. Piles of rocks moved to search for the elusive gold, made it difficult to make his way over the creek to the other side of the gulch.

They went from the alley to Main Street, past the surprisingly quiet Gem Theater and Bella Union. Must have been a rowdy night last night for them to be so quiet this morning. People were moving about in Chinatown. He tipped his hat to several as he passed the long stretch of boarding houses, dry goods stores, laundries, bakeries, gambling establishments, and opium dens. A few were working their claims along the creek. Like Daniel, and unlike many of the residents of Deadwood, he had no issue with the Chinese. They were hardworking and pretty much stayed to themselves. If the residents of Deadwood would work as hard as the people in Chinatown, they might not be so angry about the Chinese's wealth.

Finally, away from the tattered town, he nudged Chester into a trot. He had a good half a day's ride to the turnoff to the racetrack and another hour or so, depending on how hot the day became. Then he had another hour to his stable.

At the fork right outside Chinatown, King took a right and slowed as they headed into the hills. He was always careful not to overwork Chester, or any of his horses for that matter. He'd seen men abuse their horses. King had rescued a few horses after races when the owner was ready to put his property down. Call him a sap, but he couldn't see shooting a horse because he lost a race.

The farther away he was from Deadwood, the cleaner the air became. Less refuse. Less body odor. Less riffraff. With only the sound of the breeze flowing through the trees, he took a deep breath. The scent of pine filled his lungs, reminding him of home. It had been three years since he'd left Wisconsin. While there were plenty of woods out here, there was also areas of desert. Traveling through the Badlands had been an experience. How would anyone want to, or could, survive in such drastic, dry conditions?

A jackrabbit high-tailed it across the one-lane road, making Chester side-step. "Easy, there, Chester." King stopped and patted the roan's neck and nudged his sides when the rabbit disappeared. "Kinda skittish today, aren't you?"

The ride up and down the hills reminded him of his first foray into Deadwood on the stagecoach. Without any fear, the driver didn't slow for curves, hills, or fallen trees partially covering the road. To avoid the three women's screeches and the swearing of the men riding with them, at Scooptown, now known as Sturgis, they'd stopped briefly to drop supplies for the few men mining gold. He'd taken the opportunity to join the ride, which he highly regretted as the stagecoach raced down into Deadwood.

Two hours later, he stopped to give Chester a rest and a drink from a creek where water trickled from the hills. Even though he hadn't come across anything more than a few mule deer and more rabbits, he couldn't shake the feeling he was being followed. He knelt beside the creek and cupped his hands into the cool water. Chester snorted and swung his head over his shoulder. Had he sensed something, too?

Careful not to spook the horse, King took the reins hanging by his side and stood. He backed Chester up, keeping the rifle side away from the road, in case he had to grab it for protection. In front of them, a small rock slid down the hillside. Was someone moving through the woods instead of the road?

"C'mon, boy," King whispered, swinging onto the saddle. Another rock, a bigger one, this time, landed where he had been squatting. What were the chances rocks would suddenly fall exactly where he'd been? He wouldn't bet on it. Once back on the road, King resisted the temptation to search the wooded hills. Acting as if the rockfall was natural, he nudged Chester's flanks, and put him into a trot. He certainly could move faster on the road than someone could among the trees, couldn't he?

The falling rocks made his hair stand on end. Did someone want him hurt, or worse? If so, why? Did it have anything to do with the thefts? If Suzanna's description of the horses in the school's shed was correct, they were ones slated for the Army. Was someone trying to make him lose his contract with Fort Meade?

After stopping twice more for water breaks, he took the road to the racetrack. The trees had thinned out, making it more difficult for someone to follow him without being seen. With this road being straight, he was able to head Chester into a gallop. The sooner he got to his stable, the better he'd feel.

King slowed his horse as the roofs of six stables came into view. He wasn't the only one who kept a few horses here. The roofs of each stable were painted a different color making it easy to identify the owner. His was a bright green. Others were yellow, orange, blue, and one owned by a woman was bright pink. He didn't envy the poor guy who had to live and work under those colors.

Because it was so far away, many men kept employees here to take care of and train their horses. Smoke spiraled into the air from a few fires. At least once a month, King brought out supplies himself, or had one of his ranch hands do it for him.

"Mr. Winson." Sorley Jorgenson, his trainer, tipped his hat back on his head. "What're you doing here already? I don't need no supplies, yet."

King dismounted and led Chester to the stables fit for six horses. He wrapped the reins around a hitching post and shook his trainer's hand. The man had been with him for two years, first at the ranch then out here at the racetrack. King didn't mind giving ex-gold miners jobs when they asked, as he understood what it was like slogging around in ice-cold water panning for gold. Sorely was fifty years old, his arthritis was giving him trouble, and he was ready for a job easier on his body. His clothes had been ragged, his boots worn and rough from standing in the water. He smelled as if he hadn't bathed in a month of Sundays.

There were probably fleas in the long, graying beard, but King trusted him implicitly. After buying him new duds and making him take a bath, he took him to the ranch. In the past two years, the short, bandy-legged man had proved his worth many times over. The only regret he had was Sorely would not give up his awful beard. At least now he kept it clean.

Sorely's knowledge of horseflesh was impeccable. Once, when he'd had a few drinks, the trainer had let it slip he'd been head groom at a fancy horse farm in Kentucky. But the owner didn't treat his horses any better than his employees, so gold fever sounded like a good excuse to hightail it out west.

"Wanted to make sure everything is fine here. Brought supplies for you, too."

They entered the interior, passing a small room used for Sorley's personal use.

"It's funny you should do that." Sorley leaned his arms on top of a stall door and glanced at King.

"Why's that?"

"There's been some strangers poking their noses around here. There isn't a race for a month, and I'm friends with everyone here. We're kinda like a family. We even share our food and meals. So, when someone we don't recognize shows up asking questions, we wonder what's up."

"Are they talking to everyone?"

Sorley patted the nose of a pure-black horse. "That's the odd thing, too. They only talked with me. When they see the men from the other stables watching or coming over to join us, they hightail it out of here. We've talked about it over meals, but no one knows them or why they're here."

What the hell was happening? There were five horses the last time he was here and still five horses. "What kind of questions?"

"The first time they came here, they talked with everyone, asking them who they worked for." With one last pat, Sorley went outside and, keeping in the shade, leaned against the stable.

King followed, took off his hat, and fanned his face with it. It was hotter than blazes. With few trees, there was little to shade a person. "Then what?"

"After that, they always come straight to me. Asked me how often you came out here. How often you switched horses. Who you sold to. If you were going to race in the next contest. How often you supply horses to Fort Meade. Did I enjoy working for you. Things like that."

"Do you know who they are?"

Sorley shook his head. "No. And no matter how hard I tried they wouldn't give up their names. After the first few questions, I ignored them, which made the taller of the two angry. I got the impression he hated you and I should, too. Told me stories I knew weren't true."

A shiver of apprehension skittered down his spine. King pushed away from the building and scooped up a bucket of water for Chester from a water trough. Who hated him so much and why?

"What kind of stories?"

"That you mistreat your horses. You cheat the Army. You use spoiled food in your restaurant and all your beds are riddled with bedbugs."

King shook his head and set the bucket in front of Chester. Someone was really trying to harm him, if not physically then by reputation. "Anything else?"

Sorely tapped rubbed his hand over his scraggly beard reaching down to his chest. "Let's see. Your hands at the ranch are paid peanuts and dislike working for you. Hilda is tired of cooking and cleaning." He paused and snapped his fingers. "Oh, yeah. You let Asa's kid, Josiah run wild and get sprayed by a skunk."

When his horse had his fill, King led him into the cooler stable. He removed the blankets and bags, saddle and blanket, and tied the reins to a wooden bar attached to the wall. He found a curry brush on a bench outside Sorley's room. Either one of his hands was talking, or his ranch was being watched. He had a feeling it was probably both. Brushing Chester was soothing and gave him time to ponder things. He knew he paid his hands well. He had no doubt Hilda and

Paddy loved him like a son. He'd never harm a horse. If he was cheating the Army, they'd let him know. Besides, he wouldn't cheat anyone. And as far as Josiah getting sprayed by the skunk—hell, the kid deserved it for sneaking out of the house.

"So, what're you thinking, King?" Sorley sat on the bench and crossed his arms over his chest.

That was another thing, he wasn't so uppity he made his employees call him Mr. Winson. They used his first name. "I'm not sure." He went on to tell him about the thefts at the ranch and the two horses at the school.

Sorley scratched his chin through his hair. "Sure doesn't make sense to me, but sounds like someone has it out for you."

"That's what I thought." He took the curry comb, ran it through Chester's mane then lifted a hoof to check for imbedded stones. "The problem is I don't understand why."

"Well, ya know there's always those fellas who are jealous when someone is successful like yerself." Sorely handed him a hoof pick. "They're too lazy to work hard themselves and don't understand successful men don't become that way by sitting on their asses."

King released the foreleg and picked up the other. "You're right about that. I came out here with almost nothing." Except for whinnying, the stable remained silent as King finished the hooves and led Chester to an empty stall. With a pat on the horse's head, he closed the door and walked down the aisle.

"You stayin' the night?" Sorely slapped his knees and stood. "Or are you headin' for the fort?"

King went outside and glanced at the sky. Dark clouds were forming in the distance. Chester shied when thunder rolled across the sky. "The idea of riding in a storm is as appealing as bedding down with a rattlesnake. If you don't mind, I'll bed down here. I can lay out my bedroll in the haymow."

"Naw. You're the boss man, you take my bed." Sorely squinted into the western sky.

King had seen Sorely's bed when he'd walked past the room. The man may keep his physical appearance as neat as he could out here, but his room was a mess. King repressed a shudder and slapped his friend on the back. "That's all right, old man. You keep your bed. I rather like the scent of hay when I'm falling asleep."

Sorely puffed out his chest and hitched up his pants. "Who you callin' an old man, you whippersnapper?"

"Did I say that?" King raised an eyebrow and grinned. "Must have been a different whippersnapper. If you're old, then I've just left the cradle."

Sorely squinted at King as if trying to figure out if there was a hidden insult. He laughed. "All right, you can have the haymow."

Sitting on a tree stump made into an uncomfortable chair around a campfire and jawing with a group of like-minded men, filled King with satisfaction. The afternoon storm had been fierce, but brief. After half an hour of rain, a rainbow arced across the sky. Legs crossed at the ankles, he stared at the millions of stars twinkling above him while listening to the murmur of voices. Even with the full moon, they shone bright and clear.

King took a sip of whiskey one of the men from another stable provided. Except for the weekend they'd built the building and brought out his horses, this was the first time he'd stayed overnight. Usually he was in a hurry to get back to the ranch or on to the fort.

Sorely was right about the other men at the racetrack. Despite their bosses being in competition during race day, they had formed a strong friendship. What would it be like living out here if they were enemies?

"Sorely said he told you about the men coming out here," the man who'd provided the whiskey said. "We keep an eye on Sorely whenever they arrive."

"Does anyone recognize them?"

A round of no's gave him his answer. Who were these men and what the hell did they want? The fire flickered down as each man retired to their beds.

"I'm gonna hit the sack." Sorely stood and stretched his back. "I'll see ya in the mornin.'"

King set his empty tin cup on the ground. Other than the crickets chirping, an owl hooting, and the call of a coyote, the night was silent. A far cry from Deadwood. Even his ranch wasn't this quiet. He stood and entered the stable. With the full moon, it wasn't completely dark inside, but dark enough where he waited for his eyes to adjust before climbing the ladder to the loft. The worse thing he could do was light a lantern and potentially set a fire.

Thankfully he'd laid out his blankets before supper, so he only had to remove his boots and lay on his blanket. The storm had broken the heat, so he pulled another blanket over his shoulders. He turned and changed positions several times. As soft as the hay was, strands of the prickly grass poked through the blanket and his clothes. A pillow would have been nice, too. Finally, banishing his worries about the person or persons who were after him, he set his mind on Suzanna. Her sweet smile and lovely face were the last things he thought of as he settled into sleep.

"King, wake up. The stable's on fire."

Dragging himself from a dream of making love with Suzanna, he pulled his eyes open and coughed. Smoke filled the air. What the hell?

"C'mon, King. We have to get the horses out of here."

Sorely's yell jerked him to life. He yanked on his boots, pulled his blue handkerchief over his nose, and took the ladder in two strides. Sorely had already opened the first two stalls and led the horses from the barn.

King ran to Chester's stall. The horse was whinnying and rearing. He grabbed the halter.

"Whoa, boy." They were the farthest from the door, so King removed his handkerchief and held it over Chester's eyes. Coughing, and nearly blinded by the smoke, he felt his way stall door by stall door to the outside, then ran back in to help Sorley with the remaining horses.

With the six horses tied to neighboring hitching posts, he joined the other men in a bucket brigade to put out the flames. Luckily, everything was still damp from the rainfall, so the fire mainly smoldered and the damage was minimal.

King dropped to the ground, hung his head, and wiped at his burning eyes. "Did anyone see or hear anything?"

"Too dark," one man said, handing King a cup of water. "Drink this."

The horizon was beginning to turn pink and orange as the sun made its appearance.

"I didn't hear nothin' exceptin' the crackle of the fire." Sorley wiped a wet rag over his sooty face. "Damn it all to hell. Who would do such a thing? Why your horses could have been killed. Not to mention you up there in the loft."

King stood and looked over the damage visible in the early-morning light. "I believe that was the point." He walked around the building. A charred line went up the back of the building. Someone had obviously snuck around to the back of the property to start the fire. "Thank heavens for the rain yesterday."

"Ya." Sorely stamped on a stray ember. "Or you and the horses would be toast. Nothing like this has ever happened out here before. It's always pretty quiet."

"It has to be because I'm here." King went back to the front of the building. "As soon as I make sure the building is safe, it would be better if I left. If I'm gone, whoever is out to get me, will leave you alone."

"You gonna head to Fort Meade?"

"I have to. I want to find out what and if anything is being said about me there."

Sorely headed toward the stable. "I don't like you going alone, but I'll get breakfast going so you can head out."

Going alone wasn't his idea of safe, either, but what choice did he have? He'd have to be extra vigilant.

After a breakfast of pancakes, he loaded up his gear. As he was making sure Sorely and his horses were in good shape, Al, the trainer from the pink stable, came over carrying a shiny, black piece of metal shaped like those seen in books about knights. "What the hell is this?"

"It's to protect your front and back from a gunshot." Al set it on the ground and pointed to the top. "I made it myself. Instead of two pieces for the front and back, I made it one piece. It was easier for me to put on. You put it over your head."

"You're kidding, right?" There was no way he was going to wear it. "I don't see how it would stop a bullet."

Al pointed to a dent in the back. "See this here? Stopped a bullet from some rustlers back in Texas."

"Um. I'm not so sure."

"C'mon. What do you have to lose? Those critters are out there are trying to get you. Don't matter why, jest matters that they are."

The other men joined them, forming a circle around Al and King. "I wore it one day for the fun of it," a tall, thin man said. "It's kinda heavy, but these guys threw rocks at me. I felt them but didn't get knocked off my horse nor had one bruise."

Al picked it up the armor and passed it to King. "The only problem is if you do fall over, it's damn hard to get back up, but at least you won't be dead. You might want to carry your rifle instead of keeping it in your scabbard."

"How the hell do I put it on?" He hefted the surprisingly heavy item. How did knights fight in these things?

"Although it's easier to have someone help you, if you set it on a table, you can put your head and arms through the holes." Al nudged the armor with is boot. "How do ya want to do it?"

He must have hesitated too long. Sorely stepped in. "King, none of us can ride with you. You need protection. Put the damn thing on."

Letting out a deep breath and shaking his head, he set the armor on a wooden table. He bent at the waist and aimed his head at the opening.

"You might want to put your arms through first." Al raised his arms as if he were putting on a shirt. "Lift it up and slide it over your head."

King got his arms in and stood. The left shoulder banged him in the head. "Damn. Easier said than done."

"Try again. It took me several tries to get it on, and I didn't have anyone tell me how to do it. I had more lumps on my head than a toad's back."

The men's chuckles came through the metal surrounding his head. This time the right shoulder dinged him. His swearing echoed inside the metal chamber. If he ever got the damn thing on, how was he ever going to get it off?

Finally, after lining up his head with the sun shining through the top, the armor slid down and landed on his shoulders. He staggered back a few steps. The sun, now cleared of the horizon, beat down on the black metal. It wouldn't take long for it to heat up like a furnace. "How the hell do you get on a horse?"

The tall, thin trainer brought Chester to his side. "It's not as hard as it looks. The armor doesn't stop your legs from moving." He handed the reins to King.

Sorely must have geared the horse up. His bedroll was behind the saddle, and saddlebags in place. "If you say so." He took a deep breath. The armor didn't restrict his putting his foot in the stirrup, but when he latched onto the pommel and tried to swing his leg over the saddle, the metal dug into his neck. He coughed.

"I'm not sure this is going to work. I feel like I'm choking."

"Get yourself seated, and the armor will slide into place." Al grinned up at him. "Believe me, I've done it many times."

King did as the man said and, surprisingly, the contraption moved onto his shoulders and rested on his thighs.

Sorely handed King his rifle. "Sometimes we have jousting contests."

How did they do that when there was only one set of armor "You do?"

Al shrugged and the other men laughed. "We take turns riding across the grounds, while the others try to unseat the rider with poles." He pointed to the tall thin man. "Avery here is the all-time winner."

King shook his head. It was probably a fun way to bide time out here. The trainers couldn't be working every hour of the day. Anyway, he didn't expect Sorely to. They had to take a break once in a while. He adjusted the armor, so it didn't dig into his shoulders. "Now that it's on, how the hell do I get it off?"

For a second no one said anything then one-by-one they chuckled and went back to their respective stables. Only Sorely was left.

"Well?"

Sorely tipped back his hat. "Sad to say that's always the tricky part. You may want to get one of the soldiers to help you when you get to the fort."

"What?" He didn't mean for the word to come out in a squeal like a teenager boy in the throes of a voice change, but what the hell. "You're kidding, right?"

"Sorry, King. Avery is the only one tall enough to be able to bend over and let it slide off. The rest of us need help." Sorely eyed his boss. "You're almost as tall as him, so it may work for you." He patted Chester's neck. "You'd best be getting along now."

King started Chester out in a walk so he could get used to the feel of wearing the armor while riding. A few times he swayed from the weight of it. He was a short way from the track when Sorely called out to him. King stopped. He couldn't turn around to see what he wanted, so he waited for Sorely to catch up.

"Wait." Sorely held a white shirt. "Put this on. It'll reflect the sun and keep the contraption from heating up and melting your skin."

He handed his rifle down to his trainer and slipped the shirt on. There was no way he could button it over the bulk, but the idea was a good one. He set Chester into a trot. The armor banged against his thighs and dug into his armpits. Sweat poured down his face, into his neck, and dribbled into his shirt. It was going to be a long ride to Fort Meade.

Chapter Fourteen

Suzanna locked the back door of the school and ran to her and Julia's cozy, little house. Thank heavens it was Friday and she'd be free of the students for two full days. The kids had been antsy, and several were acting up. Was it the heat? A full moon? A storm coming? She was jittery, too, and couldn't shake the feeling something was wrong.

Sleeping had become an issue. The window sashes were always raised at night during the summer, letting in a cool evening breeze and fresh air. But once her head hit the pillow, every little sound outside set her on edge. Despite recognizing a mouse scurrying through the grass, a coyote's howl, or the wind rustling through the trees, she imagined the footsteps of men lurking on the schoolgrounds and horses' hooves plodding on the ground. Now she kept the windows closed.

After Monday there hadn't been other signs of anyone using the stable or stealing hay. The boys didn't see any more footsteps or horse tracks, and they'd been diligent in watching for them.

To top it off, she hadn't heard from King all week. Usually he stopped by once or twice a week to see how things were going. But not a word. He said he'd be gone two days and now it had been four. At least she had the weekend to look forward to.

When Julia had come running to the school during recess and asked her to go along with her and Daniel on a ride to help solve his case, she nearly jumped up and down. She'd always loved sleeping outdoors in the summer. At least here there were no mosquitos to battle.

She unlocked the front door and set her things on the entry bench. "Julia? I'm home."

"In the kitchen." Julia was wrapping cookies, bread, and other food in paper. "Daniel is bringing three horses over tonight so we can leave bright and early tomorrow morning."

Suzanna added a few more molasses cookies to the pile. As one of her favorites, she could never eat just one, or two, or three. "I wish I had my pants from back home. It would much easier to ride."

Over her shoulder, Julia grinned. "Daniel is going to get us some, plus better shirts, and hats."

"Uh, won't anyone question why he's buying pants and shirts smaller than what he wears?"

"Don't worry. He's getting them at Haywood's. He said he'd explain to Sadie and Colin why he needed them and the couple wouldn't say anything. He doesn't want anyone to figure out where he's going and why."

"That's good." The pile of food was growing. "Aren't you packing too much food?"

Julia took a couple of hard-boiled eggs from the icebox and wrapped them in material. "No. There's three of us and we're going to be gone for two days. Besides, you've seen how much Daniel can eat. I told him not to worry about food. We'd supply it all."

"While you're getting the food ready, I'll make up some bedrolls for us." She paused in the doorway between the kitchen and living room. "All right with you?"

"Yes." Julia perused the ever-growing pile of food and tapped a finger against her lips. "Daniel said we'd be heading up into the hills. It gets cooler up there at night, so pack an extra blanket."

"Will do." In her bedroom, she changed from her school clothes to old ones she wore when working in the garden. A bubble of excitement built inside her. It had been a long time since she had an adventure. She took a quilt from the chest sitting at the end of the bed. The women of the town certainly had provided her and Julia with everything they needed, including a chest with extra blankets and sheets. She spread the quilt on the floor and placed a sheet and a lighter blanket on top of it and rolled it into a bundle to be placed behind a saddle.

She took it into the living room where Julia had already put her quilt and blanket on the couch. Huh. Julia's bedroom door was closed. Why hadn't Julia let her get the things? When they first moved in, they'd decided their bedrooms were private and, unless given permission, were off limits to each other. Her sister had asked her to make up the bedroll, so why hadn't she let her get the things she needed?

"I had to go into my room to get something." Julia pointed to the couch. "As long as I was in there, I brought these out."

Made sense, but her answer didn't add up. Especially when Julia wouldn't look at her. She'd been acting peculiar lately. Tired. A bit irritable. "Are you all right?"

"I'm fine. Just excited about this trip." Julia's cheeks turned rosy.

Ah, so that was it. Daniel. She wasn't as excited about the trip itself, but that she'd be going with Daniel. How could she have been so stupid? She was going to be a third wheel on this trip. Of course, she'd be acting like a chaperone, but Daniel and Julia were adults and didn't have to worry about a damn contract.

As she prepared Julia's bedroll, a plan formed. She'd be disappointed to miss out on the adventure, but helping a blossoming romance was as exciting. Right?

SUZANNA GUIDED HER horse back toward Deadwood. Faking a headache hadn't been as hard as she thought, because she did have a bit of throbbing behind her eyes. Sleep last night had been hard to come by. She'd tossed and turned trying to come up with an excuse to go back home alone.

In the end, it had been fairly easy to convince Julia and Daniel she'd be fine on her own. After all, they'd only ridden about an hour and with no one else on the road so early in the morning, the idea of a woman riding alone being accosted was remote.

Even though she'd acted brave, it was a bit unnerving to be traveling by herself. This was the first time in her life she'd ever gone out on her own. Her horse, Lizzie, was a mild-mannered mare, so when she shied and skittered sideways, Suzanna's heart jumped into her throat. She knew coyotes didn't attack humans, but were there cougars out here? A bear?

"Whoa, girl." She patted the horse's neck and scanned the surrounding woods. It had better not be skunks. She'd had enough of them, thank you very much.

After a few moments, Lizzie settled down. Suzanna tapped the horse's sides with her heels to get her moving again. "C'mon, girl." It wasn't the first time she wished she was more of a horsewoman.

They went about a hundred yards, when Lizzie shied again. This time Suzanna's heart pounded so hard, she heard it in her ears. What if the horse bucked her off and raced back to Deadwood without her? Then what would she do?

Suzanna gripped the reins. Should she set Lizzie into a gallop or keep her still until whatever had spooked her disappeared? Before she could make a decision, a man stepped out from the woods.

"Well, well, well. If it isn't the lovely Miss Lindstrom."

She froze. Mr. Silverstone, the man from the stagecoach. The one who wanted to take liberties with her. She flinched and her skin prickled with fear.

"Aren't ya going ta greet me, Miss Lindstrom?" He put a hand on her ankle and squeezed. "Unlike on the stage, we're alone." He glanced around him. "You are alone, aren't you? Where is your precious Winson and Iverson?"

Should she kick him? Would she have a chance to get away before he came after her? His strong odor didn't match his dapper clothing. Obviously, he hadn't visited the bathhouse in a while. "I don't know what you're talking about." Keeping her voice from quivering was difficult, but she didn't want to show this disgusting man the pleasure of showing him she was petrified.

Silverstone slid his hand up her pant leg. "Oh c'mon, Miss Lindstrom. I've seen you and your sister wandering around town with those two. I want what you're giving them."

She jerked her leg away from him. "I have no idea what you're talking about. I'm the schoolteacher." As if it would discourage a reprobate like Silverstone.

Silverstone threw back his head and laughed. "Don't matter none. When I'm done with you, you'll only be good enough for the Gem. Besides, it'll give me pleasure to take something else of Winson's." He crept his hand up to her knee. "Too bad you ain't wearing a dress, this would be much more pleasurable." Keeping his hand in place, he turned to the woods. "Hey, Willoughby, bring the horses. We're going to have us a bit of fun as soon as we get to the cabin."

There were two of them? Bile rose in her throat. How was she going to get out of this? Why had she thought it was a good idea to head back home by herself? Until Silverstone, she hadn't encountered one person, so screaming wouldn't do any good. She had to save herself. Maybe if she applied to his ego, she could fool him.

"Why, Mr. Silverstone." Should she bat her eyelashes? No. That would be too much. Trying to keep from trembling, she placed her hand on his. "There's no need to be mean. There can be so much more pleasure if one is willing. Don't you think?" Heck, she had no idea if it were true or not, but it sounded good.

Silverstone's beady eyes lit up. His grip on her knee tightened. "Hurry up, Willoughby. We've got us a hot one here."

Think. Think. She grinned down at him. "I'm sure you two will give me great pleasure." Was that drool running at the corner of Silverstone's lip? As much as she'd love to empty her stomach over the top of his head, throwing up would only delay her escape.

The man called Willoughby, short, thin to the point of emaciation, and as foul smelling as the man smirking up at her, emerged from the woods leading two horses. Silverstone released her leg and reached for Lizzie's reins. She had to do something now. Gripping the reins away from him, she kicked at his head.

Silverstone grabbed his face, fell to the ground, and screamed. "You bitch."

Suzanna barely registered the blood coming from his nose as she kicked Lizzie's haunches and slapped the reins at her sides. "C'mon girl, Ride as if the devil is after us."

"Get her, Willoughby. Get the bitch."

Worry about keeping her seat on the galloping horse joined with fear of Willoughby catching her. She didn't dare look behind her to see if he was following. If she did, she'd certainly fall off and break her neck. She leaned forward and held onto Lizzie's mane.

"Go, girl, go." Thundering hooves pounded behind her. The buildings of Deadwood came into view, but it was still a good distance into town. Even if she made it, would anyone help her?

Her hide covered in sweat, Lizzie wheezed. What if the horse gave up? Or worse broke a leg in one of the ruts.

The closer she came to town the more people were up and about. They stared as she flew by them. She couldn't be far from home, but would she be safe there? If she made it to the house, she still had to unlock the door, get inside, and relock it. Would she have time before she was grabbed and at the mercy of a now very angry Silverstone? Before, except for him taking her virtue, she may have had a chance he wouldn't harm her. But now? He'd probably send her straight to Al Swearingen or worse—kill her.

"Help me. Someone, help me." Screaming at the men watching her fly past was like asking a she-bear to not protect her cubs. She approached the first bridge over the creek. A man was riding down the middle. Oh, lord, she was going to crash right into him.

"Whoa, there." The man waved his arms in the air. He leapt from his horse and stood in the center of the bridge. "Pull back on the reins. Pull back on the reins."

His words finally sinking in, Suzanna straightened and yanked the reins. Lizzie reared up. She was sliding down the back of the saddle. Had she ridden this far to safety, only to be thrown from the horse? When Lizzie came down on her forelegs, the man took hold of the halter.

"Easy, girl. Easy."

Lizzie's flanks trembled beneath Suzanna's legs.

The man ran his hands over Lizzie's face and glared up at her. "What the hell do you think you're doing, racing a horse until it nearly drops? You could have killed her. Take your damn hat off so I can see who I'm giving hell to."

King. She'd recognize his deep voice anywhere. He was angry. More than angry. What would happen when he found out she was the one he was giving heck to? The hat Daniel had bought for her was made for a man with a much bigger head than hers. Only the strings knotted beneath her chin kept it from flying from her head. The brim hid her face.

Before she obeyed his orders, he took the reins from her hands, led Lizzie over to his horse, and walked them back across the bridge. Once on the other side, he stopped beneath a grove of trees. Was there a reason why he wanted to be away from other people? Was he going to hit her? After all, she was dressed like a man.

"Get down. Now. Young pups like you need to learn a lesson about mishandling horses."

While still sitting high, she chanced a glance over her shoulder. Willoughby had stopped on the other side of the bridge, turned his horse, and went back the way he came. It was sure to make Silverstone angrier when Willoughby reported back to him. She didn't believe in killing a person, but she hoped Silverstone would shoot the man for not bringing her back. If she was lucky, Willoughby would shoot back and her problem with them would be solved.

Her inner thighs screamed when she dismounted and her feet hit the ground. She'd been in the saddle for more than two hours, plus she'd never been on a galloping horse before.

Hands on his hips, King towered over her. "Now, you want to tell me why you were abusing your horse?" He flicked a finger at the brim of her hat. "And I said to take your hat off."

Suzanna loosened the ties and let the hat slide down her back.

King bent down and faced her nearly nose to nose. "Suzanna? What the hell?" He shook his head. "I'm mean heck. Why are you wearing men's britches and why were you running this horse?"

"Can we please go back to my house?" She eyed the area and put her hat back in place. A few miners had stopped their work along the creek and were watching them. "I don't want anyone to know it's me."

"But..."

Suzanna held up a finger, held back a groan, and got back on Lizzie. "I'll answer your questions at the house."

Every time King tried to ask her a question, Suzanna held up a finger. Whatever it was, it had to be bad. Her face was ashen like she'd seen a ghost. After fifteen minutes of silence, they finally reached the school's stable. Suzanna rode straight into the building and sat on her horse.

King dismounted, tied Chester's reins to a post and took the other horse's reins from Suzanna and tied them off. Using two buckets, he pumped water into them from the outside hand pump, put one in front of his horse, and fed him hay. The ride from the bridge had cooled down Suzanna's horse, so he deemed it safe to give her water.

The entire time, Suzanna didn't twitch a muscle, but sat ramrod straight.

"Suzanna?" He put a hand on her boot. "You gonna get down from your horse?"

After a moment she jerked to life. "Um, yes." She looked down at him and worried her bottom lip. "Um. I might need help." A tear ran down her face. "My legs are a bit wobbly."

What the hell had happened to her? He swallowed around the lump in his throat. There was no easy way to get her down without taking her by the waist. "If you'll let go of the pommel, I'll take you by the waist and pull you off."

Suzanna widened her eyes. "Um . . . Wouldn't that be improper?"

King shook his head. "Probably, but I don't want you falling off and hurting yourself."

"All right."

Her waist was so tiny, his hands nearly went completely around it. He did have large hands, but still. Her wearing britches made the task easier, but when her right leg slid over the saddle, he had to take a step back to give her room to maneuver. He bumped into Chester. The horse bumped him back, squishing him into Suzanna. Her rear pressed into his groin. If anyone were to see them now and notice the bulge in his pants, her reputation would be ruined. He couldn't suppress a groan.

Suzanna turned around. "Is something wrong?"

Now her breasts were pressed against his chest and her pelvis to his groin. He pushed against Chester again to give them more room.

The horse pushed back. What the hell was wrong with him? Was he trying to keep them squished together on purpose?

"No. This darn horse stepped on my foot." Sounded like a good excuse, didn't it? Hopefully, Suzanna wouldn't realize his feet were facing the wrong direction to be stepped on.

She glanced down at their bodies rubbing against each other and jumped back into her horse. "Oh, my." Her cheeks turned red as she sidestepped outside. "I . . . I'd better go to the house and change."

"Good idea. I'll take care of the horses." Suzanna stomped off to her house. Men's britches did wonderful things to a woman's behind. He wasn't watching or anything, but they didn't leave much to the imagination. Releasing a deep breath, he willed his hard-on away and turned to his horse.

"What the hell is wrong with you, boy?" Chester nickered and tossed back his head. "Did you push me into Suzanna on purpose?" Chester's whinny was louder and longer. "Are you laughing at me?" Damn horse.

King uncinched the saddle and removed it and the blanket and tossed them over the hitching post. His horse hadn't been as lathered up as Julia's, so he'd wait to brush him down.

Unlike Chester, who kept swinging his tail at him and sashaying his rear back and forth until he slammed into King, Suzanna's horse remained docile all through the process of taking off the saddle and giving her a good rub down.

With the horses taken care of, King went from the dim stable into the bright sunlight. His stomach growled. It had been a while since he'd eaten this morning. Would Suzanna give him food for his poor offended stomach or would she be upset with him yelling at her? There was only one way to find out. With a deep breath, he made sure his shirt was properly tucked into his pants, slicked down his mustache, brushed his dusty boots against the back of his pantlegs, and, with her saddlebags over his shoulder, walked to her front door.

After leaving King with the horses, Suzanna practically ran to the house. While she hadn't minded Daniel seeing her in men's pants, it was different with King. And the way he'd yelled at her had been a shock. She'd have to remember not to let him get mad at her, if she ever had the chance to make him angry. He probably wouldn't want to see her again.

Women didn't dress like men. Yes, there were exceptions, like Calamity Jane. But from the stories she'd heard, Calamity didn't act like a woman, but swore, chewed tobacco, and drank until she was so drunk, she couldn't stand up straight. There was also a generous side to her, proven by her actions during the smallpox epidemic in Deadwood last year when she cared for the sick when no one else would.

Suzanna tossed the over-large hat on the bed, followed by the pants, jacket, and shirt. As much as she enjoyed the freedom allowed by men's clothes, it would feel good to get back into a familiar skirt and blouse. She undid her braid, ran a comb through the tangles, and rolled her hair into a bun. She licked her fingers and swept them over the stray hair at the sides of her head, left her bedroom, and made a beeline for the kitchen. The time for lunch had passed. Were her shaking legs from hunger, galloping on Lizzie, or from almost being attacked? Probably a combination of all three.

Would King be hungry, too? Should she prepare something for him to eat? Should she let him in the house without Julia here or take it out to him? She stood in the kitchen doorway. Why couldn't she make any decisions? What would Julia do? She shrugged. It didn't matter what her sister did. She wasn't Julia and had to forge her own life.

A rap sounded at the door. It had to be King, but she still jumped. What if it wasn't? A jolt went through her and bile rose to the back of her throat. What if it was Silverstone? Why hadn't she and Julia brought a gun from home for protection.

"Suzanna? It's me, King."

Thank goodness. She unlocked the front door. King set her bag on the floor and looked over his shoulder. "Maybe we should sit outside and talk in case someone is watching." King held the door for her and she followed him on her still shaky legs. He followed her to two chairs placed beneath a large maple tree. The two wooden outdoor chairs had been made by the father of one of her students. The bright blue they were painted was not a color she would have chosen, but one couldn't look a gift horse in the mouth.

"Please sit," King said.

"Go ahead."

"No. A gentleman doesn't sit until a lady does."

Suzanna smiled at his comment. After his seeing her race down the road dressed as a man, she'd hoped he still thought of her as a lady. "I'm hungry and thirsty. Would you like something to eat or drink?"

"I wouldn't refuse either one. Let me help."

"No. You sit. I'm only bringing out what I had in my saddlebag. It won't take long." She swept her hand to gesture at one of the chairs. "Please sit." After making sure he did as she asked, Suzanna entered the house and took the saddlebag into the kitchen. What if the sandwiches were squished and cookies crumbled? She didn't care for herself, but for King, she wanted something better. She pulled out the wrapped food and groaned. The sandwiches were like pancakes, but most of the cookies were still whole. There was still some lemonade in the icebox, so maybe that would appease him.

She shrugged, put everything on a tray and left the room. If King got upset by this, then he wasn't the man she thought he was.

King tapped a finger on the arm of the surprisingly comfortable chairs. The color was a bit bold for his tastes, and he'd thought the angled back and long seat would be awful, but they weren't. He rested his head on the high back and sighed. Exhaustion washed over every inch of his body.

The past week had been worse than he'd expected. If he ever saw another piece of armor, it would be too soon. He rubbed the raw skin on his neck where the damn piece of metal had rubbed it raw. The bruises on his thighs wouldn't be gone any time soon, either.

His stomach growled. The skimpy breakfast of hardtack, a piece of meat resembling rawhide, and black, bitter coffee had long been digested. Whatever Suzanna brought out to eat, would suit him fine. Getting back to the ranch and Hilda's cooking would be a pleasure.

The front door slammed. Suzanna carried a tray. Seeing no place for her to put it, he rolled a stump into place between the chairs. She bent over and set the tray down. Darn, she'd taken off the britches. Now he could only imagine what was beneath her skirts. If he were lucky enough to spend his life with her, he'd insist she wear them while at the ranch.

But if he enjoyed watching her rear end, so would his employees. He held back the groan in the back of his throat. Maybe he'd ask her to wear them when they went for a ride alone. She could wear a skirt over them and when . . .

"King?"

Suzanna's voice brought him from thoughts becoming too exciting. The last thing he needed was to embarrass her and himself by getting an erection. He waved a hand at her chair. "I'm sorry. I was thinking about the past week and how hungry I am." After sitting, she lifted a towel revealing a plate of sandwiches. Anyway, he thought that's what they once were.

"I'm sorry they're so flat." She picked one up and took a bite. "But they still taste good."

He wasn't going to take her word for it. The flavor of chicken and onions rolled over his tongue. This time he couldn't hold back a groan. "This is delicious."

A blush crept up Suzanna's neck to her face. "Thank you." She pointed to a small, bare patch of dirt between the house and necessary. "We built a fire and cooked the chicken over it."

"I've done that, too, but it's never tasted this good." He took another bite and let his taste buds enjoy the ride.

Suzanna shrugged. "I can't take credit for it. Julia made up a mixture of vinegar, chopped onions, sugar, and garlic from Leona."

King licked his fingers and took another sandwich. "Maybe them being squished helps the flavor."

"And maybe it tastes so good because we're hungry."

"Could be, but I doubt it. I may have to talk with Leona about making this at the restaurant."

"Julia would have to give you the ingredients and how much."

"Give?" King raised his eyebrows as he took another chunk out of the sandwich. "I'll pay her for it. By-the-way, where is she and why were you charging down the road as if the devil was after you?"

"She went with Daniel to help find out who is bringing bad liquor into town."

"That's right. I forgot. He had asked me to go, but I couldn't." He finished off his glass of lemonade and poured another from the pitcher she'd brought out. "They went unchaperoned?"

"Actually," Suzanna set her sandwich in her lap and brushed a strand of hair from her face. "I went along." Another blush crept up her face. "But I got a headache and came back."

Why would getting a headache make her blush. He grinned when it dawned on him. "You little minx. You didn't have a headache, did you?"

She shook her head and peered up at him through her eyelashes. "It was wrong of me to leave them alone, but it's obvious they have feelings for each other. I didn't want to be a third wheel."

Poor Daniel. Between the two sisters, he didn't have the chance of a snowball in hell. The man was doomed. He paused. Not doomed. Marrying Julia would be a good thing for his friend. And if he got a chance to marry Suzanna, he wouldn't be doomed, but blessed. Something else dawned on him. It made the food in his stomach harden.

"You rode back by yourself?"

Suzanna dropped her chin to her chest. "Yes." Her voice came out as a whisper.

King threw his sandwich onto the plate. "Are you crazy? Do you understand what could have happened to you?"

Keeping her eyes downcast, she nodded.

"Wait." He jumped up and raked his fingers through his hair. "You weren't being careless of your horse, were you?" He tipped his head to the sky as all the pieces suddenly fell into place. "Holy hell. You were being chased, weren't you?" He didn't wait for her to answer but knelt down in front of her. "Who? Who was chasing you? Did you get hurt?"

"I didn't get hurt, but I was darn scared." Suzanna set her sandwich next to his discarded one and told him what happened.

"Are you sure it was Silverstone?"

"Yes, and a man named Willoughby."

King slapped a fist into his palm and paced before her. "I'll kill the bastard. He's been nothing but trouble since he stepped foot into Deadwood." He stopped pacing and looked at her. "Have you met him before?" Would her story match up with Silverstone's?

"He was on the stage with Julia, Mrs. Woods, another man, and myself. He kept pestering me. Saying awful things he'd like to do to me. He probably thought Julia and I were heading to a brothel. He didn't like it when I brushed him off. How do you know him?"

Silverstone's words at the party came back to him. He had mentioned being on the stage with Suzanna. "He wanted to buy some of my horses, and I wouldn't sell."

"Sit down. You're making me dizzy." When he did as she asked, she went on. "Why wouldn't you sell to him?"

"I don't know. He rubs me the wrong way. He hangs around with Woods, the banker. He's another man I wouldn't trust with my worst enemy." He picked up his sandwich and jerked a bite from it, then put it back down. He might as well be eating sawdust for what he tasted through his anger. No sense in wasting good food.

Suzanna pointed to his neck. "What happened to you?"

Now it was his turn to share his adventures. "Do you remember those two horses in the school's stable from the other day?"

"Yes. What about them?"

"Even though you had only seen them from behind, I thought they sounded familiar. With the things happening around the ranch, I've been concerned someone is trying to ruin me. I was told on my way through town there'd been an attempted break-in at the restaurant."

"Did you just get into town this morning?"

"I got back into town late yesterday afternoon. This morning I remembered Daniel was going to head into the hills to see if he could find anyone making bad booze, so I thought I'd try to catch up with him and give him a hand."

"I thought you were going to be gone only a few days."

"Me, too. I'd intended to ride up to the racetrack and check things out there, and afterward go on to Fort Meade. I should have been back in two days. Sorely, my trainer at the racetrack told me some men have been coming and asking about me. He didn't recognize them. Someone has also been spreading rumors about me, the ranch, and the restaurant."

"It does seem as if someone is out to get you." She refilled her empty glass and set it on the makeshift table. "What does this have to do with the red marks on your neck?"

She would have to get back to that, wouldn't she? Despite the damn armor saving his life, it was rather embarrassing. He let out breath. Might as well get it over with.

"Sorely and the other trainers were worried about me. One of the men had a plate of armor."

"Armor? Like knights of the round table armor?" Her lips quivered.

Was she laughing? "Yes. Like that."

"But what does armor have to do with anything? What . . . ?"

King held up a hand to stop her questions. "Let me start from the beginning. A storm came up, so I decided to stay overnight at the racetrack . . ."

Chapter Fifteen

"A fire?" Her eyes were wide. "You could have been killed."

"I believe that was the idea." He leaned forward and rested his elbows on his knees. "Now for the rest of the story. After getting the armor on, I made it to the main road without incident. I rode about fifteen minutes when..."

Chester shied, then stopped in the middle of the road. Hackles rose up the back of his neck and sweat rolled down his back. Someone was watching him. He wasn't about to stay here like a sitting duck.

"C'mon, boy." He urged the horse with a few nudges in his sides. "We need to get out of here."

A bullet whizzed past his head followed by the report of a rifle echoing in the air. With the woods surrounding him, it was hard to tell which direction the shot came from. He kicked Chester into a canter, searching each side of the road.

If someone were riding a horse in the woods, they'd move slower than if they were on the road, and if they were hiking, they'd never catch up. But it didn't mean there weren't others hiding, ready to ambush him. Why? Why? Why? went through his head with each pounding of Chester's hooves. With each beat, the armor slammed into his thighs and cut into his neck.

Another bullet whizzed past him, barely missing his knees and entering the woods to his left. The shot had to have come from his right. He jabbed his rifle back into the scabbard and urged Chester into a gallop. In a matter of minutes, he was far enough away, the only way he could be shot would be from the back. He shivered. Was someone now aiming at him from behind?

The third shot came from his left. The shooter's aim was better than the last two. The shot struck its mark. He staggered to his right, trying to keep his seat in the saddle. He hissed in a breath as he grabbed the pommel and leaned over Chester's neck, making himself a smaller target.

His side burned like the dickens. He rode for five minutes, never slowing their pace. How many men were there? Was it safe to stop and see what damage the bullet had done? While it still hurt, he didn't sense any blood flowing from a wound. Keeping his body low, he slowed Chester to a trot, and reached beneath the armor to touch his left side.

King ran his hand up and down the armor until he hit a protrusion from the metal. A bullet? There was no blood and the stinging in his side was subsiding. He shook his head. Had the armor done its job of protecting him? What if he'd been hit in the back? Would the metal have stopped the bullet?

It didn't make sense to stop and check his side. As long as there was no blood, he'd keep going until he got to the fort. Besides, if he got off Chester now, he may not be able to get back on.

He entered the gate to Fort Meade with a sigh of relief. The hour from when he'd been hit and arrived had been uneventful. So, now he knew there had only been three men trying to kill him. It was probably a safe assumption they were the ones who'd set the fire, too. Would he have the same problems on the way home? Maybe he could convince Major Lazelle to lend him a few soldiers as protection. After all, the fort was built last year to protect settlements from Indians in the Black Hills.

He'd known Major Lazelle from the inception of the fort and considered him a good friend. But after he'd been here last, a new officer, Colonel S.D. Sturgis, had taken over command. Would he and the new man become as good friends as he and Lazelle. He certainly hoped so and could keep selling horses for the troops.

King shook his head. While he enjoyed living out here, he hated that the Indians were pushed off their own land. He didn't blame them for putting up a fight. He would, too, to protect what was his.

Soldiers stopped what they were doing and stared at him. Hadn't they ever seen anyone in armor before? Probably not. At least they weren't laughing. Not yet, anyway. Wait until they see him try to dismount with a sore side and the weight of the armor. He prayed he wouldn't fall on his ass in the attempt.

"Wait a minute, King." Suzanna turned in her chair and grimaced. "You mean to tell me you were shot in the side?"

King nodded.

"And the bullet didn't go through the armor?"

"Nope. All I got was a bad bruise. Wanna see?"

"Um, would that be appropriate?"

"All, heck, Suzanna. It's not like you're going to attack me or anything." He grinned at the blush creeping to her face. "You're not, are you?"

Suzanna slapped his arm. "Of course, I'm not. What do you take me for?"

King would like to take her for a lot of things, but that was for when they were married. His breath hitched when he raised his shirt.

"Oh. My. God, King. It looks awful." She reached out to touch the bruise forming below his ribs. "Does it hurt? You didn't break a rib, did you?"

Her fingers were cool against the large bruise. He changed positions in his chair so she wouldn't see the erection growing at her tender touch. Who knew a small bullet could create a bruise the size of an apple. "Yes, it hurts. Especially if I move too fast or laugh, so don't make me laugh." He didn't miss her lips twitching. Would she laugh because he told her not to? "And no, I didn't break any ribs. As you can see, it hit right below them."

"Where's the bullet?"

King reached into the pocket of his pants and held out his hand to show her the flattened tip. "I was lucky the guys at the racetrack forced me wear it, because it saved my life."

Suzanna touched his neck. "Are these red marks from the armor, too?"

"Yep. The top kept digging into my neck and the bottom my thighs. I have bruises on those, too." He winked and stood, fingering the button on his pants. "Wanna see those bruises?"

Suzanna jerked back her hand and shook her head. "No, I don't want to see them. Sit back down."

If only it didn't hurt so much to laugh. Her face turned red, she avoided his eyes, and fiddled with her skirt. Instead, he eased back onto his chair. "Shall I continue my story?"

"Please, do."

"I was able to ride to Scooptown and the fort without further problems..."

"King?" Major Lazelle stood beside another man at the officer's building. "What are you doing here? I thought you weren't scheduled to come back until next month."

King rested his hands on the pommel and eyed the two men who, in looks, were polar opposites. Whether their abilities to lead men were the same remained to be seen. Lazelle was tall, slender, his dark, straight hair, along with his full, neatly trimmed beard and mustache were streaked with gray.

The other man, who appeared to be a bit older than Lazelle, had dark, curly hair in need of a trim. His mustache and beard covering only his chin, were also speckled with gray. He was shorter and stockier than Lazelle. He wore colonel stripes.

"King, this is Colonel Samuel Davis Sturgis. He is replacing me as commander of this post."

Sturgis stepped forward. King tried not to flinch at the pain in his side when he reached down to shake the Colonel's hand. King raised an eyebrow at Lazelle. "You're leaving? I'd heard rumors, but I hoped it wasn't true."

"I'm taking over as Commandant of Cadets at West Point. I'll be leaving in a few days." Lazelle turned to Sturgis. "We haven't had a chance to talk about it yet, but King here supplies us with the majority of our horses. They are sturdy, healthy, and trained well. I hope the two of you continue the work King and I have done together."

Sturgis tipped his head back and grinned up at King. "I would like to talk more with you, but it might be easier if you dismounted. I'm getting a crick in my neck."

King took as deep a breath as he could, gritted his teeth, and swung his leg over back of the saddle. The armor jabbed his leg and neck. He had to get this thing off himself. When his feet were on the ground, he leaned against the saddle, willing the stars behind his eyes to go away. Now that he made it safely to the ground, the last thing he needed to do was faint. He gave himself a few seconds before walking around Chester and standing in front of the officers. Sweat ran down the sides of his face.

Lazelle pointed to King's chest. "What the hell are you wearing? I've seen one of those in my books at West Point."

"Someone is stealing from me and trying to kill me." He wiped his sleeve across his forehead. "I stopped at the racetrack to check on my horses there. Someone tried to burn down my stable—with me in it."

"That doesn't explain you wearing what looks to be—armor?" Lazelle crossed his arms over his chest and grinned.

"The men there were worried about me, so one of them convinced me to wear this thing, and I'm glad I did."

Sturgis walked around King and lifted the white shirt. "Interesting." He stopped. "Is this a bullet stuck in the metal?"

"I was shot at several times. One of the bullets hit paydirt."

Lazelle joined Sturgis. "It stopped a bullet. Amazing." He poked at the hole. "Are you injured beneath it?"

"I don't know. Hurts like the devil, but I don't feel any blood."

"Why don't you take it off?" Lazelle gestured to several men observing from a distance. "Look here, men. King is wearing what is called armor made of heavy metal. It's strong enough to stop a bullet."

Mumblings of surprise grew as more soldiers joined.

"Can you get it off?" Sturgis asked.

"Damned if I know. It took several men to get it on me." King removed the white shirt, now damp with sweat, tossed it over Chester's saddle, and tried getting his arms inside the armor to slide if off. "I may need help."

Lazelle pointed to two soldiers. "Peters and Jones, you stay here. The rest of you get back to work."

Thank goodness. He didn't need a crowd of soldiers watching the process. "If I bend at the waist and stretch my arms out, they can slide it off me."

Sturgis snapped his fingers. "Do as he says"

King bent at the waist and held his arms out. Nothing happened. "Why aren't you pulling?"

"Uh, where should we grab?" one of the soldiers asked.

Great. Looks like a couple of morons were going to help. "Each of you take hold of a shoulder and tug." The armor jerked against his chin and armpits but didn't go any farther. "What's happening? Why won't it come off?"

"We can't get it to move. It's stuck."

"Awe, c'mon guys. Try harder. I have to get out of this thing." There was more tugging and jerking. His side was screaming. His armpits felt like they were on fire, and even though he'd tucked his chin, it had to be full of cuts.

He sensed, more than heard Sturgis approach. "His body swelled up and that's why you can't get it off. Peters, go get the surgeon and the blacksmith."

King stood. His head was starting to spin. He was hot, sweaty, and thirsty. "What good is that going to do?" With the amount of sweating he was doing the damn thing should just slide off.

Lazelle handed him a cup of water. "Drink this. Maybe the surgeon will have an idea what to do."

What could a surgeon do the rest of them didn't? He was stuck, plain and simple. "What about the blacksmith?"

"If we can't slide it off, he may have to cut it off you."

Great. "You have to get it off without cutting it. Al will kill me if I return it damaged. It's bad enough there's a bullet hole in it."

Jones laughed. "Better in the armor than in your skin."

The soldier had a point, but still he couldn't let them cut it off. "There has to be a better solution."

"What's going on here?" A short, stocky man with bright red hair approached. His unkempt beard hung to mid-chest. Bits and pieces of food dotted his graying shirt. "I was told you need a doctor." He shoved his filthy hands into his pockets.

For the many times King had been at the fort, this was the first time he'd ever met the man, his initial impression was the doctor left a lot to the imagination. What good was a doctor going to do? Unless he planned on cutting off his arms.

"What do ya want me to do?" The physician glanced between the two officers. "I don't see no bleeding, or nothin.'"

"Phillips, this gentleman has a piece of armor stuck on his body." Sturgis glared at the doctor. "We were under the assumption you might be able to help, but I can see you're not in any shape to do anything."

A wave of alcohol wafted past King's nose. If this was the best the Army could get for physicians, the military was doomed. He looked old enough to have served during the Civil War. It was unhygienic doctors like this one who were responsible for the deaths of too many soldiers.

There was no way he'd let the man touch him. "Um, maybe the blacksmith will have an idea." At this point, with the white shirt off, the sun was heating up the armor. He swore his skin was melting beneath the metal. His head was pounding.

A tall, bull of a man parted the group of soldiers who had re-gathered to watch the doings. His wide shoulders and muscular biceps stretched his faded, short-sleeved shirt. Suspenders held up his blue army pants. His face was clean-shaven and blond hair trimmed until his skull nearly showed. For a man who worked a forge, his hands and nails were clean. Maybe he hadn't done any work for the day, but every time King had been at the fort, the blacksmith was clean.

Dr. Phillips growled at the blacksmith and spit a stream of tobacco juice, barely missing the man's boots. "What'cha doin' here, Bull? Aimin' to cause problems?"

Bull turned his back on the doctor. "Sirs, I was told you needed me. What can I do to help?"

King held back a chuckle at the difference between the two men. One would expect a learned doctor to have better manners, speech, and hygiene. He didn't know how much education a blacksmith would need, but by his speech and neat appearance Bull was heads and tails above the doctor. There didn't appear to be any love lost between the two men.

Lazelle pointed to King. "King has a piece of armor stuck on him."

A wide grin split Bull's face. "Hi ya, King." He stepped back and swept King from head to foot. "How the hell did you ever get into it?"

"I'll tell you later. For now, is there any way you can get it off without cutting it?"

"Not sure, but if you'll come to the smithy, I'll see what I can do."

King cringed when Phillips grabbed his arm. The scent of alcohol and his unwashed body, combined with boiling up inside the armor, was nearly his undoing. He swallowed past the bile rising in his throat and took a step back.

"I'll be around to fix ya up when Bull here takes a chunk of your skin off."

It would be a cold day in hell before he'd let Phillips doctor him. He'd let ten-year-old Josiah doctor him before this man. "I'm sure I'll be all right."

With a sneer at Bull, Phillips hitched up his pants, sniffed, and stomped back to whatever hole he'd come out of.

Lazelle shook his head at Phillips' back. "Colonel let's go to my, I mean, your, office. We still have a lot to go through before I leave in two days."

As the officers walked away, Lazelle's voice carried back to King. "I've been trying and trying to get a new physician out here. Believe it or not, the last one was worse than this one. Drunk himself right into a grave."

The rest of the conversation was lost as they entered the log headquarters.

Bull tapped King's arm. "Come on. Let's get you taken care of."

"Thanks, Titus."

They walked across the parade grounds to a wide, low building set off from the enlisted men's quarters. Smoke rose from a chimney. The closer they came the stronger the scent of hot coals and another smell King couldn't identify became.

The building was hot, hotter than being outside. "With the sweating I'm going, this damn thing should slide right off."

"I have an idea." Titus went to a cupboard set against a far wall.

King grimaced when the armor bit into his neck. "Why does the doctor call you Bull, and why does he hate you?"

Titus came back with a small tin bucket containing a gooey-looking substance. He set the bucket near the bellows and sat on a barrel next to King. Dare he ask what Titus was going to do? Did he want to know?

"We served together during the war. He wasn't as bad as he is now. He drank like he does now, but at least he kept himself clean. It was during the Battle of Stones River. The casualties on each side were horrific. I was called to help the sawbones do their jobs. I held men down. Stitched up saber cuts. Changed dressings. Watched men die. Did about everything the doctors did except amputate and wipe up puke and piss." Titus closed his eyes and shuddered. "I still have nightmares. You can't imagine the sight of men with no arms, legs, heads blown off."

King couldn't imagine it. "How did you handle it?"

Titus shrugged. "Eventually you turn your emotions off. Then it just becomes one more body. One more leg or arm being amputated. One more dead man being carried to a mass grave."

"What does this have to do with Phillips?"

"After the second day of constant casualties coming into the medical tents, he lost it. I can understand a man being able to take only so much, but to run and leave them to die?"

"He ran?"

"Yeah. I found him curled up in a ball, sobbing his eyes out. There were many times I'd felt like crying, too, but I never left the men who needed help. Some of those men were no more than boys crying for their mothers. I had to force him to man up and go back. I guess he hasn't ever forgiven me for seeing him fall apart. The next time I saw him, he was heavy into drinking and blamed me for his weakness."

Titus took a deep breath and stood. "I think the grease is ready."

"Grease?" That didn't sound good. The heat seemed to rise as Titus walked toward King, stirring the container with a long, evil-looking nail. "Um. What are you going to do with the grease? And nail?"

"Nail?" Titus eyed the item in his hand and laughed. "All I'm doing with the nail is mixing the grease. And I'm going to try to get the grease between you and the armor. Hopefully, it'll help it to slide off easier."

"Hopefully? Can you be a bit more positive?"

Titus grinned. "All right. I'm positive it might work."

Great. "As long as you're not going to harm the armor."

"I won't." Titus wiggled his fingers telling King to stand. "Can't say the same about your precious skin, though. Raise your arms."

Even through the shirt he wore between his skin and the metal, the grease was warm going down beneath his arms. The smell made him eyes burn. "What the hell is this stuff made from? Horse dung? He coughed as it slithered down his chest and his back.

"Jackson," Titus yelled making King jump. "Get your ass in here and help me. And bring Silas with you."

A lad, looking no more than fifteen, ran into the smithy, followed by another male, not much older. They were the muscle who were going to pull this damn thing off? Neither looked as if they could pick up a feather without breaking into a sweat.

"Don't let their size and baby faces fool you. They've have been working with me way before we came out here." Titus set the grease can back near the coals. "If I asked a couple of the bulkier men, they might rip your arms off. Jackson and Silas will take it nice and slow. Right, lads?"

The boys nodded. Silas' hat, at least a size too large, slipped down the back of his head to the floor.

"While I push up from the bottom, I want you each to grab a shoulder. King, you need to bend over as much as you can. Don't wiggle or move." Titus stood behind him. "On the count of three. One... Two... Three..."

They were going to pull his head off. No, his arms. No, they were going to remove his torso from his legs. Their grunts echoed throughout the building. There might have been a little swearing, too.

"Stop a minute." Titus's boots came into view as he walked around King. "We've made some progress. King, the next time we pull, I want you to suck in your breath. I'm going to help the boys pull. On the count of three."

Without waiting for the third count, they pulled. Titus pushed on King's head in the opposite direction. His body was never going to be the same if, no when, they got the damn thing off.

"How the hell did you get this on?" Titus said, giving the armor a particularly strong pull.

"It was a lot easier than this." His back was beginning to ache. The armor covered his mouth and was nearly to his ears. "Don't pull my ears off." They tugged again. "Wait." His yell sounded hollow inside the metal can. "It's stuck on my nose."

Titus' sigh blew across the top of King's head. "We're almost there. Tip your head down."

If he thought the grease smelled bad before, mixed with his sweat, it was twice as bad. He sucked in his breath and held it, contracting his stomach muscles.

"One. More. Pull." Titus put a foot on King's knee for leverage and grunted. "I can feel it sliding."

The back of the armor cracked against King's skull. Stars flashed behind his closed eyes. He let out a breath and sucked it back in again. Titus pressed King's knee. Jackson and Silas maneuvered his arms. His body popped like when his boot released from the gooey Deadwood mud. Freed from the confines of the armor, he flew backwards, his arms cartwheeling at his sides.

Lying on his back in a pile of old saddles, he moaned, opened his eyes, and drew in a deep not-so-cleansing breath. It was hotter than Hades in the smithy, but still cooler than being inside the oven-like armor.

Someone snickered. He eyed the three men, well one man and two boys. Which one was laughing? Jackson was biting his bottom lip. Silas had swiveled in the other direction. Titus held up the armor to his face as if he were inspecting it for damage.

"This isn't funny."

Titus set the metal cage on the floor. "Yeah, it kinda is." He picked up a small hammer and tapped the side of the armor, then walked to where King still reclined against the saddles. He held out his hand. "Here, you might want this as a souvenir."

King took the beat-up bullet. "As if I would ever forget this incident." Or the smell. Or heat. Or bruises. Or being shot. This had to have been one of the worse days of his life.

Suzanna stood. "I'm sorry to interrupt your story, but would you like more lemonade?"

Reliving the incident had made him thirsty. After Titus had helped him up, he'd drank at least a gallon of water and didn't have to relieve himself for a couple of hours. He was so dehydrated from sweating he swore his clothes were looser.

Suzanna handed him a new glass, set a plate of cookies on the table, and sat. "So, what happened afterward?"

"First off, I took a bath and changed my clothes."

She sniffed the air. "Are you sure you got all the grease off?"

Damn. Did he still stink? "Well, I tried."

"I can always dump a bucket of water over your head." Her eyes twinkled. She bit her bottom lip as if she were trying to keep from laughing.

"Ha. Ha."

"What happened after you," she cleared her throat, "um, cleaned yourself up."

"First I wiped down the armor. Titus banged out the dent from the bullet while I talked with Lazelle and Sturgis.

Instead of sitting behind his desk, which is where King expected to find him, Lazelle was seated at a table full of papers strewn out before him. Sturgis sat on a chair beside him. They must have been going through paperwork before Sturgis took over the fort.

"I see Titus got it off." Lazelle leaned back in his chair and pointed to an empty one across the table from him. *"Did he damage it?"*

King shook his head. "Thankfully, no, or I'd be in big trouble."

"You would have been in bigger trouble without it." Sturgis stood and poured himself a cup of coffee from a tin pot heating on a still, new-looking pot-bellied stove in the corner of the room. "You'd be dead."

"You have the right of it." King took an offered cup from Sturgis. "Titus is banging out the dent right now."

Sturgis raised his eyebrows. "Have any idea who shot at you?"

King leaned his elbows on the table and wrapped his hands around the metal coffee cup. "No. And that's what I wanted to talk with you about. Someone is stealing my cattle and horses."

"What does that have to do with the fort?" Sturgis asked.

"Has anyone else been selling you beef and horses? Or has anyone been coming around badmouthing me?"

"A couple of men showed up the other day saying they had prime beef and horses for sale, but I didn't recognize them." Lazelle tapped a pen on the table. "We have a contract with only you and a rancher north of here. We don't buy from anyone else. I told those men, the same thing." He tossed the pen down and hooked his hands behind his head. "As far as saying anything about you, they didn't directly to me, but a few of my soldiers came to me later to say they'd seen the men at a saloon in town. They were saying how your beef were nothing but skin and bones and your horses couldn't carry an infant let alone a man and his gear."

"Anything else?"

"They were pretty mad we wouldn't buy from them. Said you'd pay for that."

Why would the Army not buy from them make them angry at him? Didn't make sense. "And no one knew who the men were?"

"Nope. Not that anyone would admit, anyway. There are always a few shady characters in the Army." Lazelle tapped his pipe on a small plate, letting small pieces of tobacco fall from the pipe's bowl. "Those who only joined because they thought it would be easier than working on a ranch or getting another type of job."

Sturgis followed suit with his curved, long-stemmed pipe. "During the war, men joined out of patriotism for either the North or the South" From a packet he removed from his uniform jacket, he stuffed the bowl with tobacco and handed the packet to Lazelle. "After the war, those who stayed in didn't have any other options. There are the ones who joined simply to come west and get rid of the Indians." He lit a match and set it to the tobacco, while sucking on the pipe stem. He shook out the match and tossed it on the plate. "Those are the type of men I truly dislike. Their only goal is to kill as many Indians as they can, and brag about it. They don't understand we're here to protect settlers, not hunt and kill Indians."

"I've worked hard over the past few months to set the record straight." Lazelle lit his pipe and contemplated the smoke curling past his face. "A few have deserted because of my policy. Those are the men I'd like to hunt down. Now they're out there itching for a fight."

King refrained from waving a hand at the smoke filling the room. He'd never developed a taste for tobacco. "Could it be those renegades stealing from me?"

Sturgis shrugged. "Could be. But it wasn't any of our deserters who came here to sell cattle and horses."

"Maybe they're in cahoots with someone else." Things were getting more dangerous. King slapped his hands on his knees and stood. "I'd best be heading out. I need to get this armor back to its owner." Did he dare ask for an escort? The fort was in the middle of a change of command, so who would approve it?

"Why don't you wait until after lunch," Lazelle said around the pipe clenched between his teeth. "If Sturgis agrees, I'll send a few men with you for protection. After all, that's why we're here. Give the men another job to do besides do maneuvers. Might do them good to let off steam in Deadwood."

King inwardly cringed. That was what Deadwood needed—an influx of women-hungry soldiers. Besides, weren't there brothels in Scooptown? "That would be great, Major. I appreciate the offer. I truly don't want to have to put the damn armor back on." He stood in the doorway, drew in a breath of fresh air, then faced the interior. "Maybe whoever is after me, will think twice about firing on soldiers."

"It's settled. I'll have my aide get a few men together. Will ten suffice?"

Ten? He would have been happy with three or four. "Ten will be great. Thank you for your help." He stood in front of Lazelle and reached out his hand. "It's been a pleasure working with you, Lazelle. Good luck at West Point." After slapping him on the back, he turned to Sturgis. "My contract is with the Army, but I look forward to working with you in the future."

Chapter Sixteen

A shiver ran through her. Was his story true? "So, you didn't really learn anything during your trip?"

King blinked as if he was bringing himself back to the present. "I did. Maybe not who is stealing from me, but for sure someone is after me. What I didn't find out was why they're targeting me. If I'd had time, I would have ridden out to the other rancher who is supplying beef and see if he's lost any animals."

Suzanna cradled her glass in her hands. "What'll you do now?"

"I don't know." He removed his hat and raked his fingers through his hair. "I just don't know." He looked over his shoulder at the stable. "I don't care for the idea of you being out here alone. You should stay at the hotel until Julia gets home."

Truth be told, she didn't want to stay here by herself. What if Silverstone showed up? It wasn't a secret where she lived and worked. After all, there was only one school and one teacher.

"What will people think if they see me staying at the hotel? Won't they get the wrong idea?"

King shook his head. "I get so sick and tired worrying about what people have in their little minds. They have too much time on their hands." He slapped his hat back on his head. "I'm more concerned about your welfare than what people think about you staying at the hotel."

Neither said anything for a minute. Birds chirping filled the void. Disappointment squeezed her heart. She thought he was a gentleman, and didn't gentlemen try to protect a woman's reputation?

Maybe he wasn't the man she thought he was. Suzanna jumped when King finally spoke.

"I have to admit, if you were carrying an overnight bag, we rode into town together, and you checked into the hotel, it wouldn't look good."

Suzanna crossed her arms over her chest. "Well, you certainly can't stay here."

"I know that." King's voice was filled with more than a bit of exasperation. "Even as innocent as this is, and as much as I hate it, if someone saw us here, alone, you'd be out of a job in a flash."

"So, what do I do? I can't go into town myself. You and Daniel have drummed it into our heads enough times."

King chuckled. "I'm glad we finally got through to you. But I have an idea." He stood. "Can I use your phone?"

Phone? Why would he need to use the phone? "Here or the school?"

"In case someone is watching, give me the key to the school. You stay here."

Suzanna handed him the key. "What if someone comes while you're in the school?"

King snapped his fingers. "Why don't you sit on the back steps. I'll leave the door open, so if someone does approach, you can race inside and shut the door."

That would be better than being alone outside like a sitting duck. She didn't trust Silverstone or his cohort. "That would work." She followed him up the back steps and sat on the top one. "Who are you calling?"

"Leona."

"Leona? Why..."

King held up a finger. "I'll tell you when I'm done."

Suzanna wrapped her arms around her tucked up legs and rested her chin on her knees. What could Leona do? When would Julia return? What if her sister didn't come home until Monday and she had to stay at the hotel two nights? What if Leona couldn't do what King was asking her? Who would help? Could she ask Colin and Sadie Haywood for help?

A pounding started behind her eyes. Sitting here worrying wasn't going to help any. Maybe she should go pack a bag and be ready when King got off the phone. She rose and took one step.

"Where do you think you're going?" King's deep voice came from behind her.

"I thought I'd get a bag packed so I was ready when you got off the phone."

"What part of stay put didn't you understand?" King locked the door and handed her the key. They walked down the path to the house.

"Why did you call Leona? Why not the sheriff?"

"The sheriff wouldn't do anything. He has his hands full with the drunks in town. Daily shootings keep him busy."

"Why Leona? What is she going to do?"

"She's going to ride out here. She'll be our chaperone into town."

Suzanna stopped. King bumped into her back. He grabbed her upper arms to keep her from falling. Heavens, he was strong. Something flickered to life in her lower regions. What was that all about? After a too brief moment, King released her, leaving her aching for his touch.

"But if it isn't safe for us to walk to town by ourselves, why is it for Leona?"

"Because everyone knows Leona. Most of the men in town know she can handle herself and how she carries a gun. They don't want to take the chance of being shot. The last man who tried to accost her, was on crutches for two months."

"Crutches?" They stopped at the chairs. Suzanna put their empty glasses and plate on the tray. "What did she do?"

"He had the misfortune of accosting her near a pile of lumber. She picked a piece up and whacked him across the legs with it."

"She's strong enough to break someone's leg with a board?"

King laughed and shook his head. "Nah. Simply pure luck, but the guy didn't know that. Pulling a gun on him sealed the deal. Now, if they are walking toward each other, he'll cross the street to avoid her."

Suzanna put a hand over her mouth and giggled. "I must ask her to show me her tricks."

King raised his eyes to the sky. "Heaven help us all."

"I'll be out in a minute. She unlocked the door and giggled at King's comment. Men didn't have any idea how strong women truly were. Anyway, that's what her mother always said. While it was nice to have their protection, women were stronger and oh, so much smarter than men gave them credit for.

Once inside, she took the tray into the kitchen, and rushed through rinsing the glasses and plate in the sink. Ants would have a heyday if she left them out. In her bedroom, she pulled the bag she'd brought with her from Iowa and tossed in a nightgown, clean drawers and blouse, hairbrush, and other toiletries. After a moment's thought, she added another set of drawers and a blouse in case she ended up staying another night.

After writing a quick note to Julia telling her where she was and propping it against a jar of wildflowers on the kitchen table, she gave the house a quick once over and went back outside and locked the door. A person rode toward the schoolhouse. Her heart skipped a beat. Was it Silverstone or Willoughby? She stood closer to King who had his hand on his gun. It was hard to tell who it was at this distance.

As the rider came closer, it was evident the person wore a skirt. The hat, shaped like a man's, was adorned with flowers.

"It's Leona." King let out a breath. "Hey, sis. Thanks for coming and helping. Did you have any problems on the way?"

Leona swung down from the saddle, her motions fluid and quick. A tinge of envy swept through Suzanna. Would she ever be able to ride like she and the horse were one?

"No problem, big brother." Holding onto the halter, Leona led her horse to them. "The lunch rush was over and with it being a Saturday, I have a couple of the schoolgirls helping out. Riding out here was a nice change. Most of the rowdies know better than to harm me."

King's sister glanced between him and Suzanna and raised an eyebrow. Was she worrying that her reputation was ruined for being alone with her brother? But if that was the case, why had she agreed to accompany them back to the hotel?

Leona patted her horse's neck with a black-gloved hand. "So, does someone want to let me in on what's going on here?"

They walked to the stable while King told her about Silverstone and Willoughby.

"That damn man. His sidekick isn't any better, simply dumber." Leona kicked at a stone. "I'd sooner fight with a rattlesnake than that polecat."

"You know him?"

"He used to come into the restaurant until I chased him out with my rifle when he pinched one of my waitresses in the . . . Well, you can probably figure out where." Leona's nostrils flared. "I told him if he wanted to pinch a woman's posterior, he should either get a wife, or go to Swearingen's." She slapped her hands at her waist and raised an eyebrow at Suzanna. "And you managed to get away from him?"

"Yes, and I hope I never see him again." King gave her a leg up. She searched for the stirrup and adjusted her position on the saddle, making sure her legs were covered by her skirt. Leona's mounting the horse was every bit as graceful as dismounting.

"Unfortunately, he's not one to forget what you did to him." Leona tapped her horse's sides and they headed toward town. "I'd watch my back if I were you."

"That's why I want Suzanna to stay at the hotel while Julia is gone."

"That's right. You said last night Daniel was . . ." Leona turned in her saddle and squinted her eyes at Suzanna. "Wait. I thought you were going with them as a chaperone."

Heat crept up Suzanna's neck. "I was, but decided I didn't want to be a third wheel in their budding romance."

Leona threw back her head and laughed. "So, Daniel and Julia, huh? Well, I'll be. I thought he would remain a life-long bachelor. I've seen the way women, young and old throw themselves at him and how he ignores them all."

"Really?" What a nice tidbit to tell her sister. She grinned. And to think the last time she'd seen Julia she was dressed as a man. Maybe Daniel didn't care, but . . . she mused as she brushed a wrinkle from her skirt. She'd rather catch a man in a dress than men's britches any day of the week.

"Well, Daniel is smitten for sure." King guided his horse around a pig lying in the muddy street.

"Really?" maybe she'd better find another word to say. "I believe Julia feels the same way about him, or I wouldn't have left them together."

"Besides," Leona went on. "Daniel is a gentleman and wouldn't do anything to Julia."

The crowd picked up the closer they came to town. Suzanna swatted at a fly. It was mid-afternoon and the heat had drawn in the pesky insects to the refuse on the street. Heaven help her if she should fall into the street. Once was enough.

A movement from the corner of her eye caught her attention. She urged Lizzie closer to King. "I just saw Willoughby standing on the corner by the bank."

King glanced over his shoulder. "I don't see him."

Suzanna tried to swallow around the lump in her throat. "Honestly. He was there."

"I believe you saw him, and where he is, Silverstone can't be far behind. The sooner we get you to the hotel, the better."

"What's to stop them from coming into the restaurant?"

King slapped his hand on his holster.

Oh, brother. A man who thought he could solve problems with his six-shooter. Leona grinned and shook her head. Was she thinking the same thing?

"What are you going to do, sleep by the front and back doors?" Leona asked. "You can't do both."

He dipped his head. "I'll talk to the sheriff and ask him to keep an eye on the place. He can set one of his deputies to work overnight."

The hotel was only a few buildings away and none too soon. Suzanna's eyes were tired from constantly watching each side of the street. No one seemed to pay any attention to them, but one could never tell. A few women, escorted by men, wandered down the boardwalk. Oh, no. There was Mrs. Woods on the arm of her husband, lips pursed in a tight line and wearing a scowl that could scare the most dangerous men. Thank goodness, she'd changed from her britches to a skirt and blouse. No telling what the banker's wife would think if she hadn't.

Mr. Woods' eyes were on King and if looks could kill, King would be six feet under the muddy street.

"Why does the banker look as if you're the lowest scum of the Earth?" she asked as King tied Lizzie's reins to the hitching post.

"There's no love lost between us. I bought land he wanted before he could get his hands on it. I don't trust the man any more than I trust Silverstone." He reached up his hands toward her.

Suzanna hitched in a breath and eyed the townspeople. Other than the Woods' no one seemed to be paying any attention to them, but one couldn't be sure. "What are you doing?" she whispered down to him.

"Helping you dismount."

"You can't do that." Heart pounding in her ears, she glanced around. "What will people think?"

King dropped his arms, muttered under his breath, and glanced back up at her. "That I'm a gentleman, helping a lady from her horse and setting her on the boardwalk so she doesn't get mud on her shoes and skirt." He walked to Leona's horse. "The same thing I'm going to do with my sister."

"But I'm not your sister, I'm the schoolteacher." Barely in time, she caught herself from sticking her nose in the air, like Julia said she does when she calls her uppity. Maybe King was right. Getting her best pair of boots muddy wouldn't be good. Especially since she hadn't brought another pair with her. "All right, you may help me," she said when he'd set Leona safely on the boardwalk.

"Exactly like we did at the ranch. I'm going to take you by the waist. Swing your leg over the saddle. I'll help you down to the boardwalk."

Mrs. Woods' pursed lips meant only one thing—word would spread like wildfire that the schoolteacher was being touched by a man. Surely the woman could see King was merely being a gentleman. Couldn't she? The banker's wife huffed a breath, muttered, "Well, I never," stuck her nose in the air, and headed in the other direction. Why had she wanted to emulate the snooty lady? Why her mother had more class in her little finger than Mrs. Woods did in her entire, frumpy body.

King's hands burned through the fabric of her skirt and blouse. At least Mrs. Woods had stomped off when she did, or she'd certainly be scandalized by the heat rising to Suzanna's face. She could always chalk it up to the warmth of the day, but since certain parts of her body were responding to his touch, it would be a lie.

Once she was safely on the boardwalk, King stepped back, tipped his hat, and swept his hand toward the restaurant door. "Ladies. After you."

Leona hooked her arm through Suzanna's and pulled her through the door. "Oooh, that woman makes me crazy."

"Who?"

"Mrs. Woods." She took Suzanna's bonnet, set it behind the registration desk, removed a key from the hooks behind the desk, and slapped it onto the wooden counter. "King, put Suzanna's bags in Room Fourteen."

King saluted Leona as if she were a general in the army. "Yes, ma'am."

Suzanna giggled. Leona had sounded a bit authoritarian. Rather like Julia when she got all big sister on her.

"Brothers can be such an irritation, but I do love King dearly."

"I have a brother, several actually, so I know what you mean." Suzanna followed Leona into the kitchen.

Leona went to the stove and pressed her hand against a tall, blue and white speckled coffee pot sitting on the warming shelf of the stove. She pointed to a table in the corner of room. "Have a seat. Would you like coffee? It's still hot from lunch. And maybe a piece of apple pie?"

Suzanna's mouth watered at the mention of Leona's fabulous apple pie. The first time she'd had it, it took everything in her power not to pick up the plate and lick it clean. "I'd love some, but please let me help."

"Not a chance. You sit yourself down and relax."

Relax is what she'd love to do, but the events of the past morning and having Mrs. Woods observe her with King, made it difficult. She closed her eyes and took three cleansing breaths.

The cup clinked against its saucer when Leona set it down on the table. She opened her eyes at the scent of coffee and apple pie.

"Are you okay?"

"I will be once I have a bite of your pie." Because she and Leona were alone in the immaculate kitchen, she didn't hold back the moan of delight when the flavors of cinnamon and another spice hit her taste buds. "Oh, heavens, this is delicious."

"Thank you." Leona added cream to her coffee. "Now. No one else is here. What's going on with you and my brother?"

What? What gave Leona the idea there was something between King and her? "What are you talking about? Why do you ask?"

"I see the way he looks at you like you're better than my apple pie." Leona put a spoonful of sugar in her cup and waved a finger at Suzanna. "And let me tell you, he once ate an entire pie in one sitting. And you look at him as if he was your star pupil."

She did? Why, oh why, did she have to blush? "Um . . . there's nothing between us. Besides, I'm the school . . ."

"Oh pshaw. Those teacher contracts are just plain stupid and once men realize that, they won't have such a hard time keeping teachers who want to marry."

"That's what King has said." The conversation was getting a bit too personal. Leona was a relative stranger, and talking about marriage to a man she'd met a few weeks ago was ridiculous. It may work for Julia, but not her. Oh, but King was such a nice, handsome, man. Every nerve ending in her body tingled. Now would be a good time to change the subject. She set down her fork.

"Why did you say Mrs. Woods drives you crazy?"

Leona wrapped her hands around her coffee cup. Her grin seemed forced. "She doesn't live here all the time. Says it's too unsophisticated for her. When she is here, she acts as if the world should revolve around her, plus she tends to stick her nose into everyone's business."

That didn't sound good. "We rode in the stagecoach with her. She commented on everything, and most of it not good."

"Sounds like her." Leona leaned across the table as if she was going to impart a great secret. "You can bet your bottom dollar she'll be telling everyone King had his hands around the schoolteacher's waist."

"But he was only helping me from the horse."

"We know that, and most people won't listen to her. But there will be a few who believe it will help their station in life to be friends with a banker's wife and will listen and believe every word coming from her mouth like it's the gospel truth."

"King doesn't care for Mr. Woods, either."

Leona chuckled. "You can say that again. There is no love lost between those two. After King managed to buy up the land Woods wanted, they've been at each other's throats. At least it keeps the pompous jack . . ." Leona blushed. "I'm mean pompous . . ." She shrugged. "I can't think of a phrase a proper lady should use."

"I get the idea." She was beginning to like King's sister. While she didn't care for swearing, sometimes a swear word was the best option.

King came into the kitchen. Suzanna's heart skipped at beat at his presence.

"Would you like to join us, King?" Leona asked, nudging Suzanna in the shin and grinning.

"Sorry, but no. I put your bag in your room." He handed Suzanna her key. "I locked it, and you should make sure to do so every time, too." He kept his eyes on hers. "I'll head out to the ranch and see how things are going there."

Leona slapped her hands at her waist. "But you just got back to town. There are things you need to get done around here. Like the stack of paperwork waiting for you on your desk."

He turned his sights on his sister. "I know, but it would be best if I didn't stay here. I'll be back tomorrow. Monday at the latest." He held a hand over his heart. "And I promise to go through the bills when I get back."

"Ah, I get it." Leona bit her bottom lip then grinned.

What were they talking about? What was she missing in this conversation? "Is there something you need to tell me?"

Leona patted Suzanna's hand. "Don't worry, it's nothing bad, but if people, like nosy and nasty-minded Mrs. Woods, saw you with King and you're staying here while he is, they'll put two and two together and come up with five."

She wagged her finger between herself and King. "You mean they think King and I . . ." Heavens. Why did she have to blush so much?

"Yep."

Were people so narrow-minded? "You're kidding, right?"

Leona shook her head. "No, I'm not. It doesn't take much for a woman's reputation to be soiled."

"It's not fair, Suzanna, but that's the way things are." King leaned against the counter and crossed his legs at the ankles. "Surely you have gossip in Iowa."

Suzanna snorted. "Of course. When my father broke his leg and my mother went to the bank to try and get a loan, a rumor was spread she propositioned the banker to get the loan." She cringed at the awful memory. "The thing was, she didn't get the loan and was so busy with us kids and talking care of the farm while Dad was laid up, she barely had time to comb her hair in the morning let alone meet up with a man."

"What happened?" Leona patted her hand.

"Thankfully the banker stood up for my mother. Then, of course, people thought the rumors were true." She couldn't keep the sarcasm from her voice. "Why else would a man stand up for a woman if he wasn't spending time with her? It finally took his wife to convince people her husband and my mother were not stepping out together."

"Well, people are idiots." Leona stood, took their plates, and washed them in the sink.

King put on his hat. "I'd best head out."

"Make sure people see you leave town," Leona called after him.

Suzanna held back a sigh at his broad shoulders as he left the room. She couldn't resist adding, "And don't get shot."

King waved a hand over his shoulder. "I'll do my best."

Now what was she supposed to do? If she were back at the house, she could weed the garden, grade papers, clean her bedroom, or make supper. She drank the last of the coffee in her cup. "Can I do anything to help? I'll go crazy if I sit up in my room and I certainly don't want to wander around town."

Leona smiled over her shoulder. "I should say not. How do you feel about ironing?"

Heavens. The one chore she detested. Standing at the ironing board getting the wrinkles out of pants, dresses, and shirts wasn't her idea of helping. But, because King wouldn't let her pay for her room, she could only say yes. As long as she didn't have to press anything lacey or fancy.

"I take it by your long pause, you don't like to iron." Leona lifted a grate on the stove, stoked up the fire, added a few pieces of wood, and replaced the grate. The two sadirons were put on the heating stove.

"It's not my favorite thing to do, but I want to help." At least Leona didn't ask her to wash the clothes, too.

Leona took two chairs and placed them about four feet apart, their backs facing each other. "Good. I detest ironing." Next, she took a long board covered with cream-colored fabric from behind a set of long curtains and set it across the chairbacks.

Suzanna was beginning to like Leona more and more. Other than Sadie, whom she only saw when shopping, she hadn't made any friends in Deadwood. It would be good to have someone to talk with other than Julia. And if she and King were to marry, Leona could become another sister. She gave herself a second to daydream before banishing the idea from her mind. Leona could become like a sister without having anything between her and King.

Leona left the room and came back with a basket piled high with clean laundry. "It's only sheets and napkins." She set the basket on the table, picked up one of the sadirons, and sprinkled water on it. The sizzle meant it was hot enough to use. "Are you sure you want to do this?" she asked over her shoulder.

"Of course, I do." She closed her eyes. Would God strike her down for telling a lie?

"I appreciate this so much. This will give me time to prep for supper."

Holding back a sigh, Suzanna pulled a sheet from the basket, attached a handle to one of the sadirons, and started the mind-numbing job, one which gave her too much time to think about Silverstone, Willoughby, and King.

Chapter Seventeen

September 25, 1879

Suzanna plunked her chin in her hand and gazed out one of the schoolhouse windows. Not a whisper of a breeze fluttered the curtains. The open windows didn't help cool the stifling air. She swiped at a bead of sweat rolling down the side of her face and picked up her fan to get the air moving. At least with the children done for the day, the scent of sweaty, unwashed bodies had diminished a bit.

It was hot. Hotter than Hades. After a miserable hot and humid August, she and the residents of Deadwood were hoping for a cooler September, but so far, it hadn't been the case. The children were cranky and lethargic. Even the sweetest of kids were misbehaving. It was so bad she'd considered taking the entire student body down to the creek to swim, instead of teaching them arithmetic. Maybe dunk a few of them until they cried uncle. Their attention was shot, anyway, and holding classes outside beneath the trees hadn't helped.

People in town weren't faring any better. There were more arguments, gunfights, and with the mystery of who had been poisoning the liquor in town solved, people moved on to other topics of consideration, one which she wished people would drop.

Tears pooled in her eyes. Nasty Mrs. Woods simply had to spread rumors about her and King. Now the woman had left town leaving behind the mess she and her husband had created. The school board had called her to task. Of course, King, being a man, wasn't given any trouble. It was as if whatever they were supposed to have done was done only by her.

King had repeatedly told the board and anyone else who would listen they hadn't done anything wrong. He wasn't even in the hotel while she was there. Leona had said the same, but someone had started a rumor of Leona servicing men in her room upstairs, so no one listened to her.

It was the Haywood's and many of the parents who stood up for her and helped her keep her job. The couple was known for their honesty, which went a long way in helping her case. Parents didn't want her to be fired. Their children loved her, and had learned to love school, which no other teacher had been able to do. But there were still those narrow-minded folks who believed the worst of everyone.

The back door creaked, making her jump. Darn, had she forgotten to lock it? She eased the top right drawer open and removed the pistol King had sent her. Thankfully, with the training her father had given her and Julia, she knew how to use it. She pulled back the hammer and set the gun in her lap.

Even though there'd been no sign of neither Silverstone nor Willoughby, there'd been enough activity around the property to realize someone was watching her. Her nerves were stretched as tight as a piano string.

"Suzanna?"

Julia. She let out a breath but left the gun in her lap. Just because she knew it was Julia, didn't mean someone wasn't behind her. She twisted in her chair to face her sister.

"What's wrong? You jumped like someone put a stick of dynamite under your chair."

Only until she was sure Julia was alone, did she let go of the gun, setting it on the desk. "I'm fine. Just skittish. This not knowing the whereabouts of Silverstone is getting to me." She took in Julia's disheveled appearance. Dark circles rimmed her eyes. Her clothes hung on her already slim frame. Her sister was obviously suffering. "Haven't heard from Daniel, yet?"

Julia shook her head. "I knew what I was doing would get me in trouble, I didn't figure it would hurt so much." She cradled her stomach. "I miss him so much, and I've ruined things between us for good."

"He'll come around, I'm sure of it." She understood how Daniel felt about what he thought Julia had been doing the past few months. She had a hard time coming to grips with Julia working for a madam. But Daniel should have given Julia a chance to explain herself before rejecting her outright. Julia would never do what Daniel accused her of.

"I'm not so sure. At least with your and King's help, I can continue working." Julia picked up a stack of slates filled with sums. "Are you ready to go?"

"Yes. I hate having to be so careful all the time. I worry when the children are here."

"Would Silverstone do anything with a building full of kids?"

"I don't know."

"King says he hasn't seen or heard from the man in a while, so maybe he left town for good."

Suzanna locked the back door. "After finding out about Mr. Woods, maybe he has. I can only hope."

They made the short trip to the house. Julia unlocked the front door. "King says the problems on the ranch have stopped. So, with Silverstone nowhere in sight, he believes he was the instigator."

King says this. King says that. Obviously, King was talking with her sister, but why not her? She set her things on the entry bench. Oh, that's right, because of Mrs. Woods and her wagging, lying tongue, people were watching her closely. And what would they think if they found out what her sister was doing? They'd be run out of town on the first two-legged donkey they could find.

She missed King. Missed his handsome face, his kindness, his sense of honor and humor. Why hadn't she kissed him when she'd had the chance the day at the school? Now it looked as if she'd never find out how it felt to have his mouth pressed against hers. Anger, frustration, regret, and a myriad of other emotions she couldn't define roiled in her stomach, ready to explode. And when it did, heaven help the person in her way.

"Suzanna?" Julia stopped in the kitchen doorway. "You look as if you're ready to punch someone."

Which was honestly what she wanted to do. But who? The woman who started this whole thing had disappeared, there was no one else she could slug. "I would love to give Mrs. Woods what for. If she ever shows her face in town again, it'll be too soon."

Julia grinned. "With her husband in jail, I doubt she'll ever come back to town. Saving face is too important to her."

"Well, then, I guess I'll go punch my pillows."

"How about we go pick the vegetables from the garden. The potatoes and onions are ready to be dug up. That should take some of the built-up anger out of you."

Ugh. She didn't mind picking beans or peas and canning them. She rather enjoyed harvesting tomatoes and peppers and making sauce. But digging up potatoes and onions was not on her list of things she enjoyed doing. Wearing gloves didn't keep dirt from getting under her nails. Not only did the dirt dry out her hands, she managed to get it in her hair, which meant she'd have to wash it in the middle of the week.

But Julia was right, it would certainly get rid of her pent-up anger. Maybe instead of carrying the potatoes and onions into the cellar in baskets, she could simply toss them down one-by-one. By the time she was done, she'd feel better.

"What about your anger with Daniel?"

Julia shook her head, slapped the doorframe, and entered the kitchen. "Maybe we both need to dig potatoes. We can toss them down into the cellar and let them land wherever they want."

Suzanna snickered. "You must have been reading my mind, but I guess it would be better for our winter food supply if we're careful with it."

"Then let's have a quick supper and get to work." Julia opened the icebox and stuck her head inside. "It gets dark earlier now." Her words were muffled from inside the icebox. She backed out holding leftover chicken and pickled red beets.

"I'll get changed."

Suzanna had to admit digging in the dirt helped. It had taken them three hours to dig onions, potatoes, and red beets, rinse them, haul them into the house and down the stairs into the cellar. Tiredness replaced her anger. She came up the cellar steps, closed the trap door in the floor, replaced the rug and table over it, and went outside to join Julia.

Crickets sang their early-evening symphony. Besides being tired, dirt, clung to every spot of sweat. "Why did we pick such a hot evening to do this?" With the back of her hand, she swiped at a brown drop of sweat sliding down her forehead toward her eyes. I'm too tired to wash up, but I can't go to bed like this."

"I'm not going to bother, yet."

"Are you heading to Letty's tonight?"

"Mm-hmm."

"Who are you going as this time?" A shiver of fear skittered down her back. Sometimes she wished she hadn't found out what Julia did.

"The old man. I haven't been him in a while."

Why didn't she have courage like her sister? Yes, Julia was getting paid, but if she wasn't, she'd probably still befriend the women in the brothel. Hattie's story was truly a sad one, as were most of the women stuck in those places.

"You be careful. I have a bad feeling."

Julia stood and brushed dirt from her skirt. "I'm always careful. Being with King helps."

Suzanna clenched her teeth. It was a sad day when she was jealous of her own sister, but she got to spend time with King, while Suzanna had to act like the perfect teacher and stay away from him. Julia might have her heart set on Daniel and dressed in different male costumes to hide her identity, but she still was with King.

"I'm exhausted." Julia glanced up at the darkening sky. "I hate it when it gets dark so early. I guess I should wash up, change clothes, and work on the corset for Hattie."

"I'm going to stay out here a bit. Tell me when you're done cleaning up." The door slammed behind Julia, leaving Suzanna alone with the increasing night noises. What was making her so skittish? Why did she have a feeling something bad was about to happen? Her grandmother had the ability to sense upcoming events. She never knew what they were. At the time, it had always sounded like the ramblings of an old woman, but there were too many times her thoughts came true.

In her mind, it was easy to say *something* was going to occur without being specific and later say it was what she meant. Suzanna did have to admit when she'd had premonitions, it freaked her out when they came true. She only wished her premonitions were more specific.

Was Julia safe tonight? Should she say tell her more than to *be careful*? But it wouldn't do any good because she didn't understand what was making her antsy. Julia would simply tell her she was being silly. Or maybe it was King who was going to be in trouble. Would Julia be in a position to help him?

In the distance an owl hooted. What little breeze there had been when digging, was now gone. Everything was still. Too still. Like the universe was holding its breath in anticipation . . . Suzanna shook her head. Nothing was going to go wrong. Anyway, nothing more than had been for King and her.

When Julia poked her head out the front door, Suzanna rose and went in to clean up. She still had work to go over for tomorrow. It was so warm out, the cool water from the kitchen pump was refreshing. It was late enough in the evening to don her nightdress. Her long, wet hair dampened the back of her nightgown which further cooled her off. She sat on the couch, legs tucked to her side and went over the students' sums—twice as her mind kept wandering to Julia and King's trip into town.

At nine o'clock, she stood and stretched. "I'm going to bed." It had been a few weeks since she'd ventured out to the necessary before bed. Worries about who may be lurking made them switch to using their chamber pots in their rooms. And instead of Julia heading to Hattie's on her own, King now met her at the bottom of the hill and escorted her to town.

Julia set down the bright purple corset and smiled. "Sleep well. I'm going to stay up until it's time to leave. It's so much easier now that you know what I'm doing. I hated having to lie and sneak out."

"And I don't have to wonder why you were always so tired."

"Stress can do that to a person." Julia grinned. "That and not getting to bed until all hours of the morning."

Suzanna leaned down and kissed Julia on the cheek. "Be careful. Please."

"Don't worry about me. I'll be careful."

From her sister's mouth to God's ears.

Chapter Eighteen

Early Morning, September 26, 1879

"Julia, where are you?" Suzanna uncovered her face and peered through the heavy smoke. Nothing but smoke and more smoke. And where were King and Daniel?

The ground beneath her shook as another explosion filled the air, masking the screaming and yelling of Deadwood's residents. She stood and walked toward town, then turned back to the house. What should she do? She stepped on a rock with a bare foot. Whatever she did, she needed to get dressed and put on shoes.

She ran back into the house. Once in her room, she put on a skirt and blouse, forgoing the usual petticoats and corset. It was too hot for them and fripperies would only get in the way.

Standing in the middle of the living room, she turned this way and that. Why couldn't she decide what to do? At one point she thought she'd heard someone yell to go to the hills. If Deadwood was burning, would that be where everyone went? Should she go up the hill behind the house and try to find Julia or would she get in the way. She had no idea how to put out a fire, and surely the fire department was doing their job. Before long, they'd have the fire under control. Wouldn't they?

Maybe it would be better if she stayed here and prepared . . . but prepared what? While indecision plagued her, Suzanna rolled her hair into a bun at the back of her neck. She had no idea how bad the fire was. It could be only one building. But she'd heard three explosions. It could only mean things were more serious.

Food. People always needed food in an emergency. She raced into the kitchen and looked over their shelves. Because it was only the two of them, they didn't have a lot. Between what they had and what others in the community would share, people wouldn't starve.

Someone pounded on the front door. She jumped and dropped a jar of tomatoes on the table. Who would be coming to the house at this time of the morning? Julia had a key.

"Suzanna? It's me, King."

Thank heavens. Ignoring the tomatoes and juice splattered on the table and running onto the floor, she raced through the living room. What happened for King to be here? It had to be bad. Before opening the door, she peeked through the side window. It looked like King, but with his sooty face, it was hard to tell.

"King?"

"Yes, it's me. Let me in."

She unlocked the door and stepped aside. He reeked of smoke. Small holes dotted his clothing. His hat was gone. "What's happened?" She peered around the door. "Where's Julia?"

Instead of answering, King drew her into his arms. A shudder passed through his body. "It's awful, Suzanna. Deadwood is gone."

Suzanna pulled back and looked into his red eyes. "What do you mean, Deadwood is gone?"

King raked his fingers through his hair and flinched. "A fire started and before we knew it, it raced through the downtown destroying everything in its path. It wouldn't have been so bad if containers of gunpowder hadn't exploded. Almost everything is burned to the ground."

"And what about Julia and Daniel? Where are they?" She clutched King's arm. "Are they hurt?"

"No. We ran into him outside his building. We got Hattie and her girls out and up the hill where everyone else in town went. We sat up there and watched the town disappear into ashes."

Not worrying about the mess he'd leave behind, Suzanna guided King to the couch and pressed him to sit. She knelt before him. "What about your restaurant."

King shrugged and buried his face in his hands. "It was too hard to see, but I can only assume it's gone, too."

Suzanna took his hands in hers. Tears rolled through the soot on his face, leaving white streaks. "You have burns on your hands."

"I'm fine." He huffed a breath. "It's probably not the only place."

"Let me get some water and clean you up." She rose to her feet.

King shook his head and stood. "I can't. I need to get back to the people on the hill and see if anyone is missing. I wanted to come here to make sure you were all right."

"I am. I was about to gather food and supplies." She let him hold her again. His scent made her eyes burn, but it was nothing compared to what he'd gone through. "I couldn't figure out what else to do."

He kissed her forehead. "I can tell you one thing right now. After things get back to normal, I'm not waiting a year to let everyone know how I feel about you."

Warmth poured through her system. "And what is that?"

"Hell, woman. I can't believe I've fallen in love with you so fast. I missed you and want to spend my life with you."

"You do?" She widened her eyes when he cupped her cheeks. His breath blew across her face sending shivers down her spine. Was he going to kiss her?

"Yes, I do." He caressed her skin with his thumbs. "I don't care about the damn contract. Life is too short. Do you understand me?"

"I missed you, too. I don't care about the contract, either. I want to be with you." Before she knew it, he leaned down and pressed his lips against hers. In that moment she knew why Julia didn't want to talk about her first kiss from Daniel. It was too precious. Too special.

Too private. Too marvelous. Too . . . for a teacher she couldn't come with any more adjectives, she simply leaned in and enjoyed the kiss.

Much too soon, King broke the kiss. "I need to get back up the hill."

It took a second to remember why he was here. The fire. That's right, the fire. "What can I do to help?"

"Be ready for an onslaught of people. With the school being safe and the fire having gone in the other direction, this is where people will converge. Gather blankets, sheets, and any food you can spare. The only thing people have is what they are wearing. And for some, it wasn't much. Be prepared, but keep the doors locked. I'll get back to you as soon as I can."

With another swift kiss, he left. In a daze, she locked the door, leaned against it, and pressed her fingers against her lips. Goodness. Her first kiss. It was so warm, so delicious, and way, way too brief. And he loved her and wanted to spend their lives together. It would end her teaching, but so, what. She'd be with the man of her dreams. When would they get married? If Daniel and Julia worked things out, would they have a double wedding? Where would they live? If she wasn't teaching, they couldn't use this house. The restaurant and hotel were gone, and presumably Daniel's living quarters, too.

The ranch? She'd love living at the ranch. But . . . her reverie was broken by a shout from outside the house.

"Suzanna, it's Julia. Let me in."

Suzanna pushed away from the door and unlocked it. When Julia came into the room, she grabbed her sister and held her, tears streaming down her face. "Even though King said you were safe, I thought I'd lost you." She stepped back and searched her sister. Like King, she smelled like smoke and was covered in soot and ash. Burn holes peppered her clothing. Unlike King, parts of her hair were singed.

She took Julia's hands. Blisters dotted the skin. "You must be in pain. Let me pump water in the sink so you can wash up."

"Lock the door first." Julia's voice quivered. "You wouldn't believe how crazy people are acting. The flames aren't completely out, and the sun is barely up to see the devastation, but already people are complaining about what they're going to do. Asking me what to do. Asking me for help. There was nothing I could do, so I came home.' She dropped to the couch. "It won't be long and I'm afraid they're going to descend upon us and anyone else who didn't lose everything. It's going to be chaos."

"We'll do what we can, Julia."

"I know. But even the men are acting like fools. I'm afraid there's going to be a lot of looting going on." Julia picked at her ruined pants. "I need to get out of these clothes. No one noticed I was wearing men's britches. But once they start coming to their senses, it won't take long for some of the old biddies to wonder why I'm dressed like this."

Suzanna pushed the pump handle up and down, filling the basin with water. She set a towel, washcloth, and bar of soap next to the sink. The curtains over the sink remained closed from the evening before. "Well, get in here and get those clothes off."

"We should burn these." Julia dropped the old-man clothes on the floor and kicked them across the room. "I never want to wear them again."

"You won't have to, if Hattie's place is gone."

Julia shook her head. "That poor woman. To lose everything she owns twice to fire. If I were her, I'd go live in a lake."

Suzanna picked up the clothes and holding them out before her, took them into the living room, and tossed them into the stove. "I'll get you clean clothes." Once she'd learned of Julia's side business, her room was no longer out of bounds. She took Julia's garden skirt and a fresh blouse, plus clean drawers and camisole into the kitchen.

"Here." She set them on a kitchen chair. "Want me to wash your hair for you?"

"No. I have a feeling it's only going to get smelly again. Besides, everyone else is going to smell, too."

While Julia finished, Suzanna wiped up the spilled tomatoes, which Julia thankfully, hadn't noticed. She wasn't about to share what transpired between her and King. She may have pestered her sister for details about her first kiss, but she didn't want Julia to reciprocate.

When Julia was done, they gathered what quilts, blankets, and sheets they had. After all, they were supplied by the town anyway. They piled food into baskets and set everything out front and waited for the people to arrive.

The wait wasn't long. First one family arrived, then another, and before they had a chance to help them, others arrived, begging for help.

"This isn't going to be good, is it?" she whispered to Julia as the last quilt was given away.

"No. And it's only going to get worse."

Truer words were never spoken.

Chapter Nineteen

King couldn't take his eyes from the empty lot where his hotel and restaurant once stood. All his hard work, gone up in smoke. If he ever smelled smoke like this again, it would be too soon. The scent of the fire at the racetrack was nothing compare to this.

Even though it had been two days since the town burned down, he swore the ground still smoldered and was warm to the touch. He glanced up and down the street. A few saloon owners who'd set up business by throwing up tents and slapping boards between whisky casks delivered from Lead. Many of the men had their own priorities and drinking was one of them. Unburned bank vaults stood as sentinels among the rubble. A few brick walls remained standing. But other than that, the land, covered in white ash, was bare.

Over the course of those two days he'd done what he could to help others. There were times the residents' helplessness drove him crazy. Was it laziness or the overwhelming sense of vulnerability that made people unable to act?

He'd left the makeshift camp before people began stirring. He twisted to relieve the ache in his back from sleeping on the ground. Unlike others, he at least had a tent as shelter. Paddy had arrived yesterday afternoon with a wagonload of blankets and food. With the number of people without anything to their names, the supplies disappeared fast. Word was that supplies from Lead and other towns would show up soon.

King released his breath. Standing here wasn't going to get anything done. He pushed up his sleeves and took the shovel leaning against the wagon Paddy had left behind. His foreman would have stayed to help with cleaning up, but someone had to run the ranch. Besides, what a perfect opportunity it would be for someone to steal his stock when a large portion of his crew had come to town to help.

He viewed the area. The best place to start was . . . anywhere. Hell, he couldn't even tell where he was standing. The dining room? Kitchen? Reception area? He jabbed the tip of the shovel into the ash, stopped, bent over, and pulled out an ash-covered plate., Was he in the kitchen or dining room? He set the plate aside. One down, too many more to go.

The sun had nearly crested the trees when Daniel appeared at his side.

"Were you able to salvage anything?" Daniel glanced between King, the empty lot, and the wagon.

"The stoves are intact." He pointed his shovel toward a pile at the corner of his lot. "From what I can tell, so are most of the plates, cups, and silverware. They'll need a good scrubbing. It seems anything made from ceramic like sinks survived. Beds, dressers, tables, and anything else made of wood were burned. I have no idea where to start."

"We're here to help." Julia looked at him but shifted her eyes everywhere but at Daniel.

Suzanna stood next to Julia, her cheeks rosy, a rake in one hand and bucket in another. "Tell us what to do."

The women appeared no older than twelve or thirteen. They each wore handkerchiefs over their hair and had their skirt hems tucked into their waistbands. Knee-high rubber boots covered their lower legs.

"Well?" Julia said, directing her question to King.

"I'm appreciative, but shouldn't you be helping those staying on the school property? When I left this morning, more tents were going up."

"There are enough people to help," Suzanna said. "Besides, we were getting tired of the whining and crying from some of the women. You'd think they could get off their lazy backsides to help out."

Shaking her head, Julia leaned on the handle of her rake. "After things were stolen from the house, the sheriff set guards to protect what we have left. There's been a lot of looting, so he asked General Sturgis to send in soldiers to protect property not damaged by the fire. After he left two men to protect the house and school, we hightailed it out of there."

King rubbed the back of his neck. "I'm still digging for anything useable. You could help while Daniel and I fill the cart with junk." He jerked a thumb over his shoulder. "I have a pile started over there."

SUZANNA TWISTED AT the waist in an attempt to relieve the pain in her back. They'd only been at it for an hour or so and already she was tired. She hadn't had much sleep. But while working, she was totally aware of King's presence. How could she not be? With each shovelful of debris he tossed over the sides of the wagon, his shirt stretched across his broad back. The muscles in his bare forearms rippled.

"Seems like a hopeless task, doesn't it?" Julia set another fork on the growing pile of cutlery and other utensils.

She set a blue coffee pot beside three others and found a tarnished spoon. "I'm not sure how everything is going to get cleaned, or if it can be cleaned enough to use again." A yell from down the street caught her attention. A wagon with one man driving a team of horses and four other people riding in the back came toward them, the horses kicking up ash in their wake.

As soon as the wagon stopped, Leona jumped over the side, ran to King, and held him in a hug. "What are we going to do, King?" Tears streamed down her face.

"The choices are to leave town or rebuild." He draped an arm around her shoulders. "I'm glad you decided to go to Lead for the night, or you would have been caught in this."

"Was anyone killed?"

King shook his head. "Only the man who was deaf and didn't hear the fire bells. As fast as the fire spread, we're lucky not to have lost more."

A sob built in Suzanna's chest as the siblings viewed the destruction.

Leona rested her head on King's shoulder. "What are you going to do?"

He glanced down at his sister. "If you're willing to stay and help me, I'd like to rebuild. This will be a good opportunity for the town to rebuild stronger and better than ever."

"I'll stay."

King kissed the top of Leona's head. "Thanks, sis."

Suzanna closed her eyes and let out a breath. Thank goodness. If Leona had decided to leave, King would probably have sold his property and left, too.

As if he were holding back his emotions, King cleared his throat and turned to the wagon.

"Who are these fine folks, and what did you bring with you?"

"King, Suzanna, Julia, and King, these are my friends, Madeline, Tessa, Conrad, and Taggard. They've come to help. And as far as I know, more will be arriving later today and tomorrow."

"It's nice to meet you, Suzanna." Conrad took her hand and held it longer than was proper. "I'm sure we'll get along fine."

Suzanna tugged her hand from his. King stood beside her and put an arm around her waist.

"Let's see what they have in the wagon, shall we?"

Conrad grunted and walked away. Had King given the man a sign she belonged to him? Julia raised an eyebrow at her. She was certain to get the third degree later, but right now, they needed to get to work.

"We brought some large tents we can set up as a kitchen," Leona said, walking to the wagon full of supplies. "If we can get them up today, the dishes, pots and pans washed, and stoves scrubbed tomorrow, we should be able to start cooking by the following day."

"That's wonderful, Leona," Julia said, wiping an arm across her face.

It may sound wonderful, but it was an awful lot of work to get done in a day and a half. Did anyone know how to put those tents up? And there were still people at their house causing chaos.

Julia nudged her in the side. "We can take these things back to our house to wash them tonight. Leona and her friends can stay with us tonight. With the extra hands, it shouldn't take long to clean things up.

Was she kidding or had she gone crazy? There were a lot of dishes and pots and pans to be scrubbed. Not to mention finding tables and chairs. At least the stoves had survived the fire, and because they were already black, there was no need to scrub them until they shone.

She drew her attention to King who was hitching a mule to the wagon full of debris. "Where are you taking the wagon?"

"I was told there's an empty field on the edge of town where we can take our rubble." He climbed onto the seat and smiled down at her. "I don't know what is going to happen to it after that, nor do I care."

KING PULLED THE TEAM to a stop where the restaurant used to be and glanced at the sky. While he was gone, dark, ominous clouds filled the sky. A rumble of thunder echoed into the valley. Unless they were lucky, it wouldn't be long before they were doused with rain.

It had taken longer to dump the wagon than he thought. Someone had organized the field, letting only so many wagons in to dump. While it kept chaos from ensuing from everyone being anxious to bring back another load, it made the process slower. Speaking of progress, he jumped down from the wagon and whistled.

"Well, I'll be damned." King stood next to Daniel. "How'd you get those tents up?"

"See those women over there? The ones covered in dirt?"

"It's hard to tell, but do you mean Suzanna, Julia, Leona, and her friends?"

Daniel grinned at him. "Yep. They labored like work horses to get the tents in place."

"You're kidding."

"Nope. I guess growing up on a farm helped them build muscles." Daniel wiped a forearm over his forehead. "Too bad you weren't here to see it."

"Yeah." King shook his head. "Hell, if there was a restaurant around, I'd buy everyone supper."

Daniel chuckled. "Speaking of food," he glanced at the sun hanging low in the sky, "we should quit for the day. Everyone's exhausted. We can load whatever needs to be washed into the wagon and haul them to Julia and Suzanna's."

King shoved his hands in his back pockets. "Sounds fine with me. You going to stay with me tonight?"

"I don't know."

"A tent has to be better than wherever you've been sleeping the past few nights." King didn't miss the way Daniel kept staring at Julia. "Hell, man. Swallow your pride. Get on your knees. Tell her how you feel." King grinned, his heart pounding in his chest. Dare he admit what he'd told Suzanna? "I did."

"What?" Daniel clenched his fists and took a step toward King. Anger filled that one little word.

King backed off. "I didn't say it right. What I meant was I told Suzanna how I felt about her. I love her and want her to be with me the rest of our lives."

"Seriously?"

"Yep. When I went to see her while you were up on the hill. I realized life is too short to abide by stupid rules. And saying a teacher can't marry is plain stupid."

Daniel shrugged. "I can't argue with that." He rubbed a hand over his stubbly face. "I figured out what I have to do about Julia."

With a grin, King slapped his friend on the back. "And what would that be?"

"Grovel, my brother, grovel."

"I wish I could be there when you do, but I guess it should be a private moment between the two of you."

Daniel eyed the sisters. "Amazing. We'll be brothers-in-law."

He hadn't considered it, but in two seconds he realized he liked the idea of forever being tied to his best friend. He swallowed around a lump in his throat. Before he did something stupid like hug his friend or cry, he clapped his hands together. "Okay, everyone. Looks like we have a storm approaching. Let's get the wagon loaded and to the schoolyard. Maybe we can get the tents up before it hits."

Chapter Twenty

If there was a muscle in her body that didn't hurt, Suzanna couldn't figure out where, unless it was her brain, and she wasn't too sure about that, either. Three days of putting up tents, washing dishes, raking ash at the restaurant, helping set up makeshift tables and benches.

The worse part of having people camping by their house was the noise. Children playing, adults arguing, card games starting up. Why weren't they helping themselves, instead of sitting back and waiting for aid? Especially the women who a few days ago considered themselves the cream of society, such as it was in Deadwood. They looked down their noses at anyone they considered inferior—especially the prostitutes, and it was those ladies of the evening who stepped in to help others.

The first day they'd come back from downtown, Julia found the fence around their garden had been ripped down. Julia argued with the women who dug up their food. Telling people there was food arriving every day from outlying towns didn't stop them from taking what they wanted. What made it more irritating was she knew for a fact some of the people taking handouts still had lodgings and their belongings. Thankfully, someone besides herself reported them to the sheriff, who promptly sent them on their way and made them replace the food, blankets, and clothing they'd said they needed.

The biggest surprise of the first day was the arrival of Mrs. Woods. Considering what her husband had done and how she had lost everything in the fire, it was surprising she continued to act high and mighty and expected to sit on her big backside and have others do her bidding. Her reaction to the prostitutes was beyond sickening. But Daniel put her in her place. The woman seemed to have settled down to the point of watching the younger children while their parents tried to rebuild their lives or making preparations to leave Deadwood for good. She also helped some of the balcony girls wash clothes and hang them to dry on ropes strung between the trees.

The whole fire incident had certainly shown her the unethical, un-Christian, underbelly of people. She'd always sought to see the good in people, but now she knew many of the so-called good people were putting on a show.

Since no one knew when people would either leave town or start rebuilding, the school board decided to close school for the rest of the year and use the building for food distribution. People didn't want to make the trek downtown where the food had originally been taken.

"Are you coming, Suzanna? Leona and the others have already left."

Holding back a groan at what would surely be another exhausting day, she locked the front door, nodded at the guard, and linked her arm through her sister's. "Are you as tired as I am?"

"Probably." Julia stopped, tugged off her boot, turned it upside down, and tapped a stone out. "I'm not sure how I got out of bed this morning." She held onto Suzanna's shoulder while she slipped the boot back on. "Which reminds me. I forgot what a bed hog you are."

"Me? If I'm a bed hog, then you're a blanket hog."

Julia giggled. "I've missed sleeping with you."

Suzanna hugged her sister's arm to her side and grinned. "Me, too."

This was the first time they walked to town unescorted. Besides the contingent of soldiers sent to Deadwood to protect thieving, most of the men were too busy and tired to accost women. With every brothel and the saloons burned to the ground, it didn't take the owners, with the help of the single men, to start rebuilding them.

"So, you and Daniel have patched things up?"

Julia blushed. "Yep. He asked me to marry him."

Suzanna squealed. "He did. What did you say? What did you say? C'mon, don't leave me in suspense."

"If you be quiet for a minute, I'd be able to tell you I said yes."

She squealed again. "You and I both getting married is so exciting."

Julia stopped and pulled Suzanna to do so, too. "What do you mean? You can't get married."

Through her tear-filled eyes, Julia's ire was evident. Hands on her waist, eyebrows nearly meeting. Lips stretched into a grimace.

"King came to see me the night of the fire to make sure I hadn't ventured into town. He told me he loves me and wants to spend the rest of our lives together."

"But . . . but, you can't. Your contract. We'll lose our house."

"We aren't going to say anything for a while, but King is going to force the board to let me keep teaching and live here. After all, who is going to want to come to a burned-out town to teach—especially when so many families are talking of leaving and not coming back." Suzanna took Julia's arm and propelled her forward. "Besides you and Daniel aren't going to want to live with me, anyway. You'll want a place of your own."

They reached the beginning of Main Street where the fire hadn't reached. Although blackened in places, a few buildings still stood. The trees that managed to escape the blaze had scorch marks on the sides facing town. Between the rain and ash, everything was now a dull gray. If someone was enterprising enough, they could collect the ash and use it to make soap.

"Ladies. So nice to see you again."

That voice. The voice of the man she and King thought had left town. Three men, guns drawn, stepped from the trees and faced them. Silverstone and Willoughby. She didn't recognize the third man. She jerked Julia's arm. "We need to get out of here. Run."

The few seconds it took for her words to register with Julia was all it took for the men to grab them.

"Don't scream," Silverstone said, his voice a deep, threatening growl. "We're going for a little ride."

A fourth man came from the woods, leading two horses. "You ready, boss?"

"Get them on the horses, and for Pete's sake, protect your man parts. These two *ladies* are sneaky."

Julia kicked, slapped, and bit the man who had his hand around her mouth, making them struggle to get her on the horse.

With his arm around her stomach, Silverstone dragged Suzanna to the other men. "Damn it, tie up her hands and feet, and make sure to gag her."

"How are we supposed to get her on the horse if'n her feet are tied together?"

Silverstone paused as if he hadn't thought about that part. "Well . . . well, tie her hands and throw her across the saddle. Then tie her feet together under the horse's belly."

"You can't do that to me. Daniel will be here any minute and when he does . . ."

Silverstone laughed. "We've been watching you closely and know damn well King and Iverson have left. So have his sister and her friends." He looked Julia up and down. "So's it's just you ladies," he doffed his hat, "and us. So, what'll it be? Sit on the horse like a nice little girl or lay across the saddle. It's not very comfortable." His brown teeth showed when he grinned. "What'll it be? It's up to you."

Julia yanked against the men holding her. "If it's up to me, I choose to be let go."

His grin slipped. "Not a choice. Men, put her across the saddle."

"No, no wait. I'll behave."

As Julia was put on the horse, Silverstone ran the gun's barrel down her cheek. "What about you? You gonna' behave?"

Suzanna nodded. She may agree now but find a way to escape as they traveled... to wherever it was they were going.

"Good girl. I will, too." His sneer belied his words. "Put gags on them anyway."

Willoughby sauntered up as if he hadn't a care in the world. "This the one who got away from me?"

Even standing six feet away, his hot breath smelling of old tobacco and beer made her stomach roll.

Silverstone hitched up his pants and puffed out his chest as if the action made him appear more manly. "Yep. And we're gonna have us some fun later. First, let's get them to the boss."

Boss? Who was the boss and what did he want with her? As far as she could recall, neither she nor Julia had done anything to anyone.

With her and Julia between the two men in front and Willoughby and Silverstone in the rear, they wound their way down a narrow path. It didn't take long for the sounds of civilization to fade and disappear. Where were they going? She swallowed around the cloth in her mouth trying not to gag. Willoughby had pulled the cloth from his back pocket. She grimaced. How many germs were on this thing? Best not to worry about it.

As the scenery passed, her mind flitted from idea to idea on how to escape. The path was too narrow to kick the horse into a gallop. And with her hands tied to the pommel, how safe would she be? Pretending to faint and falling off the horse wouldn't work either. Again, with her hands tied, her arms would be pulled from their sockets. Besides, she glanced at the ground, she was awfully far up.

She'd not only have hurt her arms, but would probably break her neck, too.

The narrow path opened up into a field where a herd of black cattle chomped on grass. She squinted against the sun now high in the sky. How long had they been riding? An hour? Two?

"Let's stop here for a break." Silverstone rode up beside her. "We have at least an hour to ride yet. If I untie you, do you promise not to cause any trouble?"

Trouble? If she knew where they were, she'd give the man so much trouble, he wouldn't know which way was up. But she had no idea where they were. Putting up a fight wouldn't do any good. "I promise."

"Good. Willoughby, get the other dame from her horse."

Suzanna jerked back from him, when he reached up for her.

"Take it easy, I'm only gonna help."

King had helped her down from her horse numerous times, so she was quite aware a man didn't have to touch the sides of her breasts nor put his hand on her backside during the process. Bile formed in the back of her throat. With the gag in place, if she were to throw up now, she'd choke to death.

"I'm going to take off the gag so you can take a drink of water. I want you nice and healthy for later on. Remember screaming won't do you any good out here. There's no one but us and the beef."

Willoughby jerked Julia to her side. "You all right?" Julia's face was red. From the heat? Anger? Lack of water?

"Yes. I need to . . ."

Silverstone interrupted them. "You gals can go into the brush and . . ." He flapped a hand. "Do what it is you ladies do." A pink hue rose to his face.

Suzanna nearly laughed. The man was blushing? As tough as Silverstone acted, he couldn't say 'go to the bathroom' or 'relieve themselves?'

With their hands free, they searched for a place to do their business and not be seen by the men. Finally, they located a few scant bushes well away from the horses.

"I'll hold out my skirts so for sure they can't see us." Julia glanced over her shoulder. "Then you can do the same for me."

She dropped her skirts and changed places with Julia. "Do you have any idea where we are?"

"Not a clue. Do you recognize any of the cattle?"

Suzanna snorted. "Now, why would I be able to do that? They look the same to me—black. I didn't see any marks on them, so they might be King's."

"That's what I thought, but why would they be out here?"

"I don't know, unless somehow we're close to his ranch." She peered through the bushes. "King did say he had a herd of cattle in a field somewhere. Maybe this is it."

"Could be. Do you have any idea why they took us?"

Suzanna shook her head. "Not a clue. I told you about how I got away from Willoughby and Silverstone."

"Yes, and I still feel awful for letting you go back home by yourself."

"It wasn't your idea."

"Ladies," Silverstone yelled, "get a move on. We don't have all day. I'm going to count to ten and if you don't come out, I'll come in and get you, done or not. One. Two. Three.

"Don't argue. What happened, happened. Let's try to figure out how to get out of this situation."

Even though they were ready by the count of two, they didn't step into the pasture until Silverstone got to nine. No sense in letting the man believe he was completely in control. Suzanna stepped around a cow pie. "We should wait to try to do anything. Maybe once we're where they're taking us, we can come up with a plan to get away."

"What if they are more men? There are only four of them now."

Suzanna eyed their captors. "By any chance do you know where we are?"

"Good point."

Before they could discuss their situation more, Silverstone came closer and shoved a canteen at her. "Drink, then mount. I'm sure you have no idea where you are, but I need to re-tie your hands and replace the gag."

"Really? Why?" Why did she have to sound like a whiny four-year-old.

"Don't you worry why." Silverstone wrapped the rope around her wrists, spun her around to tie the gag behind her head, and hoisted her to the horse. If she thought it would help their cause, she would have kicked him in the face when he ran his hand down her leg and grinned up at her. "Later."

All but one of the men got on their horses. The cattle ignored him as he led his horse, not to the visible trail, but to a spot to the left. He dropped his horse's reins and pulled back a bush.

Another trail? Julia raised an eyebrow. "Where does it go?" she mouthed.

Suzanna shrugged. The men mounted and one-by-one, they entered the wooded trail. When they stopped a brief time later, she glanced over her shoulder. Willoughby was replacing the bush, hiding the trail once more. It didn't seem possible, but this trail was narrower than the last.

Unlike riding on the last trail where the men joked with one another, this time not one word was uttered. Before they traveled at a decent clip. This time the horses plodded along, their hooves making little noise on the ground.

Her horse's slow cadence, the lack of sleep over the past few nights, and the stress of being taken hostage, made her drowsy. Several times her body jerked upright as she began to fall asleep.

"Wake up. We're here."

Silverstone's gruff voice jerked her awake. She opened her eyes. Several scraggly men surrounded a large firepit in an area not quite the size of the pasture they'd left. Even from where she sat on the horse, their smell burned her nose. At first count, there were three, then four more emerged from the decrepit, once-white canvas tents edging the area.

"They finally here?" The group parted, making room for a stocky man. If his gray hair, reaching nearly to his shoulders had been combed in the past month, she'd be surprised. The sleeve of his black and white striped shirt was torn at the shoulder. The only thing holding his pants up over his protruding stomach was a pair of suspenders.

It took a second to recognize the man. Mr. Woods? Did his wife know he was back in town? With his thumbs tucked into his suspenders, he strode to Julia.

"Well, well, well. If it isn't Miss Julia Lindstrom? Not so high and mighty now, are you?" He rolled back on his heels. "Willoughby, get her down."

Suzanna held in a gasp when, without a care for her sister's well-being, Willoughby yanked her from the saddle and tossed her to the ground. Woods walked around her, eyeing Julia as if she were a piece of meat.

Woods jerked his head toward Suzanna. "Get her sister down, too. And untie their hands and remove their gags. We don't have to worry about two helpless women, do we Willoughby?" He stalked up to Silverstone's partner and slapped him across the face. "That's for letting the schoolteacher get away from you."

Woods stood in front of Silverstone, missing the glare Willoughby tossed at him as he wiped the blood from his lip. Obviously, there was no love lost between the men. Was there a way she and Julia could use it against Woods?

"What do you have to say for yourself, Silverstone? You're as bad as your partner." He stood in front of Suzanna and lifted a long curl that had escaped from her chignon. "Letting a little slip of a thing like this escape your clutches."

Without thinking, Suzanna slapped his hand away. Little slip of a thing? She lifted her chin and glared down at the shorter man. "Keep your hands off me, you oaf." No sooner had the words left her mouth then Woods backhanded her, sending her sprawling to the ground.

"You ass." Julia rushed to her side and knelt beside her. If looks could kill, Woods would have been dead in the time it took it took to blink. "Are you all right?"

Even though her ears rang, she accepted Julia's help to stand. Were the trees swaying more? Had the number of men doubled? She brushed at her skirt. "Nothing. I'm fine, but he won't be," she whispered.

Julia faced Woods. "What are you doing here? Why aren't you in prison?"

Woods' grin could have scared the devil. "It's amazing what a few coins can do to help a person escape." He swept his hands to stumps surrounding the fire. "Now, why don't you ladies have a seat. It's time we have a little discussion."

Chapter Twenty-One

King set down the pencil on top of the drawings for his new establishment. His "desk" consisted of two boards laid across two barrels set up at the rear of the restaurant tent. Light came from the back flap pulled up. He checked his pocket watch. Ten-thirty. Where the hell were Suzanna and Julia? His sister and her friends had been here for hours. He'd spent more time leaving the restaurant tent to search the streets for them than he did working out his plans for a better building.

He owned the lots on either side of the former restaurant. Now would be a good time to expand. A larger restaurant, cigar shop, dress shop for Julia, and more rooms. Some thought he should have a card room, but he drew the line at gambling in his place. The saloons could handle the gamblers. He wanted an upscale place.

"You sure the girls were following you?"

Leona put a tray of rolls into the stove and wiped her hands on her apron. "They said they were. I guess I was too busy to worry about them."

Sometimes his sister could be rather cold. He raked his fingers through his air and down the back of his neck. Something didn't feel right.

"Maybe they decided to make the cookies they'd talked about last night." Leona wiped down the counter used to serve customers, while her friends took care of the tables scattered around. Yesterday, the men who had accompanied Leona, went to Lead and brought back tables and chairs. Not as many as they had before the fire, but enough to start back in business.

"But why didn't they c . . ." What an idiot. Of course, they couldn't call. Even if their phone was usable, the ones in town were destroyed. Once again, he left the tent and searched the area, ignoring the pounding hammers, men yelling, and wagons filled with wood creaking down the street. No sisters.

At one of the side streets, a kiln was already spitting out bricks. The town leaders had met and decided Deadwood had a chance to start over. Re-building would be done under new rules. No more buildings put up haphazardly. No more having Main Street meandering crookedly past buildings. There would be order and structure. Several of the saloon owners balked, but when faced with the possibility of another fire, they agreed using bricks was in their best interest.

He, and Daniel, were all for the new rules, but it would take time. Time to get enough bricks. Time to get supplies. Hell, his wasn't the only place needing furniture, lamps, bedding, towels, food, dishes, and the thousands of other items needed to be in business. The only thing not in short supply was liquor. It amazed him how quickly the improvised saloons had popped up with enough liquor to keep the men happy.

The one thing he did like to see was people helping each other. He'd even heard of men stopping their gold hunting to lend a hand.

"King?" Leona interrupted his musings.

"What?" He re-entered the dim interior of the tent. The scent of roast, potatoes, rolls, and Leona's famous pies filled the air. His stomach rumbled.

Tossing a towel over her shoulder, she approached. "Can you help serve? Even with my friends here, I'm short-handed. My other girls are helping their own families. Once people realize we're open, we'll be swamped."

"How are we going to keep people from storming us?"

"Right now, the entire front of the tent is exposed, but if we close it more and make a doorway, that should help."

"Won't it be too dark in here?" He glanced into the interior of the tent. "And hot? What if we tie back the sides, and string rows of ropes to stop access?"

Leona smiled at him. "Good idea." She glanced at the watch pinned over her left breast. "We have half an hour before we begin serving. Will it be enough time to put up the ropes?"

"Should be. I'll put some of my men to work."

It took an hour and a half for the food to be gone. King thought a riot would break out when he announced to the line of hungry people still waiting to eat. To make things fair, he tore up pieces of paper and wrote numbers on them and handed them to the people remaining in line. Tomorrow they could line up according to their number.

There had been a few men who tried to go over the ropes, but his crew from the ranch held them back. Why didn't people realize there was only so much food to be had in town. Just because this was a restaurant didn't mean he could snap his fingers and food would magically appear. Many of them thought the food should be free, too. Didn't they realize *he* had to pay for the supplies? The merchants from other towns certainly didn't give their supplies away for free.

As busy as they'd been, thoughts of where Suzanna and Julia were always on his mind. Several times he wanted to shove people out of his way and run to their house to see if they were safe. To top it off, he had no idea where Daniel was. He hadn't seen the man since last night when he'd bunked in his tent. He'd already been gone when King woke.

The tables were cleared and chairs resting on top of the tables. Leona and her crew were discussing what to make for tomorrow to stretch their supplies. Until more food was delivered, they would only be able to serve one meal a day. Which suited him fine. There were too many things to get done to play waiter three times a day.

King untied his apron and tossed it over a rope. He needed to find the sisters. Worry about them was like an itch he couldn't scratch. "Leona? If you don't need me, I'm going to the school."

She waved a hand over her shoulder. He was halfway down the street, when he stopped and went back and approached Asa, who was stacking clean dishes.

"You're doing dishes, Asa?"

Asa scowled. "Your sister is a taskmaster. I was set to stand around and watch for thieves like you told me to." He shook his head. "But no. She told me if she could do ten things at once, I could certainly do two. How do you put up with her?"

King chuckled. "I have to, she's my sister. Don't let her get to you. Keep an eye on things."

"Sure thing, but I'd rather be mucking out stalls than doing woman's work."

"I hear ya. By the way, I haven't seen Josiah today."

"He didn't want to come into town. Said he had better things to do than sweep up ash or be ordered around."

"Leona?"

"Yep."

"Doesn't he realize Hilda will put him to work?"

"That's different." Asa grinned. "He knows Hilda will feed him."

"Someday he'll have to eat one of Leona's pies." He paused. "Say, you haven't seen the schoolteacher and her sister today, have you?"

Asa averted his eyes and scuffed his boots into the ash. "Can't say as I have."

"Well if you do, can you tell her I'm looking for them?"

"Sure thing."

King stood at the entrance to the tent and glanced back at Asa. There was that itchy feeling again.

The number of people at the schoolyard had dwindled. Many of them had gone back to their properties for the day, digging for possessions that may have survived. Last night discussions ran from who were staying to rebuild to who were leaving for good.

Daniel sat on the ground, going through some papers.

"What are you doing and where did you disappear to this morning?"

"Going through stuff for the town. Need to make sure their ideas are legal."

"All right. That answers what you're doing, but not where you disappeared to this morning."

"Yesterday I bumped into one of the deputies from Lead who was guarding supplies coming into town. He swore he saw Woods."

"Woods? Isn't he in prison?"

"Supposed to be, so I went to Lead to see what I could find out."

King's stomach dropped. Maybe there was a good reason for this sense of doom. "And?"

"Two hours from here the prison wagon turned over. The driver and guard riding up front were killed. By the time the guards riding behind them could do anything, the three prisoners who'd survived overtook the guards." Daniel wiped a hand down his face. "They strangled them with their chains, found the keys, and they took off in different directions."

King tipped his head to the side. "I'm confused. If everyone was dead, how do the authorities know this?"

"The guard riding with the driver actually survived but played dead."

"Smart man." King slapped his hat against his leg. "Let me guess—Woods was one of the men who got away."

Daniel tapped the papers together and put them in a satchel. "Yep. I'd be more concerned about him coming after Julia if I didn't know she was safe here."

King tipped his head back and closed his eyes. "Shit."

"What?"

"Suzanna and Julia didn't show up at the restaurant this morning. They were supposed to follow Leona, but they didn't."

"Maybe they're in the house baking?"

King glanced at the house. "That's what we thought and why I came over here. I would have checked right away, but I thought I'd talk to you first. I'm sure they're safe in the house."

"I don't like this. Let's go."

Daniel knocked on the front door. "Julia? Suzanna? Are you in there? It's Daniel and King. We need to talk to you." When there was no answer, he pounded on the door. "C'mon girls, we need you out here."

King ran around the house, checking each window. He returned to his friend. "I don't see them inside." Sweat poured down his back. His heart pounded in his ears. Where could they be?

"Let's check the schoolhouse." Daniel raced down the path to the other building. "The doors are locked. Maybe someone saw them."

"Most people have left for the day, but I'll check with those still here."

"I'll head back to town and ask around."

"Meet back here in twenty?" King checked his pocket watch. "That would be two o'clock."

Daniel barely nodded before racing toward town.

The soldiers guarding the schoolhouse and tents had no answers. Everything had been quiet all morning. A familiar woman came from one of the tents. He'd forgotten she was here. Her face was white, her lips trembling. Tears slid down her plump cheeks.

"Mrs. Woods? I take it you heard what Daniel said?"

"Yes." She dropped onto a scorched bucket. "I had no idea he'd escaped."

King squinted at her. "Are you sure about that?"

"Yes."

"And he hasn't contacted you?"

"No." Her voice was barely a whisper. "Even if he had, I would have reported him. I hate him." She pounded her fists on her thighs. "I've always hated him."

Speechless, King ran a hand down his face. She hated him? "But you two always acted so lovey dovey."

She raised her tear-filled eyes to him. "All an act. He was, is, a mean man. If I didn't do as he said and help keep up his reputation in town, he'd . . . he'd." She shivered.

For a woman he'd always disliked, his softening toward her surprised him. "I believe you. But right now, we have to find Julia and Suzanna."

"They're missing?"

"Yes. Julia helped Daniel get your husband arrested and we've always hated each other. I'm afraid something might have happened to them. If Woods escaped, he may have kidnapped them."

"I wouldn't put it past him. He's big on retribution against anyone who defies him." She rubbed her arms as if trying to wipe away a memory.

Had Woods physically harmed his wife? "Do you have any idea where he might have taken them?"

Mrs. Woods shook her head. "No. I never paid any attention to what he was doing. And if I asked . . ." She closed her eyes. A shudder went through her. "Well, let's just say, it wasn't pleasant." She opened her eyes and looked up at King. "If I had any idea where he is, I'd certainly tell you." She stood and put a hand on King's arm. "If there is anything I can do, please let me know."

"Thank you." He turned to leave, then stopped. "Wait. You know most of the people who are staying here. Can you see if they've seen the sisters? You could report back to Leona."

"I certainly can. I'll go right now."

"I'll escort you to town."

Mrs. Woods smiled. "Why thank you, King, but I believe I can make it by myself. I doubt anyone will accost me and if they do," she picked up a rock and hefted it in her hand, "I'll make sure they see the error of their ways." Without another word, head held high, she strutted down the path toward town.

Now what? Where else should he look? Who else could he ask? There was no one left around the campsite. A thought occurred to him. The school's stable. What if the girls were taken by the people who were using the stable? He ran around the school. The rain would have washed away any tracks, so any new ones would be obvious.

He searched the area. Nothing. No horse or human tracks neither around the stable nor heading into the woods. Maybe they'd been taken while they were walking to town. He followed the path everyone took meaning seeing anything out of the ordinary would be impossible. He punched his fist into his palm. Damn. Where could they be? The longer it took to find them, the worse it would be for them.

Daniel raced toward him. "King," he yelled between pants. He stopped and rested his hands on his knees."

King waited as Daniel tried to catch his breath, but he couldn't wait forever. Suzanna and Julia's lives may be at stake. "Well?"

"Someone saw the girls talking with two men this morning."

"Do they know who the men were?" *Please don't let it be Woods.*

"They recognized Silverstone and Willoughby."

Damn. They were as bad as Woods. "Are the three somehow connected?"

Daniel spun on his heel and walked back toward town. "Seeing as how we've have seen them together, you bet your bottom dollar they're connected. And I wouldn't be surprised if they weren't involved with your missing cattle and horses."

"They probably had their hands in setting the fire at the racetrack and the things happening at the ranch." King followed his friend combing the edge of the road, his heart in his throat.

"No doubt." Daniel stopped and pointed to the ground. "Here, take a look at this. Doesn't it look as if someone was standing here?"

King knelt in the dirt. Sure enough. Several sets of large boot prints were intermingled with two pair of smaller ones. They led into the woods where there were multiple horse hooves. He stood. "This has to be where they were taken."

"I agree. We need to follow and see where they go." Daniel charged into the brush.

"Daniel, wait." King chased after his friend and grabbed his arm. "Think this through. We can't go after them half-cocked. We don't know how far they've gone. We need water and food." He touched his gun. "Enough ammunition."

"Horses?"

King paused and surveyed the path going through the thick brush. "No."

"Why not? We'd make better time on horseback."

King shook his head. "No, we wouldn't. Look how narrow the path is. They'd have to move fairly slow to get through this. It would be easier on foot."

"Make sense. Let's get supplies and head out."

"I'll have Leona pack some food and fill canteens. You go see if you can find ammunition. We'll meet back here in twenty minutes." Running past people still digging through the rubble, King prayed they wouldn't be too late to help the sisters.

Chapter Twenty-Two

Woods stood in front of Julia. "You're the one I want to see." He glared at Suzanna. "Actually, both of you."

It made sense why he'd be mad at Julia, but why her? "Why?"

"You're King's gal. And I hate anything King has." With his hands clasped behind him, he rolled back on his heels. "No. I despise anything King has."

Woods' smile didn't reach his eyes. He nodded to the men. "Tie them to the tree over there. And be careful. I've seen what they can do to a man. Don't underestimate them for a minute."

Struggling did no good when they were outnumbered. Before any of the other men could approach, Willoughby tied Julia's hands behind her back while Silverstone did the same to her. Without any thought to their well-being, they were shoved to the ground. At least they were next to each other. A rope was wrapped around the tree, lashing them into place. The tree bark dug into her back.

Silverstone knelt before her and ran his hand up her leg. "Now I have you right where I want you."

Anger boiled inside her. "What? Tied to a tree. Not much you can do to me here is there?"

Julia nudged her leg. "Shush, Suz. You'll only make him angrier."

She narrowed her eyes at Silverstone. "So what? He *thinks* he's going to have his way with me. He *thinks* he has the upper hand, but the only way he's been able to handle me is to tie me up. A real man, he is."

Even though it shouldn't have, the slap came as a surprise. Stars flickered behind her eyes. Her cheek hurt as if a dozen bees had stung her.

"Shut up." He drew his hand back again.

"Enough," Woods grabbed Silverstone's hand. "We don't want to hurt them . . ." he smirked at Julia, "yet. Only want to draw out Iverson and Winson. But first I have a few questions for this one." He pushed Suzanna's foot with his boot.

"Me? What could I possibly know?"

With a snap of his fingers, one of the men rolled a stump over and placed it in front of Suzanna. Woods sat down and rested his elbows on his knees. "Now, Miss Lindstrom. Where does Winson keep his papers?"

Papers? "I have no idea what you're talking about. Besides, why would I know where King would keep his papers?"

"Now, now, my dear. You and him are sweethearts. Cozying up outside your house. Staying at the hotel with him."

Where had he gotten that idea? "We are far from being sweethearts." Woods squeezed her knee. She bit her lip against the pain.

"Don't lie to me. I'm sure he's told you his secrets while you're in bed together. Most stupid men do." He puffed out his chest. "But I'm too smart for that. My stupid wife has no idea the things I've done."

The man had to be crazy. "First of all, King and I have never been together. Second, I don't understand what you're accomplishing by taking Julia and myself."

Woods' laugh proved he was a bit on the crazy side. "I'm taking back everything King took from me and paying Daniel back for sending me to prison."

Julia squinted her eyes. "Daniel told me how you wanted the land King bought. But you never owned it to begin with, so he couldn't have taken it from you, now could he?"

This time Suzanna nudged Julia's leg. The sarcasm in her voice was only going to make Woods angrier.

"Listen here, girlie." Woods pointed a finger in her face. "Every bit of land he bought should have been mine. I was going to run this town. In order to do that, I needed land, lots of land. Winson came along and stole it from me. But once I get my hands on those deeds and get rid of him, everything will be mine, including that damn ranch of his."

Silverstone scowled and tossed a chewed piece of grass to the ground. "What do you mean it'll be yours? You mean it'll be mine, don't you? As soon as you show your face, you'll be arrested." He hooked his thumbs in his vest. "So, who'll run the town then?"

Woods rose and faced Silverstone. He was shorter by several inches but still poked Silverstone in the chest. "Listen here, you brainless piece of horse dung. If it weren't for me, you'd still be mucking stalls at your family farm. I'm the one who pulled you from the life of poverty and I'm the one who can put you back there. Once I have King's land, I'll be the one running the town, not you. You don't have the brains it takes to muck the crap you came from."

"Yes, sir."

Suzanna didn't for a minute believe Silverstone's backing down so meekly. There was a power struggle going on. Maybe she and Julia could play on it.

"Right now, I want you to go into town and see what Iverson and Winson are up to."

He turned his back on Silverstone, missing the hatred crossing his face. So, there was no love lost between the two men.

"And don't go near the ranch. Also, find out if anyone is interested in the beef. There's so little food in town, we'll make a killing on them. Take Willoughby with you."

Once the two men were out of sight and Woods was back in his tent, Suzanna gave their surroundings a better look. A man pulled out a deck of cards and called to two of the others. In short order, they were seated around a table fashioned from two boards set across sawhorses, playing poker. Another man lay on the ground, his hat over his head. No one paid them any attention.

"Julia," she whispered. "Can you loosen the ropes around your hands?"

"I'll try."

"Keep working at it. Somehow we have to get out of here."

Beside her Julia wiggled. "Then what? There are too many men here to get away."

Suzanna worked at her bindings, her mind spinning with ideas, none of which made any sense. Julia was right. Even if they were to get free, getting away would be difficult. Woods came from his tent, hitched up his pants, and stared at them.

"I have an idea." Suzanna stopped working the ropes. Her wrists were getting sore.

"What is it?"

"Just play along with me." As she continued to tug at her bindings, she perused Woods. Head down, hands behind his back he strutted back and forth like a king contemplating his kingdom. "Julia, how much would you trust Silverstone and Willoughby?"

"About as far as I could throw them."

Suzanna shook her head. "Yeah, me, too. Mr. Woods must have complete faith in them to send them to town."

"I imagine a smart man like Silverstone would have money put away somewhere." Julia grinned at her. "Why, I bet he hasn't ever once given all the money he's collected to Mr. Woods."

Woods jerked his head up. "What do you know about Silverstone?"

"Why nothing, Mr. Woods," Suzanna said keeping her tone innocent, which was easy to do. She didn't know anything about the man, except he was awful and scared her. "All I'm saying is you have an awful lot of trust in him, which is a good thing, since it sounds as if you'll have to run things while in hiding." She shook her head again. "Why, who knows what he's up to when he goes to town."

"And because Willoughby is *his* right-hand man, the two could be doing anything." Julia nudged Suzanna in the side.

"Right. Why they could be . . ." Well, what could they be doing? "With your bank burning down, they could be digging through the rubble to find coins or other valuables. Maybe get the safe open. He doesn't have the combination, does he?" Suzanna bit back a smile at Woods' scowl. They must be getting to him. "Why, they might not come back."

Woods spun on his heels and pointed to the three men playing cards. "Go follow Silverstone and Willoughby. And make sure they come back." He stomped to his tent, pulled back the flap, and glared at the sisters over his shoulder.

The three men saddled their horses and went down the trail after Silverstone and Willoughby, grumbling about having to do Woods' bidding and not getting paid.

When they were out of sight, Julia giggled. "Good idea, Suz. We're down to one man, and he's sleeping."

"I wouldn't let him fool you." She bit back a moan when the rope cut into her wrist, but she wasn't going to give up on her plan of getting herself and Julia free. "Why did they have to tie these so darn tight?"

Julia snickered. "I don't know—to keep us from getting loose?"

"You don't have to be sarcastic about it." She stopped struggling. It was no use. The ropes weren't any looser. She dropped her head against the tree trunk and closed her eyes. What was King doing? Did he or anyone else realize they were missing? And if they did, would they figure out where to look for them?

"Don't worry, someone will find us," Julia said as if she'd read her mind. "Someone has to notice we didn't arrive at the restaurant." Her stomach growled. "It has to be well after the lunch hour, doesn't it?"

Suzanna's stomach answered. "Must be. I'm quite hungry."

"They'll come."

"I know." *King, where are you?*

Chapter Twenty-Three

King put up a hand. "Shh. Someone is coming." They'd been on the trail for over an hour and a half. He was hot, sweaty, and thirsty. They'd only stopped once for a quick drink of water. "Hide in the brush."

He hadn't been hiding for more than a minute when two riders appeared. Obviously, they felt safe enough to talk between themselves. Their conversation was loud and clear.

"Damn, Woods. Who the hell does he think he is? I have half a notion to take the money I kept for him, sell off more of the cattle we stole from Winson, and take off for California."

"Yeah, and if he found you, you'd be a dead man."

Woods? The voices were familiar. King eased back a branch to get a good look. Silverstone and Willoughby? So, he was right. Silverstone was in cahoots with Woods.

The two men weren't bothering to keep their voices down, so King didn't have to worry about being overheard, but he still whispered to Daniel. "When they are in front of us, you jump Willoughby and I'll get Silverstone." Like Daniel, King slid his rucksack containing supplies from his back and eased a few feet away from Daniel giving them room to attack.

When the two horses were in front of them, King nodded at Daniel. At the same time, they jumped from the brush.

"What the . . ."

Silverstone didn't have a chance to say anything more before King punched him in the face, sending him into the bushes. The men's horses took off down the trail, giving them room to maneuver.

King didn't pay attention to Daniel as he gave his man a few more blows. Silverstone fought to keep standing in the tangle of brush. Branches poked and stabbed at them. Silverstone struggled to stand. King tried to get him onto the trail where he would be easier to handle. He swung at Silverstone and missed and tripped over a branch. As he tried to keep his footing, he pushed Silverstone to the trail.

Silverstone, got to his hands and knees, then his feet. He prepared to run, then dropped to his knees again, giving King time to extricate himself from the bushes. Silverstone rose again and limped down the trail.

Huffing and puffing, ankle throbbing from tripping, King pursued. Within a few yards, King grabbed the back of Silverstone's shirt and gave him a shove, making him land on his stomach. King sat on his back and pulled his arms behind him. Silverstone bucked.

King pulled his gun from his holster, pressed it against Silverstone's back, removed the man's gun, and tossed it behind him where Silverstone couldn't reach it. "Lay still or this gun may accidentally go off. I'm going to stand up, and you're going to slowly rise and turn around. Any sudden moves, and you'll be wishing you were never born."

Behind him, things were quiet. Before he got off his man, he glanced over his shoulder. Daniel already had Willoughby's hands tied behind his back and was shoving him forward. He dropped Willoughby's gun next to the other. Using Silverstone as leverage, King stood, pushing Silverstone's face in the dirt. After what he tried to do to Suzanna, the temptation to beat the man to a pulp was strong, but he needed answers first.

King tied Silverstone's hands and jerked him upright, inwardly grinning at the man's grunt. Daniel pushed Willoughby down so the two men were seated side by side. He wiggled his jaw back and forth. For a man in his late thirties, Silverstone still could pack a punch.

"How're you doing?" Daniel poured water from his canteen over his raw knuckles. "I haven't had a brawl like that in ages." He grinned. "Felt damn good."

"Yeah, but we won't feel so good tomorrow." He wiped his hand over his mouth and glanced at the blood on his hands. He turned his attention back to the trussed-up men. "Now talk."

Silverstone smirked and blew out a hiss. His lip looked as bad as King's felt. Hopefully it hurt worse.

"About what? Can't a man and his friend take a ride if'n they want?"

"Not if the ride happens after one man escapes from a prison transport and two women disappear."

Willoughby's eyes grew wide. "How'd you know Woods escaped?"

Silverstone kicked him. "Shut up, you ass."

"Ouch, that hurt."

"Not as much as you'll hurt when we get out of this." Silverstone turned his attention back to King. "So, what's this about women missin'?"

King squatted down before Silverstone. "You know damn well the Lindstrom sisters were taken this morning, and who they are with." He poked the gun in Silverstone's side. "Now where did you take them?"

No answer.

King pulled back the hammer while Daniel held his gun on Willoughby.

"I . . . I . . . I only done what I was told to do. I'm not the boss of this outfit, so you jest leave me alone."

Leaving his gun trained on Silverstone, he turned his attention to the other man. "And what were you told to do?"

"Woods. It was Woods. He had us steal your cattle. And . . . and . . . other stuff, too."

Daniel kicked Willoughby in the foot. "And what other stuff?"

"You jest shut up, Willoughby. Don't tell them anything or Woods will . . ."

"Woods will what?" King clenched his jaw and flinched from the pain. Time was wasting. If Woods had the sisters, no telling what he would do to them. "We have all day, you know. Besides, Daniel and I could drag you into the woods, tie you to a tree and leave you there. No one would know where you were. No water. No food." His knees cracked when he stood. "Why who knows how long you'd be there."

Daniel also stood. "What we need to do is follow this trail and it will lead us directly to Woods and the girls. Am I right?"

Silverstone shook his head. "Don't rightly know where it might lead."

"C'mon, Daniel, let's get them into the woods." King pulled a hanky from his back pocket. "First, let's gag them so they can't scream for help." He knelt behind Silverstone. "Did the girls scream when you took them?" He slipped the hanky over Silverstone's mouth and tied it behind his head, giving it a good yank before standing.

When Daniel went behind Willoughby, the man kicked at the dirt again. "Wait. Wait. I'll tell you everything. Please don't leave me out in the woods."

King chuckled. "You scared of the boogeyman Willoughby? Why don't you tell us what we want to know and we'll think about not tying you up." Like that wouldn't happen.

"Okay. Okay. Woods and Silverstone have been partners for a long time. Woods found him at a ranch in Kentucky, and they came out here together. Woods had other deals going on."

"We know why he was arrested, but what else was he doing?"

"Well," Willoughby licked his lips. "He wanted the land you bought. Thought it should have been his. Wanted to run Deadwood. Every time you got property he wanted, he got madder and madder. He's jest plain mad, you know, like crazy?"

Silverstone kicked at his partner again, mumbling behind the gag. Willoughby glared at him and went on. "He was having us steal your animals, setting fire to things. I didn't want nothin' to do with taking the schoolmarm, but I had to do what I was told."

King tipped his hat back on his head. "And why did you have to do what you were told?"

Willoughby hung his head. "I got caught trying to steal from Woods. Silverstone caught me, took me to Woods. Instead of killing me, they said if they let me live, I'd have to do their bidding."

"Did you follow me on the road to the racetrack?"

"Yes."

"Did you shoot at me on my way to Fort Meade?"

"Uh-huh. Me and some of the others who work for Woods."

Others? Of course, there had to be more than just these two idiots. "How many work for Woods?"

"Besides us two," Willoughby closed his eyes. "uh, there are . . . um . . . four?"

Daniel shook his head. "You believe him?"

"Yeah. He's too stupid to make that up, but I'm concerned he can't count that far and there might be more." An idea came to him. "Do any of the men work for me at the ranch?"

Willoughby kept his eyes downcast. "But I don't know who it is, only that he reports to Woods every few days. Tells him when you're gone. Who's staying there. That's how we know you and the schoolmarm are lovers."

"Lovers? We aren't lovers."

"Well, Woods thinks so, that's why he had us grab the girls. Besides taking someone who is yours, he wanted the other sister for helping Daniel."

Daniel grabbed Willoughby's shirtfront and yanked him to his feet. "Did you hurt them? Did Woods hurt them?"

Willoughby shook his head. "I didn't hurt no one." He lifted his chin to Silverstone. "But he slapped the schoolmarm."

A rage unlike he'd ever known flashed through him like the tornados ripping through his home state. He pulled back the hammer on the gun again and pressed it against Silverstone's temple. "You slapped a woman?" He dug the gun deeper into his skin. "You hit Suzanna? What kind of man are you?" He rested his finger on the trigger.

"King?" Daniel put a hand on his shoulder. "You don't want to do that. Remember I'm still a sworn deputy. If you kill him in cold blood, I'll have to arrest you." He eased King's gun away from Silverstone. "Besides, he's not worth it."

King took a deep breath, released the hammer, and slid the gun into his holster eliminating the temptation to put the bastard six feet under. "You're right, he's not worth it." He turned back to Willoughby. "Now where is Woods hiding?"

Once King was satisfied Willoughby had maybe told them the truth, he turned to Daniel. "Gag him and let's get them into the woods."

"But you said you wouldn't." Willoughby's words came out like a stuck pig. "You did."

"I said I'd *think* about it, which I have." He dragged Silverstone to his feet. "We don't have time to take you back to town, so into the woods you go."

Once they had the two men secured and the brush back in place, they picked up their rucksacks and started back down the trail. Neither said a word, but his thoughts were racing like one of his thoroughbreds.

Who from his ranch was working against him? Was Johnson retaliating because of his son? Most of the other men had been with him for a year or more, but they could have been reporting back to Woods before he was arrested and after his escape.

Lost in his thoughts, he hadn't realized they'd reached a wider part of the trail, nor did he hear the men coming toward them until Daniel put a hand on his arm. They slipped into the brush. It wouldn't be as easy taking down three men as it had two, but to save Suzanna and Julia, he'd move heaven and earth if he had to.

"You move up the trail about twenty feet. I'll stay here. When the first guy is near me, I'll step out in front of him. You go out behind the last man. I'll raise my arm when I'm ready."

King nodded and slipped away. Like Silverstone and Willoughby, the men were talking loudly. As the men passed before him, he kept Daniel in his sights. His friend dropped his arm and came out from the bushes.

"Stop right there, or I'll shoot."

The first man laughed. "You gonna take down three of us?"

"Nope." King stood behind the last man. They glanced over their shoulders, then back at Daniel. "He has help."

The lead rider laughed again. "That's still three against two."

Daniel shook his head and kept his gun on the man. "Not if I shoot you and King back there shoots the last man. That would leave two against one, wouldn't it? Now, I want you to slowly take out your guns and drop them to the ground. Afterward, keep your hands on your pommels."

King let out a breath when the first and last men did as told.

"Sam, duck," the middle rider yelled. Sam ducked, giving him a shot at Daniel.

Without giving it a second thought, King jumped around the last man and pulled the trigger. The horses shied, the middle rider fell from the saddle and landed with a thump to the ground.

"Don't shoot no more." Sam yelled, raising his hands in the air. "Don't shoot. We don't want no more trouble. Let me get down and check on Rusty."

"Me, too," the third man said.

Daniel waved his gun at Sam. "Go ahead and get down. Nice and easy."

Once on the ground, Sam ran to his friend and turned him over. "Ah, hell."

King's stomach sunk. He'd never killed a man before. "Is . . . is he dead?"

Sam stood. "Nah. It's only a flesh wound to his arm. The idiot fainted. Can Charlie help me with him?"

Thank the heavens. He didn't want a man's death on his conscience. He waved his gun at Charlie. "Go ahead, get down, but don't make any sudden moves. I'll shoot and maybe this time one of you won't be as lucky as Rusty."

While Daniel kept an eye on the men, King picked up the guns, removed the bullets and put some in each of his shirt pockets and handed the rest to Daniel. Sam and Charlie had put a bandage around Rusty's arm and splashed water on his face to rouse him. He motioned for the men to stay on the ground.

"Now that we have your attention. I have some questions for you."

"What questions?" Sam raised his chin a notch. "We don't know nothin'. We're just out for a ride."

King raised an eyebrow. "On a hidden trail?" Before he went on, they needed to secure the men. With Rusty injured, it was still three against two. Was Daniel feeling the effects of their last fight like he was? Did they have the energy to haul three men into the woods? He took a rope from Charlie's horse and tossed it to Sam. "Bind Charlie's hands and tie them to his feet."

When he did as instructed, King tossed him Rusty's rope. "Now him."

Rusty cussed and swore about hurting an injured man until Sam told him to shut up and quit acting like a simpering old lady.

Two down, one to go. King holstered his gun, removed Sam's rope and secured him. When the three were seated several feet apart, Daniel put his gun away and folded his arms over his chest.

"How many men are left in your camp?"

"Ten."

Daniel kicked Sam in the foot. "How many? And, by the way, Silverstone and Willoughby are back a ways, tied up nice and snug."

"They told us quite a nice tale, so I'd suggest you answer us properly." King put his hand on his gun. "How many men are with Woods right now?"

"One."

Daniel raised an eyebrow at King. "One? There's only one man besides Woods?"

Sam glared. "Yes."

"Who from my ranch is supplying Woods with information about me?"

The three men shared looks.

"Well? What man is helping Woods?"

"Ain't no man." Charlie said.

A woman? The only woman at the ranch was Hilda. No way would she be against him. Would she? His heart sank. Were she and Paddy involved. "A woman?"

Rusty shook his head. "Nah. A kid. Can't remember his name. Skinny thing about ten. Smells like skunk."

Sam laughed. "Yeah. Whenever he comes into camp with food and information, we have to cover our noses. Said you were to blame for it."

Josiah. The little brat. "Was his father involved, too?"

"Nah." Charlie shook his head. "Never saw no one from your ranch except the kid. He was kinda a smart ass. Didn't really care for him."

Rusty kicked at a rock by his foot and flinched. "Kid got a kick out of fooling his pa and you and a guy named Paddy and his wife."

That was a relief. "Daniel, we need to get going."

"What about us?" Sam asked. "You can't leave us tied up out here."

Daniel leaned into Sam's face. "How did you leave the women?"

"Tied up," Sam mumbled.

King pulled Charlie and Rusty's bandana's over their mouths and tightened the knots, checking to make sure none of the men would be able to get loose. He stood before Sam. "You'd better hope someone knows about this trail or you'll be sitting here until we get around to sending the sheriff for you." He slapped each horse, sending them galloping in the direction of town.

"Hey, you can't . . ." Sam's words were cut off when Daniel pulled the bandana over his mouth.

They took off at a jog toward the pasture, the one he'd been planning on showing Suzanna the day of the picnic. The pasture he thought was safe. He was so wrong. "At least we won't be outnumbered when we get to Woods' camp."

Daniel puffed beside him. Sweat poured down the sides of his face. "Unless he has more men than those guys know about."

"I doubt it." They reached the edge of the clearing and, not bothering to see how many cattle he had left, wove through them to the other side. The entrance to the trail was so obvious, a blind man could have found it. "Looks like they thought they didn't have to cover their tracks."

They paused for a drink of water.

Daniel slapped the canteen cork back in place. "Makes it easier for us."

Knowing there would only be Woods and one other person with the women, they didn't worry about coming across anyone else. They ran, walked, and ran some more. King swiped at the salty sweat stinging his eyes. His shirt beneath the knapsack was drenched, but, as much as he wanted to dump it, there were things in there that might help. Including... he stopped.

"What's wrong??" Daniel halted short of ramming into King.

"What if they're lying about how many men were left behind? They're Woods' men, so it's in their best interest for Woods to survive." King slipped the sack from his shoulders and set it on the ground. "We have their guns and bullets." He opened the sack and, one-by-one, lay the guns on the ground. He retrieved the bullets from his shirt pockets and loaded three guns while Daniel loaded the other two.

"Between ours and these, we have forty-two rounds." King sat back on his haunches and put three of the guns in his knapsack. "That should be enough, shouldn't it?"

"Hell, I hope so. If not, we're in deep trouble." Daniel put two of the guns in his sack and slung it on his back. "Let's get going. At this rate, it'll be dark before we get there."

"Wherever there is." He picked up speed, praying they'd make it in time to save Suzanna and her sister.

Chapter Twenty-Four

Suzanna caught movement from the edge of one of the tents. Had someone come to rescue them? The figure came farther into the camp.

What in heaven's name was he doing here? "Josiah?"

Josiah stopped at the sound of her voice and set a burlap sack down. "Miss Lindstrom?" He ran over to her. "Why are you tied up?" He glanced around the area. "Where is everyone? Where is Mr. Woods?"

"Young man, you tell me right now why you're here. Why aren't you with your father?"

Josiah puffed out his skinny chest. "I'm helping Mr. Woods and his friends. He said he needed me."

"Don't you realize Mr. Woods is not a good man?" This boy was going to be the death of her. And, unfortunately, it could be literally. "So are Mr. Silverstone and Mr. Willoughby."

"They are not. They're only trying to take back what Mr. Winson stole from them."

Suzanna shook her head. "Is that what they told you? It's one thing to pull pranks at school and another to help men who cheat and steal. Does your father know what you're doing?"

"Nope. And I ain't tellin' him, neither."

Now would not be the time to correct the boy's grammar, but she cringed anyway. "Josiah, you need to help us get out of here."

The boy simply stood and glared at them. "If'n you're tied up, it must be for a reason." He turned and walked to Woods' tent. "Mr. Woods. It's Josiah."

Woods threw back the tent flap. "What the hell you doin' here, boy? I told you not to come back for three days."

At Woods' yell, the sleeping man, rose, and disappeared into the woods.

"I brought some of Hilda's chicken and rolls for you. I thought you'd be hungry." He smiled at the ex-banker. "And why are Miss Lindstrom and her sister tied up? What did they do wrong? You shouldn't be tying up a schoolteacher."

"Who are you to be telling me what to do?" He backhanded Josiah, sending him flying to the ground.

"Woods, that was uncalled for." If only she could get loose and pummel the pompous ass. "He's only a boy."

Woods rounded on her. "You shut up. No one tells me what to do. You hear?" He slashed his hand through the air. "No one." He kicked Josiah in the leg. "You get on back home now. And don't tell anyone about this. You hear?"

Tears streaked down Josiah's dirty face. He crab-walked away from Woods, picked up the sack of food, stood, and headed back the way he'd come.

"Wait, boy."

Josiah turned, hope on his face. "Yes? You want me to help you?"

"Yeah, give me the sack of food. Then get out of here."

"You really are a piece of work, aren't you?" Suzanna said between clenched teeth. "You must feel like a real man tying up women and hitting children. Huh? Does it make you feel powerful?"

"Shut up."

Julia's stomach growled.

"Sounds like you're hungry, girlie." Woods held up the sack. "Want some chicken? Hilda makes the best fried chicken around these parts."

"That would be quite nice, but you'll either have to feed or untie me."

Woods sauntered over, sat on the stump, opened the bag and pulled out a chicken leg. "Mmm... Hilda does make good fried chicken." His words were slurred as he talked around his full mouth. Next, he removed a biscuit.

Recalling how delicious Hilda's chicken was, Suzanna closed her eyes against Woods' torture, because that was exactly what he was doing—torturing them. Except for her rumbling stomach, Julia remained silent. After a few minutes of chomping and chewing loud enough to scare the birds away, he quit eating, stood, and wiped his hands on his pants.

"Well, ladies, I'm going to retire to my abode." He patted his stomach and belched. "I'm full." Leaving the remaining chicken and rolls laying on the sack, he left them.

Suzanna's mouth watered and stomach gurgled. They hadn't had anything to eat since their meager breakfast early this morning.

"That man is a bastard." Julia said.

"Julia Marie Lindstrom. What would Ma and Pa say if they heard you swear like that?"

"Well, Ma and Pa aren't here and I'm calling it as I see it." An ant crawled over Julia's leg on its way to join his comrades at the feast on the ground. "Woods is a . . ."

"Even though I agree, don't say anything more." Suzanna settled her head against the tree. "I'm not sure how we're going to get out of here. And when those men come back . . ." She shuddered.

"I know. My wrists are sore from trying to get loose."

"Mine, too." She tried to look around the tree trunk. "Where did the other man go?"

Julia shrugged. "Probably headed for the hills when he heard Woods yelling."

"Psst."

"Did you hear that?"

"Psst."

Julia twisted her head back and forth. "You mean like someone is trying to get our attention?"

"Yeah."

"Maybe it's King and Daniel?"

"I sure hope so."

Suzanna caught a movement between two tents. "It's Josiah."

"Now why would that awful child come back here?"

Josiah ran between two more tents, obviously trying to avoid Woods'. For a few moments Suzanna lost track of him.

"Miss Lindstrom?" Josiah whispered behind them.

"Why are you back here?" Her irritation at the boy knew no bounds. If they ever got out of this dilemma and school started again, she'd have him doing more than writing on the board. He'd be mucking the stable, hauling wood, changing the water in the water bucket in the school every half hour so it was cool and fresh, washing the windows, and anything else she could come up with. "Coming to help your *friends*?" The ropes tugged at her wrists.

"I'm sorry, Miss Lindstrom. I thought he liked me and no one likes me. Not at school. Not at the ranch. Nowhere." He sniffled.

Was he crying? For a brief moment her heart melted for the boy, but she squashed it. Now was not the time to explain to him why no one liked him. "What are you doing back there?"

"I thought I could untie the knots, but they're too tight, so I'm sawing the ropes. It's going to take a bit. My knife ain't too sharp."

He was cutting them loose? "Why?"

"'Cause men shouldn't treat women like Woods and Silverstone and Willoughby treated you." He grunted as he talked and cut.

"Woods doesn't like me anymore than anyone else. He only needed me for food and information."

At least now he understood. "What will happen once you've cut the ropes?" She wiggled her nose. Was that skunk she smelled? Goodness.

Julia nudged her. "Look."

"Josiah," she whispered. "Hide. There's a man coming."

"Oh, him? That's just old Pete. Give him a few minutes. Only thing he does is sleep."

She believed him as it was all the man had done since they had stopped. The ruckus of men talking and leaving on horseback hadn't roused him. Pete lay on the ground and plopped his hat over his eyes. Hopefully, he'd stay asleep.

"Suzanna? What should we do once we're free?"

"Josiah, how far is it to King's ranch from here?" The rope around her wrists slackened.

"About a half-hour walk. For me, anyway. Might take longer with women along."

Suzanna held back a laugh. Goodness, for a young boy, he sure sounded like a man. "Don't worry about us. We can handle ourselves."

Her eyes sparkling, Julia, bit her bottom lip, and shook her head. "We're used to roughing it, Josiah."

"I'm almost through your rope, Miss Lindstrom."

At his words, the rope fell away. When she brought her arms from behind, her shoulders screamed. She bit back a groan and rubbed her raw, chafed wrists. "Move slow when Josiah cuts your rope. My shoulders hurt like the dickens."

It didn't take as long to get through Julia's ropes. Josiah worked at the one tied around their bodies holding them to the tree.

"Wait," Julia whispered. "Woods is coming from his tent. Put your arms behind you again."

Ignoring the pain in her shoulders, Suzanna thrust her arms back in place. Where had Josiah gone? He wasn't in sight when Woods approached them.

"What the hell is all the chattering about? Can't you women ever shut up? How's a man supposed to sleep?"

Suzanna tipped her chin toward Pete. "He doesn't seem to have any problems."

"Oh, hell. Pete could sleep through an explosion if it happened right next to him."

Woods sat down on the stump. "So, Miss Schoolmarm, are you ready to tell me what I want to know?"

"I told you I have no idea about King's businesses or papers or anything."

Without looking at the food, he picked up an ant-covered chicken wing and took a bite, smirking at them, taunting them.

"What the hell?" He jumped up and spit out the chicken. He grabbed the ladle from the water bucket, poured water into his mouth and spit it out. After repeating the process three more times, he stood in front of them, hands on his hips, face red, tongue swollen.

"'Y didn' 'u 'ell 'e 'ood 'overed ants?"

Julia giggled. "Ants got your tongue?"

Woods swung back his arm to strike her. Josiah rushed at him. His thin body was no contest against the stout banker. Woods staggered sideways but didn't fall down. He picked Josiah up by the collar and tossed him aside.

Josiah jumped up again and started for Woods. "You leave Miss Lindstrom alone." Woods held him off with one hand on his shirt.

With his back to them and her hands untied, Suzanna slid from beneath the rope and lifted it for Julia to escape. She lunged at Woods. In the collision, he released Josiah, giving the sisters a chance to attack Woods.

The man was stronger than he looked. Even with the two of them struggling, they couldn't get Woods to the ground.

"Hold it right there, ladies."

Suzanna stopped tugging on Woods' vest and glanced over her shoulder. Sure, now Pete is awake. Not only awake but pointing a shotgun at them.

Woods straightened, arranged his vest over his portly stomach. "Thank you, Pete." He grinned. "Looks like you've been thwarted, ladies. Pete keep an eye on them. I'll be right back."

Josiah jumped up from the ground and ran to Pete. "You have to let them go. Mr. Woods will kill them. You can't kill two women. You jest can't."

Pete ruffled Josiah's hair. "He won't kill them. Maybe rough them up a bit, but he won't kill them. Doesn't have the guts." He glared at the women. "Oh, he may have me do it, but he won't do it himself."

Suzanna grabbed Julia's hand. What were they going to do now? There was no doubt Pete would shoot if Woods ordered him to.

Woods returned, carrying a pistol. His swagger didn't do anything to bolster her hopes he would leave them alone.

"Mr. Woods. I'm sure I can get King to tell me where he has his papers and sign the properties over to you. All you have to do is let us go."

"Do I look stupid? If I let you go, you'll send help. Besides, Silverstone, Willoughby, and the others should be back soon. I have no doubt he'll have what I want with him." He waved the gun at them. "Now, if you'll sit yourselves back down, we'll wait here for them." He pointed the gun at Josiah. "Join them." Woods held out his empty hand. "But before you do, I want the knife you used to cut the ropes."

Julia moved first and sat down beneath the tree. As Suzanna followed, she searched the area for a way to escape. A branch to knock the gun from Woods' hand, or maybe a rock to knock him out. But the area was clear of any potential weapons. She sat beside Julia. Not that it helped any, but at least they weren't tied up again. Josiah positioned himself between Julia and herself. Now all they had to do was wait.

"WHAT DO YOU THINK?" Daniel whispered.

King eased aside the brush. "Looks like Woods' men were telling the truth. Besides him, I only see one other man."

"Yeah, but they have guns aimed at the girls."

Daniel was right. And what the hell was Josiah doing here? None of them were tied up, but from here the bruise on Suzanna's cheek was plain as day. "I have an idea."

"Better be a good one."

"I'll go in and pretend I'm by myself. Maybe I can give them the idea that I have the upper hand. You can join us later."

Daniel shook his head. "I have a better idea. We go in and make sure they realize they don't have the upper hand."

"Either way, they could easily shoot the girls and Josiah." As much as he disliked the kid, he didn't want him hurt.

"Woods is a coward. One time when he was in his cups, he told me he'd never shot a gun. Never wanted to shoot a gun."

That was interesting information. King grinned. "So actually, we do have the upper hand. You go around behind the guy with the shotgun. I'll come in from here. When I give you a signal, you come out."

"Sounds like a plan."

King gave Daniel a few minutes to get in place, then walked into the clearing, his gun in his right hand. "Hello, Woods."

At King's voice, Woods swung around, his eyes wide. Suzanna grinned, Julia stood, and Josiah took several steps backward.

"What're you doing here, Winson? You gonna save these little gals by yourself?" As if King was no threat, he turned back to Suzanna and Julia. "Now, Miss Julia, did I give you permission to stand? Pete, keep an eye on them. And ladies, in case you don't know nothing about shotguns, one blast can do damage to the three of you."

King walked farther into the campsite. "Besides kidnapping, are you going to add murder to your other crimes?"

Woods chuckled. "By the time I'm done, no one will dare defy me. Once you hand over your properties to me, including your ranch, I'll have my men dispose of each one of you. There won't be anyone left to remember my crimes. Even my stupid wife will be gone."

The man was delusional. Did he really believe the business owners of Deadwood would forget? Not in a million years. "You'd have to get rid of every saloon and brothel owner in town."

"Over time, it could be done. I have plenty of men who are willing to aide me. They know how rich they could be if they stick with me. Right Pete?"

Pete nodded, but didn't say anything.

"Are you talking about Silverstone, Willoughby, and those other men you sent to town?"

"So, Silverstone talked to you, did he?" Woods stared at his boots and shook his head. "I take it he didn't get the papers. Stupid fool. He never was good at taking orders."

"Oh, he talked all right. Told me about your big plans." King pushed his hat back on his head. "To tell the truth, it was Willoughby who spilled the beans. Guy's a real talker."

"Another idiot. So, they're still in town?"

"No. They're back on the trail, trussed up like a couple of calves waiting to be branded." King winked at Suzanna. Her smile set his pulse racing. He turned his attention back to Woods. He couldn't let her distract him. "And don't forget the three men you sent after them."

"You saw them, too?" Woods' mouth fell open.

"Saw, tied up, and left them stewing on the side of the trail. I imagine their horses are in town by now, though."

"Ha. You lie. There's no way one man could take down five men by himself."

King raised an eyebrow. "Who said I was alone?"

Woods licked his lips and searched the surrounding brush. "I don't see anyone else, so you're bluffing."

"Am I?" He chuckled to himself when the banker took a step back and did another sweep of the area. Daniel had hidden himself well. At his nod, Daniel appeared behind Pete and wrapped an arm around his neck. Pete dropped the shotgun.

"What . . . You . . ." Woods' face turned red.

"Wasn't bluffing, was I?" He waved his gun at Woods. "Now put down your gun. You don't have a chance against two armed men. No one can help you, and I'm standing in front of the entrance to the trail."

King pointed to Josiah, who would get a thrashing he'd never forget once they were out of here. He didn't care what Asa said. "There must be a path to the ranch for the kid to come here, but if you try to escape to the ranch, I imagine Paddy and my other hands will be able to stop you. So, you see, there's no way out."

Before he realized what Woods would do, he reached down and grabbed Suzanna by the hair. She screamed and kicked at him, but he yanked her hair and pulled her against him.

"Let her go." He didn't have a good shot because Suzanna's body protected Woods.

Woods pressed his gun into her side. "Not a chance. You won't shoot your lover. Get out of my way and drop your gun. Iverson, you too." He inched his way around King. "Now, I'm going to take this little lady with me." He glanced at his remaining man. "Pete, grab your gun and follow me."

"You won't get away, Woods."

"Ha. Once I get my men released, it'll be you who won't get away."

Afraid Woods would shoot Suzanna, he stood helplessly as he dragged Suzanna down the path with Pete covering his back. She dug her heels into the dirt, making it difficult for Woods to move.

When they disappeared, he swiped up his gun. Julia ran to him and grabbed his arm.

"You have to go after them."

Blinded by rage, he threw off Julia's hand and charged toward the trail.

"King. Wait." Daniel stood before him. "Give them time to get down the trail. We can cut across the woods and cut them off at the pasture."

King ran a hand over his face and holstered his gun. "You're right. We'll give them ten minutes, before we take off." He walked over to Josiah and clenched his fingers. Josiah cringed back against the tree. Tears streamed down his face. The boy should be afraid, very afraid.

"What do you have to say for yourself, boy?"

"I . . . I . . . I want my father."

King reached down to pull Josiah to his feet when a shot rang out, followed quickly by another.

Julia screamed and ran to the trail. "Suzanna."

Daniel grabbed her. "Wait. We can't go charging in. You stay here with Josiah. King and I will see what happened."

The hadn't gone more than a few hundred yards when they came upon Bertha Woods holding a gun at her side. Her husband lay on the ground with Suzanna on top of him. Two feet away, Pete lay motionless, a red stain growing on his shirt.

Keeping an eye on the banker's wife, King knelt beside Woods and Suzanna. The banker had a whole in the side of his temple. He pressed a shaking finger on the side of her neck and let out a breath when her strong pulse beat against his skin. He glanced up at Daniel. "She's alive."

Suzanna's eyes fluttered open. "King?"

"I'm here, Suz. Thank God, you're all right."

"She shot them. Mrs. Woods shot them both."

"We know." He reached to pick her up.

"I can stand." She held up her hand for help.

Once on her feet, he held her in his arms. How could he stop her shaking when he couldn't stop himself? If he had lost her? It was unthinkable.

The banker's wife hadn't moved a muscle, simply stood, staring at the ground. Keeping his eyes on her, King approached. When she didn't respond, he removed the gun from her hand. Like a crazy woman, her hair hung in damp strands over her face. The shoulder of one sleeve was ripped, the other sleeve completely gone. Her skirt was torn, and one stockinged foot peeked from beneath it.

"Sit down, Mrs. Woods."

At Daniel's soft words, she came to life. "That bastard." She kicked a clump of dirt at Woods. "That slimy, no good-for-nothing bastard." She spat on him "I spend my entire marriage putting up with his beatings, letting him carouse with prostitutes. Followed him to this god-forsaken place." Dry-eyed, she dropped to the ground. "I knew he was bad. Knew he was real bad, but I didn't know what to do. I was glad when he was arrested. Glad I didn't have to put up with him anymore. Thought I could sell our house and head back East to my family. But now everything is gone." She looked at Suzanna. "I'm sorry he took you and your sister."

"How did you know where he was?"

Bertha glanced up at Daniel. "I didn't. I heard you and Mr. Winson talking at the restaurant, so I followed you. I don't stand for anyone kidnapping women."

"You followed us?" Why hadn't he and Daniel heard her?

"I kept well behind you." She grinned. "Watched you take down Silverstone and his cohort. Got a chuckle out of the way you handled the other three. But it was when I saw J.W. dragging the poor schoolteacher with a gun in her side that I knew I had to do something. I had found this gun in a sack, so I took it. Old J.W. was a bit surprised to see me, wasn't he, Miss Lindstrom?"

"I'll say. I never heard a man squeal so loud."

"He threatened to kill her unless I got out of the way." Bertha shook her head. "In all the years we were married, he never knew I was a crack shot." She slapped her hands on her thighs. "So, what happens now? Do I get arrested?"

Before he could answer, Julia came running toward them, Josiah on her heels. She yanked Suzanna from his arms. "Oh, my God, Suz. I thought he'd killed you." They held each other for a moment before Julia took in the bodies. "What happened?"

Bertha stood. "I killed them." Her voice was flat.

"You? But . . . But . . ." Julia shook her head as if it would clear her mind.

"No one would believe old stuffy Bertha Woods could shoot someone, would they? There's a whole lot people don't know about me." She held out her arms to Daniel. "Well, are you going to arrest me? You're a deputy, aren't you?"

Daniel shook his head. "It appears to me you saved a life by killing two wanted criminals. You should be rewarded, not arrested."

For a few minutes no one said anything. In the distance a crow called out. Julia and Suzanna sniffled. He swatted at a fly buzzing around his ear. Josiah kept his eyes on the ground, while Daniel knelt beside Pete and checked his pockets. He glanced up at Mrs. Woods and raised an eyebrow. At her nod, he ruffled through her husband's pockets, coming up with a ring of keys, a wallet packed with bills, and a picture of a woman who bore no resemblance to his wife.

"What now?" Suzanna asked.

King looked up at the sky where, surprisingly, the sun still shone through the trees. "Josiah, how far are we from the ranch?"

"With the women with us, about half an hour."

"That's closer than going back to town." King looked at each woman. "Are you up for it?"

"Huh. We can do it in twenty minutes," Mrs. Woods said.

Well if she could so could the rest of them.

Julia pointed to Pete. "What about them?"

"When we get to the ranch, I'll send a couple of men back here to haul them out. Can't leave them out here overnight." King took Suzanna by the elbow and walked toward the campsite. "We'd better get started. You can stay at the ranch tonight."

Suzanna glanced at the dead men and shuddered. "But what about the men you left tied up in the woods?"

Daniel chuckled. "A night in the woods will do them good. I'll send some men for them tomorrow. With the jail gone, I'm not sure where we'll put them anyway."

"Maybe the soldiers can get them in the morning and take them back to the fort." Ignoring his aching, tired body, he took Suzanna by the elbow and followed the others to the ranch.

Chapter Twenty-Five

The next morning, Suzanna dragged herself from the bed she and Julia shared, her body aching in places that had never ached before. She stretched and nearly fell back into bed.

"What are you doing up so early?" Julia mumbled from beneath the blankets.

"Couldn't sleep anymore." She wrinkled her nose at her mud-covered and torn clothes from yesterday. It had been late by the time they'd arrived at the ranch, told and re-told the story to Paddy and Hilda, and ate supper, then Hilda had insisted everyone take a bath.

A subdued Josiah had been hauled off by his father. Maybe he'd learned his lesson and would be better behaved. She shrugged her shoulders. She could always hope.

She buttoned the last button on her blouse and stood at the bedroom door. "I'm going down to eat breakfast." Vague mumbling came from the bed. Obviously, Julia wasn't getting up anytime soon.

Following the smell of bacon, she took the back stairs to the kitchen. The men, Hilda, and, surprisingly, Mrs. Woods sat around the table. Empty plates, coffee cups, and a plate with two muffins covered the top. King pulled a chair out for her.

Hilda stood and put a cup of coffee in front of her. "Can I make you fried eggs? I kept bacon warm for you and your sister."

"That would be wonderful." She took a sip and nearly groaned with delight. "What were you talking about?"

Daniel pushed his plate away from him. "King sent a couple of his men into town with the bodies. Because of the heat, they'll be buried right away."

Suzanna turned to Mrs. Woods, who sat next to her. "Don't you want to be there for the burial?"

"Huh," was all she said.

"I sent a letter along with my men asking the Army if they could spare a few soldiers to collect the other men and take them to the fort." King handed her the salt and pepper. "This morning we found records in Woods' tent documenting the stock he stole from me and where he sold it."

Hilda set a plate of bacon, eggs, and warm, buttery biscuits in front of her. With everyone watching, she refrained from shoveling the food into her mouth. The stuffed wallet sat in the middle of the table. She pointed her fork at it. "Is that his money?"

Mrs. Woods huffed again. "It's King's money. Anyway, I imagine most of it is."

Daniel smiled at her. "King and I talked about it this morning. From the records, we can tell how much is King's. Where the rest came from is a mystery. So . . ." He raised an eyebrow at King, who tipped his head. "The rest is yours, Mrs. Woods."

Tears pooled in her eyes. She slapped a hand against her large chest. "Why . . . Why . . . I can't take it."

"Why not?" As far as Suzanna was concerned it was. "Who else is it going to go to?"

King put a hand on the older woman's arm. "Consider it payment for putting up with your husband for so long. It'll help you get back East and start a new life."

"I'm speechless. Thank you."

Suzanna wiped her mouth on her napkin. "Will you go back East?"

Mrs. Woods' eyes twinkled. "Maybe, maybe not."

"What about Josiah?" Surely the boy would be reprimanded for his role in helping Woods.

Daniel wrapped his hands around his coffee cup. "Right now, he's with his father, who I'll be speaking with this morning. Hopefully, Asa finally realizes his son is out of control."

"I can only hope he'll be different when school is up and running again."

King stood. "If you're done, Suzanna, could I talk with you outside?"

Whatever could he want? And why was he taking a chance on being alone with her with Mrs. Woods around?

Once outside, King took her hand and led her the far end of the wide front porch. To her delight, he pulled her into his arms and kissed her forehead. Her heart melted. She sighed into his chest. This was exactly where she belonged.

"I'm so sorry this happened to you. It's my fault," he said into her hair.

She leaned back and took in his scowl. "No, it isn't. It's Woods' fault and no one else's."

"But if it weren't for me..."

Suzanna put a finger against his lips. "You didn't do anything wrong."

"But I could have stopped him."

"How? You didn't know who was stealing from you." He tried to speak, and she pressed her finger to them again. "You may have had an idea, but you can't have a person arrested for his ideas. When did you find out he had escaped?"

"Yesterday morning. Daniel told me when I went looking for you and Julia at your house."

"See? Are you able to read minds?"

"Well, no."

"Then you can't blame yourself." She ran her fingers down his shirt. "What did you do when you found out?"

"Nothing at first, but when we found out you hadn't shown up at the restaurant, we realized what must have happened. I've known for years that Woods hated me."

"Again, you can't arrest a man for hating you. You are an honest, caring man, and I'm proud of what you did to rescue us."

"You sure you don't blame me?"

She stood on her toes and kissed his cheek. "I'm positive. And don't you dare blame yourself. After hearing how Woods treated his wife, I'm happy she's free of him." She kissed his cheek again, surprised at how bold she was. "And giving her the money was an honorable thing to do." She smiled when his face turned red.

"Thank you."

He led her to a bench hanging from the porch ceiling by stout chains. She sat, marveling how it was like a swing for two. King joined her. Her insides flipped and twittered when his leg brushed against hers.

"There's something else I want to talk to you about."

He rested his arm across the back of the swing and toyed with her hair, sending shivers down her spine. "What's that?"

"Remember the day of the fire when I said I didn't want to wait until your contract was up to court you?"

"Mm-hmm." It felt like weeks ago but was only three days. Where was he going with this? A contract was a contract.

"I meant it. And, after yesterday when I thought you'd been shot, I mean it doubly so. Life is too short. I'm going to talk with the school board about changing the contract."

Dare she ask the question was burning in her brain and heart? What if she was wrong? Like her mother said, nothing ventured, nothing gained. "Umm..."

"Yes?"

King's breath was warm against her cheek. "Are you asking me to marry you?"

"After a courtship, and I mean a very brief courtship, yes. I love you and want to spend the rest of my life with you."

"You wouldn't care if I kept teaching after we're married?"

"What else would you do during the day?"

"Where would we live?"

"Here. Or if the board allows at your house." He paused and caressed her cheeks with his thumbs. "I do have a question for you."

"Yes?"

He took a deep breath, held it for a second, and let it out. "Do you love me?"

The front screen door creaked. A stout woman stood before them. Heavens. Mrs. Woods. They were in trouble now.

"I have one, or maybe two things to say to you." She folded her arms over her chest.

Suzanna gulped. "Yes?"

"First of all, I'm sorry for the trouble I caused."

Had she heard right? Mrs. Woods was apologizing?

"Next, you'd better say you love him."

What?

"Also, I agree it's stupid a woman can't teach after marriage. I'll put a word in with the school board. And lastly . . ."

"Yes?" she and King said at the same time.

"For heaven's sake. Kiss the girl."

And so, he did.

Excerpt from "The Balcony Girl"

Shouting, screams, and bells ringing jerked him from a dream of kissing Julia. He peeled his eyes open. He rubbed them with the back of his hand and squinted across the room. The room was hazy, making the lantern light barely visible. Smoke? He coughed and sank to the floor.

Voices yelled from the street. "Fire! Fire! The town's on fire."

Shit. It had to be bad if there was smoke in his room. As he stood an explosion rocked the building, sending him flying to the floor. What the hell? It sounded like cannons going off. Had they gone to war again while he was sleeping? He crawled across the floor, grasped the doorknob, and twisted. Nothing. He jerked the knob. Stuck. Damn landlord. The angry, swirling smoke thickened. He needed to get out of here before he couldn't see or breathe, stuck doorknob or not.

He kicked at the door. Luckily, he'd left his boots on. On the third kick, the door crashed open. There'd be hell to pay when his landlord saw the damage. Taking the steps three at a time, he got to the street in record time. People were running toward the hill, carrying whatever they could hold in their arms. Horses ran wild down the street. Over on Sherman Street, flames shot into the air, making the night sky glow. From what he could tell, the fire was heading toward downtown.

King ran down the street toward him. Soot covered his face. "The fire set off kegs of gunpowder at Jensen and Bliss' Hardware Store."

The old miner Daniel had seen on and off ran up alongside King. Gone was the stooped back. His hat was absent, revealing blonde hair draped over his shoulder. Daniel did a double take at the miner. Long, blonde hair? His face was as dirty as always, but beneath the grime, womanly features became apparent.

"Julia?"

She nodded.

"What the hell are you doing here dressed in those old clothes?"

King glanced over his shoulder. "There's no time to question her. Right now, we need to help people from the buildings and up the hill."

"I'll go to Hattie's and help them get out."

Daniel captured her elbow. "You'll do no such thing. Go back to your house. The fire isn't headed toward it."

Julia yanked her arm from his hand. "I'll do no such thing, Daniel Iverson. You can't tell me what to do." Without another glance, she ran toward Hattie's.

"Damn woman," he muttered, chasing after her.

"You got that right," King said, racing behind him. "A damn *fine* woman."

Daniel had no idea fire roared. In a fireplace, flames snapped and crackled cheerfully, but the fire hot on their heels snarled and growled like a hundred bears being attacked by thousands of bees. A woman, dressed in nothing but a sheer nightgown, screamed as she raced past them, a cat wrapped in her arms.

"Head to the hills," he shouted after her, praying all the other residents of the town would make it to safety.

The heat seemed to sear through his clothing. Taking a chance, he looked over his shoulder. Flames were devouring buildings three doors away. How was anyone going to get out alive? He and King threw open the doors to Hattie's as Julia disappeared up the stairs.

Shit. Now he not only had to help the women, but make sure Julia was safe, too. Already windows were bursting from the heat.

When they reached the second floor, Julia had already pounded on the first two doors to the right of the stairway.

"You follow Julia, I'll take these rooms." King nodded in the opposite direction. "Fire! Get out now," he yelled, pounding on the first door.

Hattie's girls popped from their rooms holding thin wrappers to their chests, some followed by men wearing nothing but their long johns.

In front of him, Julia coughed, still yelling for the women to get out. "Run! Fire! The entire town's on fire!" She shoved two of the girls toward the back stairs.

"Hattie," a woman he recalled was Dorrie, shouted. "You have to get Hattie out of here. She took something to help her sleep."

"We'll get her out, Dorrie. Help the other girls. You don't have much time to get to the hills before the entire town is gone."

He pounded on a few more doors, making sure the inhabitants escaped, barely registering that one of the emerging men owned the haberdashery, was married, and had five children.

"Hattie! Wake up! The town's on fire." Julia beat on the last door and tried the doorknob. "It's locked. Hattie!" She turned to him. "You have to help me get her out."

Like he'd done in his room, Daniel kicked at the door, sending splinters of wood flying.

"She's not going to be happy about us breaking her door down," Julia said, entering the darkened room.

The scent of lilacs mixed with smoke hit him when he raced behind Julia to the still form beneath a pile of blankets.

Julia shook the woman. "Hattie," she coughed. "Hattie, wake up."

Daniel pushed Julia to the side, threw back the blankets, and scooped Hattie into his arms. The woman didn't weigh more than a bird, making his task easier. The window shattered. Cinders struck the drapes, instantly setting them on fire.

"Toss a blanket over her," he shouted over the increasing roar. Fire raged outside the window, lighting up the city like it was high noon. "Put one over your head, too, then let's get out of here."

Making sure Julia was in front of him, they ran down the smoke-filled hallway. "Where's the back stairs?"

"Here," Julia called then disappeared into the darkness.

"It figures she'd know where to go," he muttered to himself, hoisting the limp Hattie over his shoulder, giving him a free hand to follow the railing down the stairs.

"This way," Julia yelled, emerging from the building as a large beam swung down from above, blocking the stairwell behind them. She seized his hand.

With all the smoke, it was difficult to follow the shadows of people charging up the hill. At the top, out of breath, eyes stinging and legs burning, he lay Hattie on the ground. The smoke stung his nose. Would he ever be able to stand the smell of smoke again?

"What the hell?" Hattie whispered, her eyes fluttering open. "What am I doing outside?"

Julia sat beside her. Tears made muddy rivers down her sooty face. "The town is on fire." She stared in the direction of the schoolhouse. "The school looks safe. I hope Suzanna is."

Daniel eased himself to the ground. He rested his elbows on his raised knees. Around him people cried, calling for friends or loved ones. Had everyone gotten out? Down below, the fire raged, consuming building after building like a starving monster. Buildings men had purposely burned as a firebreak hadn't stopped the conflagration. Like children playing hopscotch, the blaze skipped from building to building, eating everything in its path.

About the Author:

Tina Susedik is an award-winning, multi-published author in both fiction and non-fiction. She is published in history, military, romantic mystery, erotic romance, and children's books, with over thirty books to her credit. Her books are in both print and eBook format. She lives in northern Wisconsin with her husband of forty-seven years. She also writes spicier romance as Anita Kidesu. Tina hosts a radio show, "Cover to Cover by Tina," where she interviews authors of all genres.

Where to find Tina
Twitter: https://twitter.com/TinaSusedik
Website: www.tina-susedik.com
Facebook: https://www.facebook.com/TinaSusedikAuthor/
http://www.pinterest.com/tinasusedik/
Goodreads: https://www.goodreads.com/photo/author/1754353.Tina_Susedik
Newsletter: http://tinasusedik.us11.list-manage.com/subscribe?u=874ff86e3f10f756a138fbc3a&id=1cfdf516fc[1]

Other Books by Tina

---

1. https://l.facebook.com/l.php?u=http%3A%2F%2Ftinasusedik.us11.list-manage.com%2Fsubscribe%3Fu%3D874ff86e3f10f756a138fbc3a%26id%3D1cfdf516fc&h=ATNAjGtIpC7Tz8vdC3sYYLhcCiMepWFUb2h2JGkoXHipuBjGtBon-oPOJNT8ryII0xPdQdtB-Jp01wQoYRyT_JC_6CvbgLOMSr4-8PMAEG_1Syqofne1NDlmYxT_RnORX3jB9VQ

Riding for Love
All I want for Christmas is a Soul Mate - Anthology
My Sexy Valentine
Sizzle in the Snow
Never With a Rich Man
The Trail to Love: The Soul Mate Tree Collective
Missing My Heart – A Chandler County Mystery
Missing Innocence – A Chandler County Mystery
A Photograph of Love – Hell Yeah!
Love With a Side of Crazy – Hell Yeah!
The School Marm – Wild Deadwood Tales Anthology
The Home Front – Destiny Whispers Anthology
The Balcony Girl – Book One in the Darlings of Deadwood Series
Saving Ellis – Darlings of Deadwood Short Story

Writing as Anita Kidesu
South Seas Seduction
Surprise Me
Surprise Me Again
Double the Surprise

Children's Books by Tina Susedik
Uncle Bill's Farm
The Adventures of Peanut and Casey on Uncle Bill's Farm
The Hat Peddler

Made in the USA
Monee, IL
29 July 2022